Oak and Mist

Volume One of The Ambeth Chronicles

Helen Jones

For Marcus and Isabelle,
who make it all possible.

CONTENTS

ACKNOWLEDGMENTS

With thanks to Lucy York for her editing expertise, to
Rich Jones at Turning Rebellion for the beautiful
cover design, to David Ryan for slogging through the
ridiculously long first draft and being gracious about it, to
Pam, Nicky, Lin, Neralie, Mandy and Louise for reading
and loving the story so far, to bloggers far and wide for
sharing their knowledge so generously, to my family and
friends for their love and support, and to
my beloved Marcus and Isabelle, for coming on this
journey with me.

The Valley

Spotting the path turning through the trees, she dropped her bike at the edge of the bushes and left the others behind, eager to find something new. Dead leaves and brambles crunched underfoot as she made her way through the darkening wood. She emerged onto a slope that led down into a tree-filled valley, her feet slipping on the sandy soil. She paused, sensing something wasn't quite right. As she peered down cautiously into the shadows, low-lying mist curled out to obscure her view. Her stomach fluttered and flipped as her sense of unease increased.

Then the scream came, loud and ragged with pain, arcing up from under the pines. The clash of metal and strange scraping sounds echoed in the cool autumn air and a huge shape moved in the darkness, followed by a grunting noise and a soft thump, as though something had fallen. A soft silver light flared under the trees and she flinched, her red hair falling in her face as she slowly backed away, one hand to her mouth. Turning in panic she fled along the forest path and burst out into the park, relieved beyond anything to see Sara waiting for her.

'Alma! Where did you go? I've been looking for you.'

'Um, nowhere, just got lost. C'mon, let's go.' She jumped on her bike and rode away, not daring to look back. Sara followed behind...

Nightmare

5 years later

'Ow!'

Alma slammed into the row of lockers, banging her shoulder hard and dropping her books as she fell.

'Watch where you're going.' The other girl sneered down at her, then sauntered off. Outraged, Sara rushed over to help her friend up.

'What the hell was that?' Alma was completely shaken by the sudden attack. 'Ellery!' she shouted after her. But she was gone.

'Are you all right?' Sara handed Alma her books, her brown eyes crinkled with concern.

'Um, yeah, no, I don't know. What is her problem?' Alma was breathing hard, a pain in her chest and tears threatening, but there was no way she was giving in. Seeing the curious looks from the other students as they tapped on their phones, she brushed herself off, shaking out her long hair.

'Show's over,' she said, linking her arm with Sara's and starting down the hall. She tried to act like it was no big deal, though she could feel her face was red.

'Are you sure you're OK? What a bitch!' Sara looked back to see if Ellery was following them. Alma fought to calm down, not wanting to seem like she cared, though she knew Sara would see right through her.

'I know, right? It's like she thinks the world owes her something, just cos of how she looks.' Breathing deeply, she managed to smile at Sara. 'Don't worry about it, OK? Let's just go to class.'

But she was troubled for the rest of the day. Ellery was beautiful, everyone knew that, but she had a personality that could strip paint. And now she had taken a dislike to Alma.

Alma pulled her chair up to the kitchen table, the legs scraping across the tile floor. She sat down and started to pick at her meal, ignoring Toby and Aidan who were having one of their usual mealtime disagreements. Across the table her mother and father were already eating. Alma ignored them too.

'So, Alma, how was your day?' Eleanor asked, smiling at her daughter. Alma scowled.

'Fine, I guess.'

'Really?' Eleanor glanced at Graham, who just shrugged.

'Yeah – hey!' Toby banged into Alma, pushed by his

twin, the argument escalating. Both of them carried on shouting and shoving each other, prompting Eleanor to intervene. Alma threw down her cutlery with a huffy sigh and sat back, rubbing her sore shoulder as she looked out through the French doors. In the garden leaves were turning from green to gold, bright in the setting sun.

'I think I need to go for a walk,' she announced to no one in particular. Then, focusing on her mother 'May I be excused?' Eleanor nodded, though she darted another glance at her husband as Alma got up and began to rinse her dishes noisily at the sink.

'Where are you going?'

'Out,' said Alma as she strode past into the lounge and scooped her bag up from the sofa. 'To the park. I'll be back later.' Her voice drifted down the hallway followed by the sound of the side door closing.

The sky still held the last of its light as Alma stepped outside, the cool air carrying the autumn scents of wood smoke and dead leaves. Hands in pockets she started to walk, her head down and feet scuffing the pavement. One thought was on her mind: What the hell was going on with Ellery? At the end of her street she stopped at the wooden gate and looked up at the vast oak tree standing next to it, its branches spreading across the sky. She could still remember putting her arms around the trunk when she was small, pressing her face to the rough bark and hugging it close as she listened. She'd felt sure she could hear the tree talking as the wind swooshed through its branches. She leaned her head on it now, one hand resting on the rough trunk, but it remained silent, offering no answers for her troubled thoughts.

After a few moments she went through the gate into the sloping meadow bounded with hawthorn. She skirted the old millpond with its fringe of rushes and wildflowers then crossed the road under an old stone bridge to arrive on the edge of the Armorial Park. The sun was setting over its green expanse, shadows stretching beneath the trees and her mood lifted at the familiar sight. She weaved her way through the dog-walkers and joggers, past the tennis courts and playground and the small cafe, its lights shining golden in the dusk, and headed for the woods on the other side of the park where dark copper beeches massed like thunderclouds against the lighter gold of oak and horse chestnut. She had always loved coming to the park, first with her parents then later with friends, playing in the fields and woods. Now she would come here when she needed to sit and think. Her favourite spot was a bench carved from a gnarled and ancient piece of wood, rubbed smooth by the many people who'd rested there over the years. It was empty now and Alma sat down, leaning forward with her elbows on her knees. As the shadows lengthened, she twiddled the bracelet on her wrist round and round. The silver links caught the last of the fading light as she rubbed her fingers across the smooth gemstone, something about the action calming her after the strange events of the day.

It was her fifteenth birthday. Alma followed Eleanor's slight figure up to her bedroom where she opened her jewellery box, lifting the top tray to take out an object tied in a scrap of faded silk.

'Happy birthday,' she said with a smile, holding the little package for a moment before giving it to Alma who took it and looked at her mother with raised eyebrows.

'It's from your father's family, Alma. He always wanted you to have it.'

'From my-'

'From your real father,' said Eleanor, her voice catching on the words. Alma's father had died before she was born. She had only learnt this a couple of years earlier, overhearing a whispered conversation in a darkened garden between her mother and grandmother. It had freaked her out for a while but in the end Graham was her dad, the only one she had ever known.

'Really?' Her blue eyes, the same as her mother's, widened as she carefully unwrapped the piece of silk to reveal a bracelet, a thick silver chain fastened by a hook clasp, the metal engraved all over with tiny curling leaves. A blue stone was suspended between two of the links and as she turned it in the light it seemed to shimmer with gold threads, colours swirling across the surface like oil on water.

'Wow,' she breathed, holding it carefully, her hands shaking slightly. 'It's beautiful, Mum.'

Eleanor looked fondly at her, her eyes suspiciously bright. 'Here, let me help you put it on.' Taking the bracelet, she placed it around Alma's wrist and fastened the clasp. As she went to close her jewellery box, the lid slipped through her trembling fingers and banged shut, making Alma jump.

'You okay, Mum?' she asked, frowning.

Eleanor turned around, smiling, though her mouth shook a bit. 'I'm fine.' Then she looked at Alma and her face softened with love. 'Really, I am,' she said. 'It's... just been a while since I've seen the bracelet, that's all.' She reached out to touch the links for a moment. 'It suits you.'

'I love it.' Alma gave her mother a hug and Eleanor squeezed her tight before pulling back to look at her daughter.

'Good,' she said, 'I hope you'll wear it then.'

Smiling at the memory, Alma turned the bracelet on her wrist once more, somehow feeling closer to her unknown father. Which was weird, seeing as she'd never met him. Resting her chin in her hand she watched a group of boys kicking a football, the War Memorial looming like a golden tower behind them. Her thoughts drifted along with the patterns of movement and colour they made against the green grass and golden leaves. Then she stiffened and sat up. Long legs, long dark hair and a flash of bright red jacket over the skinniest of dark jeans. It was Ellery and, by the speed at which she was walking in Alma's direction, she had seen her. Great.

Flanked by two other girls, Ellery marched towards Alma and stopped a few feet away, her arms folded and her face hard. 'I've been looking for you.'

Alma stood up, fists clenched at her side. She was damned if she was going to just sit there and take whatever Ellery decided to dish out.

'So? I don't know what your problem is, Ellery, I've done nothing to you.'

'Oh, I know you haven't done anything,' Ellery said in her clear voice, her green eyes cold. 'I've just decided that I. Don't. Like. You.'

The way she said it, each word enunciated so clearly, hit Alma like a blow. But there was no way she was giving Ellery the satisfaction of seeing her react.

'Why? Like I said, what's the problem?'

Ellery looked briefly surprised, then she jerked her head and the other two girls moved to stand behind Alma, fencing her in. Dee and Nicole, runners up for the top bitch award and always hanging with Ellery. This was not going to be good. Her stomach flipped but she refused to give in, facing Ellery defiantly. 'So, what are you going to do?' Her long red hair blew across her face and she pushed it back angrily. One of the girls snickered.

'I've decided,' said Ellery, 'that we're going to beat you up a bit – you know, just for fun.' She smiled but there was no warmth in it. Despite her challenging stance, Alma felt dizzy with fear, her heart racing. Still she refused to back down.

'Why?' she asked again, her blue eyes fixed on Ellery.

'Because I feel like it!' Shocked by the other girl's sudden anger, Alma couldn't help taking a step back. 'I don't need a reason – stop questioning me!'

She reached out to grab Alma but wasn't quite fast enough. Alma jerked her arm free and darted between the other two girls. She grabbed her bag and ran, but Ellery and her friends soon cut her off. First one girl bumped her, then another as they jostled her towards the edge of the trees. Alma gasped for breath, more frightened than she'd ever been before but determined not to go down without a fight. Pushing back, she managed to throw one girl off balance, but the other two closed in, their hands rough as they shoved her and pulled at her clothes.

Ellery grabbed at her again and Alma struck out, surprised to see the other girl recoil as though stung. Feeling a pain in her wrist Alma looked down to see the stone in her bracelet glowing golden, burning hot against her skin. What the hell? But there wasn't time to worry about it now. Alma glanced up and saw she was near to a gap between two oak trees, beyond which she knew was a track that would take her to the edge of the park and home. But before she could move Ellery pushed her so hard she almost fell, stumbling into the space between the trees. There was a split second flare of light, and she was gone.

The other two girls turned to look at Ellery, who was breathing hard and furious.

'What…What was that?' said Dee, confused.

Nicole peered through the gap in the trees. 'She's gone – I can't see her at all.'

Regaining her composure, Ellery flicked her dark hair back from her face. Then, using certain powers she had at her disposal, she looked each girl in the eyes and told her to forget all about Alma and what they had seen today. They did as they were told – just like they always did.

Darkness Wakes

Deryck woke and stretched, feeling his muscles moving against the down pillows. The servants had already been in to set the fire, his clothes for the day were laid out for him and breakfast was waiting on the small table by the window. All he needed to do was get up. He smiled, green eyes narrowing to slits as he thought of what was to come. His father's great plan – today was the day it would be set in motion, that the Dark would start to rise again, to take the power that was rightfully theirs. Sitting up, he ran his hand through his golden hair, pushing it back from his face as he swung his legs over the edge of the bed. Time to get on with the day.

After eating, he dressed quickly and was soon in the gardens, moving down the Long Walk. His green velvet cloak swirled around him as he walked through the patterns of light and shade made by the trees and topiary shrubs lining his path. White gravel crunched underfoot as he strode along, nodding to the occasional acquaintance, seeming nothing more than another member of the Court enjoying the gardens on a beautiful day. Smiling to himself, he quickened his pace. Only a few minutes more and he would have her – the Child of the Prophecy. Deryck couldn't wait to see the look on Thorion's face when the High King realised the Light had failed and the Dark were ready to take control. Reaching the edge of the gardens he stepped onto the ancient path that wound white across the green meadow, leading to the door between the worlds. But then a voice rang out, calling his name. He stopped, his face twisting with annoyance. He dare not ignore a summons from the High King. Composing himself Deryck turned to face him, bowing as was proper, waiting for the King to speak. Thorion smiled at him, the sun glinting from the gold circlet around his brow.

'I need to talk with you, if you please, Deryck. Will you walk with me?'

Deryck and Thorion walked through the gardens together, the King taking one path after another as he talked. Keeping pace with him, Deryck nodded in response to yet another question about the upcoming festival, trying to keep his temper. Then he realised the King was waiting for an answer.

'Well, ahem.' He cleared his throat, his desperation choking him. 'I think the group who play in the Hall most evenings would suit. They seem to be popular with everyone. I know my father enjoys their music.'

Thorion nodded, seeming to be deep in thought. Then he smiled. 'A good choice, I think. And the refreshments?'

Deryck shook his head, frowning a little. 'I don't know,' he muttered, unable to conceal his lack of interest completely. Thorion glanced at him, one eyebrow raised. Deryck pulled himself together, straightening his shoulders. 'I mean, my Lord, whatever they normally serve at such things will be more than sufficient, I'm sure. Would not some other courtier be better placed to tell you? I confess I do not notice, other than the wine.' He smiled, but it was more of a grimace, his hands clenching briefly as they moved further away from the Gate.

To his surprise Thorion laughed, clapping him briefly on the shoulder. 'Too true,' he said, smiling at him, though his eyes were midway between blue and grey. 'Perhaps the Lady Adara would be more helpful in that regard. Still, I do appreciate your input, Deryck,' the High King went on, his tone still pleasant. 'It is vital that both sides contribute towards the shape of the festivities, especially with things as they are, don't you agree?' He turned along the path leading back to the palace. Despite his frustration, Deryck felt bound to follow.

'Yes, my Lord,' he replied, fighting to keep his tone moderate. 'If that is all…?'

'Well, there was one more thing,' started Thorion. Then he stopped, considering. 'No, I think I've kept you long enough. You may go, with my thanks, Deryck.'

With a muttered reply, Deryck bowed to the King, then turned on the path and started back towards the woods, aware that he must not run, must not be seen to hurry or else he would give the game away. With an inward curse, he realised he wasn't going to make it – he was too late.

Gate of Oak

As she staggered between the trees, Alma felt so dizzy she didn't know which way was up. Light seemed to swirl around her, sparkles moving across her vision and blinding her. She stopped and sank to her knees, putting her hands on the ground. Really, on top of everything else, fainting was the last thing she needed to do. As the spinning sensation gradually decreased Alma scrambled to her feet, ready to run. Then she took in her surroundings and stopped short.

Something was terribly wrong. It was no longer autumn. The air was warm and blossom drifted around her, swirling in delicate drifts to settle softly onto the leafy forest floor. And she was not alone. A boy stood watching her, dressed in tunic and breeches of green and brown that echoed the colours of the forest.

'Hello,' he said, nodding his head, an amiable expression on his face. Alma stared at him a moment before looking behind her, expecting to see Ellery and her friends pushing through the bushes in search of her. But instead she saw only more forest.

'Where…where am I?' she stammered, starting to panic. 'Where is the park?'

The strange boy moved closer, smiling, and held out his hand. Not knowing what else to do, Alma took it.

'Caleb's the name,' he said. 'I've been waiting for you'.

Thorion made his way along the winding paths he knew so well, the gardens stretching green around him. He chose not to see the flirtatious glances thrown his way by both male and female members of the court, indifferent as always to their romances and intrigues. There were rumours, of course, that he had once loved someone, that she was lost and that he grieved for her still. But today as always, Thorion kept himself apart, murmuring only the occasional word of greeting to those he passed. As he trailed his hand across the feathery tops of wild grasses, Thorion recalled his studies many years before and the words of his old master, Merios…

'Since the dawn of time we have been here,' the ancient Elder said, his deep voice rumbling, eyes bright in his wrinkled face. 'Guardians of the great life force, always at odds with each other. The Dark always seeking to gain an advantage over the Light, yet both sides in their own way working to maintain the Balance so necessary to the world as we know it.' His eyes twinkled as he looked around the Great Hall at the eager young faces, avid for the knowledge he could impart. Slowly getting to his feet, he paced the floor, gesturing animatedly with his hands as he talked. 'Understand, if you will, that both sides studied the skies at first – watched the stars as they burned and wheeled through the heavens, traced the paths of the planets, followed comets as they streaked across the skies. This knowledge was sought and recorded by both Light and Dark, each working towards their own goals, yet weaving together perfectly so that there was a Balance in all things.'

He stopped, looking back for a moment to a time long gone. One of the original Elders of their realm, his age was immeasurable. Returning his gaze to the roomful of rapt acolytes he went on.

'Then the first of the humans was born. Child of Light and Dark, conceived unknowingly, cast out, unwanted in our perfect world. Dark of skin and hair she was, as beautiful as night, so who could blame her when, belonging neither with Light nor Dark, she found love with the only other one of her kind, born soon after she was, an outcast himself. But blame her they did. The Elders banished them both to the wilderness beyond the Gates, to find their way in the other world alone.' For a moment his ancient lined face was filled with sorrow and the students held their collective breath, waiting. 'There are those who mourn that decision still, laying flowers at the Gate each Feast Day, regretting the lost chance to forge a closer relationship with the humans who, surging in numbers, created a society that both feeds us and feeds from our lands.' His voice grew stronger as he went on. 'Humans are linked back to us, Light and Dark, by their original ancestors. As they love and worship and are born and die, as they murder and fight and hinder and heal, their human energy becomes part of the great life force – all that is positive flowing to the Light, all that is negative bringing power to the Dark.' Loudly now, marking each of them in turn with his bright glance, Merios finished his lesson. 'This is why preserving the Balance is so vitally important. This transfer of energy is circular and unbreakable, flowing from humans to Ambeth, then from Ambeth back into the human world. If the Dark are allowed to gain the ascension, we all suffer, while if the Balance prevails, life is as it should be, with enough Darkness allowed in that we may appreciate the Light. Truly, we are all connected and have been so from the very start.'

'Ah well,' Thorion sighed to himself, his stern expression causing a lady of the court to sigh in response as he moved past her. 'What will be will be. We can only shape events so far before they happen.' Then, turning with purpose down a narrow path running alongside a tall hedge, he prepared himself to meet one who could be the saving of them all.

'Um, I'm Alma.'

Caleb shook Alma's hand gently, his smile fading as he took in her agitated state. 'Pleased to meet you, Alma. And please don't worry,' he added. 'I'm here to look after you – to show you around.'

'Show me around? But...where am I?' asked Alma, her voice rising. What was happening to her?

'Why, Ambeth, of course,' replied Caleb, his hand warm as it held hers.

'Of course...' whispered Alma, her knees suddenly weak. Letting go of Caleb's hand she sank down to a sitting position, putting her head down as dizziness washed over her again. Caleb squatted down next to her and placed a gentle hand on her shoulder.

'It's going to be all right, I promise. You're safe with me. Trust me.'

Alma peeked from behind her hair to see Caleb's concerned face close to hers. She shook her head, still unsure.

'Come with me,' Caleb urged. "I'll explain all I can, I promise.' But Alma could only stare at him. She started to shake. 'You are safe with me, I promise you,' he went on. Please, come with me and I can help you.' He sounded really worried now. He had a nice face, she decided. The way his blue eyes crinkled at the corners when he smiled, you could almost see his good nature coming out through his skin. Realising she didn't really have any other option she smiled uncertainly, taking his hand as he helped her to her feet. She brushed the leaves from her jeans and tried to pull herself together.

'I'm sorry, this is all so strange – I mean, I still don't understand.'

'I know,' he said, sounding sympathetic, rubbing a hand through his unruly blonde hair. 'But, will you walk with me? I'll try to explain.'

'Wait – where to?' asked Alma, looking around nervously.

'It's OK,' he said again. 'Really it is. Just come with me and I'll show you.'

Sure, why not. Feeling as though she had fallen into a dream, Alma started through the woods, keeping close to Caleb. Tall trees stretched to the sky all around her and flowers filled the air with their sweet scent. It was beautiful. Wondering if perhaps she'd hit her head and passed out, she pinched herself hard on the arm and then grimaced in pain. Well, wherever she was, it was definitely real. Caleb shot a concerned glance at her and she shook her head, smiling, not wanting him to think she'd lost it completely. He grinned back but said nothing, though he kept glancing in her direction as they walked.

After a few minutes the trees started to thin out. Beyond the edge of the forest lay a huge open field covered with closely cropped grass, the greenest Alma had ever seen. A white pathway curved through the meadow towards expansive gardens and a distant blue smudge of ocean. The fresh breeze carried the scent of ozone and green growing things. At the centre of it all stood a building so magnificent it stopped Alma in her tracks.

'Wow,' she breathed. 'That building... it's amazing.'

She gazed at it in awe, forgetting her worries for a moment. From out of an immense structure of white stone came towers topped with tiles that gleamed like mother of pearl. Stained glass windows glinted beneath soaring arches set into the thick walls. It shone so brightly in the sun that Alma blinked, shading her eyes.

'It is the Palace of the Elders,' Caleb said, sounding pleased. 'You'll get to meet them, next time you are here.'

'Wait. N-Next time?" Her fear returned, swirling around her stomach and she looked at Caleb, her eyes wide. 'But... I don't even know how I got here.' She stopped, feeling weak at the knees again. 'I don't even know who you are, other than your name.'

Deryck struggled to stifle his rage as he walked through the gardens towards the forest. Of all the bad luck, to run into Thorion. Realising he couldn't possibly make the intercept he started to slow down – what the hell was he supposed to do now? His father would be furious with him. Hearing voices approaching, he stepped quickly behind a tree. He needed time to think. Peering out from behind the trunk, he watched as Caleb and a girl he didn't recognise walked slowly along the path. He smirked – so Caleb had finally found himself a girlfriend. Looking at the girl his mouth relaxed, curving in a half-smile. She was strangely dressed and almost as tall as Caleb, her long red hair cut with a fringe that fell in her eyes so she was always pushing it back with her hands. Her skin was pale and her eyes blue in her heart-shaped face. As she spoke to Caleb, the way she moved her arms lent her an impression of grace that was strangely appealing to Deryck. Overall, a very pretty girl, much better than any he imagined would ever be interested in Caleb. Once they had long passed he stepped out from his hiding place and walked away in the opposite direction, deep in thought.

No Place Like Home

'Please sit down and I'll try to explain. It's always weird, the first time you cross over. At least, that's what I've been told.'

Caleb gently took Alma by the arm, leading her to a nearby bench set against a tall green hedge. He took the seat next to her as she sat down slowly, trying to take it all in.

'Cross over?' Alma was in a daze. She thought of pinching herself again, then thought better of it. But this was like every story she had ever read rolled into one, only rather than reading of finding doorways through wardrobes or secret knowledge hidden in tree trunks, she was living it. Caleb was still talking to her, so she made an effort to take a deep breath and relax. She wasn't terribly successful.

'Yes,' said Caleb patiently, his kind face still concerned, 'you have crossed over. From your world, the human world, into Ambeth.'

'Amb-' Alma started, but Caleb interrupted, his eyes

starting to twinkle.

'Yes, this is the Realm of Ambeth, and you're not going to repeat everything I say, are you? It's just, it will make everything take so much longer.' He nudged her with his elbow and Alma grinned at the familiar gesture, starting to feel more like herself again. She started to relax.

'Okay, okay,' she said, hands up, laughing. 'I promise I won't do it anymore. I'm… just a bit confused.'

Caleb laughed too then and the sound was reassuringly normal. He offered her a bottle made of silver metal, beautifully engraved with spiralling patterns.

'Would you like a drink? Oh, don't worry,' he said, seeing Alma eye the bottle doubtfully. 'It won't turn you into a frog or anything – at least I don't think so.'

He winked and Alma realised he was teasing her again. Taking a breath, she raised the bottle to her mouth and took a long draught. The drink tasted like strawberries and mint and she handed the bottle back to Caleb, wiping the rim. 'Thanks,' she said, grinning. 'Yep, still me, no frog's legs,' she went on, then blushed at her feeble joke. But Caleb laughed out loud, nudging her with his elbow again and all it once it was like they'd been friends for years.

'So, shall we-' he started, but Alma lifted her hand to stop him before he could speak.

'Sorry, Caleb, before we go anywhere else I need some answers. Like, how did I get here, and how do I get back?'

Caleb looked at her strangely, like he didn't understand. 'You passed through a Gate, the Oak Gate, to get here. Didn't you know…?'

'Wait, passed through? I... don't even remember.' Caleb waited, watching the emotions cross her expressive face as she figured it out. 'So, it was when I went between those two oak trees...?' Alma frowned at Caleb and he nodded. 'But... I still don't get it. Is it like... magic?

'Well, I guess,' started Caleb, starting to frown as well. Then he noticed her wrist and his eyes widened.

'Where did you get that?' he asked, awe in his voice.

'Get what?' asked Alma, mystified. Caleb reached out a careful hand to touch her bracelet and they both jumped as a couple of golden sparks shot out of the stone. Alma snatched her arm back quickly.

'Wh-what did you just do?' she stammered, eyes wide.

'I don't know,' said Caleb, looking equally astounded. 'I really don't. Seriously, where did you get your bracelet?'

'Um, my mum gave it to me – it's from my father's family, an heirloom,' Alma said, rubbing her fingers slowly across the gemstone.

'Really?' said Caleb, still looking puzzled. 'I've only ever seen one other like it and it was here. They are quite rare and precious. I wonder how it came to be across in the human realm?'

Alma stared at him, her mouth open. 'You mean my bracelet came from here? But... that's impossible.'

'Impossible or not,' replied Caleb, 'that's what I mean. Are you sure you don't know anything else about it?'

'No,' said Alma. 'All I know is what I've told you.' Her voice increased in volume without her meaning it to. This place was just so confusing. All at once she wanted nothing more than to go home, even if Ellery was waiting for her. Then another voice spoke, deep and strong.

'Well met, Caleb.'

Alma looked up to see a tall robed figure silhouetted against the sunlight. She blinked, dazzled by the glare, while beside her Caleb stood up and bowed, deeply, from the waist. Alma stood up as well, bobbing her head awkwardly, feeling ridiculous. The figure moved into the shadow of the hedge and then Alma could see his face. She suppressed a gasp. His smile faded for a moment as he looked at her, a frown wrinkling his perfect brow. He looked almost shocked, thought Alma, though she couldn't imagine why. Then he recovered, holding out a hand to her in greeting.

'Welcome,' he said. 'My name is Thorion.' Alma took his hand, trying to control the pounding of her heart. But he was just so good looking! Shoulder length dark hair framed high cheekbones, a long straight nose and smooth lips that curved above a square jaw. Sea-blue eyes smiled at her. Realising she hadn't spoken and was still holding Thorion's hand, she dropped it quickly and introduced herself. Good grief.

'Alma,' said Caleb, grinning as though highly entertained. 'Thorion is our High King, Lord over both Light and Dark.'

'Uh, wow,' said Alma, blushing furiously. Thorion seemed amused by this.

'Thank you Caleb,' he said, nodding at the boy, 'and Alma, it is a pleasure to meet you. We were not sure, you see, whether you would make the crossing or not.'

'Wait – you were… expecting me?' Then she remembered – Caleb had said as much when he met her in the woods. 'But… how did you know? And why?'

Thorion smiled at her again and she almost forgot what her question was. 'Suffice to say for the moment that you were expected, which is why Caleb was waiting at the Gate,' he replied. Then his expression became serious and his blue eyes shifted colour, becoming stormy and dark. 'What is unexpected, however, is that you are wearing a talaith bracelet. It is a rare gift, a treasure of our Realm and you are lucky to have it.'

'But wait,' said Alma. 'How would I have this bracelet anyway? And, like, this is another world, like in a fairy tale? And…' She stopped as a laughing Thorion, his eyes back to sea blue, raised his hands as though to defend himself. As he did the sleeves of his blue robes fell back to reveal strong muscled arms. But really, what did they expect? Here she was, in a strange place surrounded by strangers (even if they were ridiculously handsome). A few questions were definitely in order. Folding her arms, she waited, resisting the urge to tap her foot.

'Yes, this is another world, Alma. Ambeth is home to the Lords of Light and Dark, lying adjacent to your human world. In fact, several of your fairy tales are based on mortals visiting our realm,' replied Thorion, a twinkle in his eye.

'But what about my bracelet?' She held out her wrist to him. The stone glowed a serene blue and the sunlight picked out the silvery links binding it to her wrist.

'I cannot tell you everything today, Alma, but I

promise you, I will tell you,' said Thorion gently. He bent his blue gaze on her again and she suddenly felt the urge to cry. She rubbed her hands over her face and through her hair before emerging to squint at Thorion. What was wrong with her? She shook her head.

'But I don't understand,' she whispered. 'My mother gave it to me,' she repeated, her tone becoming insistent as she looked from Thorion to Caleb. 'I think, maybe,' she went on, trying not to panic again, 'I should just go home.' She looked pleadingly at Caleb. 'You said you'd help me - please will you take me back?'

Caleb stepped forward but Thorion stopped him, a gentle hand on the boy's arm. 'Alma,' he said, his face full of compassion. 'We will not keep you here if you do not wish to stay. And do not worry about getting home. Your bracelet will help you – tell me, did you notice anything about it when you came through the Gate?

'I, um, well, the stone was, er, glowing, I guess,' she replied, frowning as she remembered the panic of her entry.

'Good,' said Thorion, smiling. 'That means it is still active. When you go back, take a moment to think about when you would like it to be, and you will get back at that time. It cannot be earlier than when you crossed over, that is all.'

'When I'd like it to be?' repeated Alma, folding her arms. 'Really?' This sounded a bit much.

'Really,' echoed Thorion, his lips twitching slightly. 'Go now, if you feel you must, but will you come back to us? We would very much like to see you here again. And hopefully, next time, we can answer some more of your questions.'

Alma looked at the High King and then at Caleb, both smiling expectantly at her. She looked around at the beautiful gardens, the gleaming Palace – were they serious? Despite her confusion, she realised she wanted to come back, to know more. This was beyond anything she had ever experienced before.

'Yes, I mean, that would be great,' she said, butterflies dancing in her stomach. 'But when?'

'Whenever you wish,' said Thorion, his smile even more glorious than before. 'You are always welcome here, Alma. Caleb will meet you at a time of your choosing. Until then.' With a nod of his noble head, he bade them both farewell before disappearing back into the garden. Alma gazed after him as he went.

'Is he always like that?' she asked, her eyes wide as she turned back to Caleb, who seemed to know what she meant.

'Thorion is somewhat…'

'Overwhelming?' said Alma, still recovering.

'Well, yes, that I suppose,' frowned Caleb. 'No, I was going to say mysterious. He doesn't mean to sound that way, he just does. He will keep his word, though. You will find out all that you need to.'

In spite of Alma's protests, Caleb insisted on taking her on a more meandering route back to the Gate.

'Thorion wouldn't lie to you,' he insisted. 'Your bracelet will take you back home in time. Besides, don't you want to see more of the gardens?'

Alma, wringing her hands as she looked around her, finally gave in. She was already really late – a few more minutes wouldn't make any difference and she did want to see more, she couldn't deny it. Besides, she still wasn't sure that any of this was real. So, squashing her worry down she wandered through the gardens with Caleb, taking winding paths past flowerbeds and sections of green lawn. Hedges rose around them like a maze and every corner revealed something new – an intricately carved stone bench next to a fountain, a small wooden bridge leading to a summer house perched on the edge of a pond, a perfectly circular green lawn strewn with colourful cushions.

'This place is… amazing,' Alma sighed. 'You could spend days exploring, I guess.'

'The Gardens are very old and constantly changing.' Caleb smiled, pride in his voice. 'They are a wonder of our world.'

Finally, they reached the meadow path and Alma fell silent, lost in thought. 'Oh, I'm sorry,' she said, blushing a little when she eventually came out of her reverie. 'I'm being rude. It's just, there's so much to take in.'

'I know,' said Caleb, grinning at her. 'And you're handling it really well, you know.'

Alma laughed. 'Thanks. I think it'll hit me later, you know? It's all just a bit… surreal at the moment.' She looked down for a moment, hands in pockets, then up at Caleb. 'So, can I ask some more questions?'

Caleb nodded. 'Ask away,' he said. 'I told you I'd explain as much as I could.'

'Okay, so…' Thinking hard, Alma framed her first question. 'Have you always lived here, in… Ambeth? Did I get that right?' she asked, stumbling over the unfamiliar word.

'Yes, always,' said Caleb, seeming amused. 'I was born here. And yes, you got it right.' He nudged her gently with his elbow and she grinned, finding his presence oddly comforting as they walked through the field under a sky not her own.

'And, are you one of the Light, or-or the Dark?' She was sure she already knew the answer; Caleb just felt so right, she knew he had to be of the Light. But his response surprised her.

'I'm neither. Well, my allegiance lies with the Light but actually, I'm half human.'

'How… what?' Alma couldn't think of any way to ask the question that didn't seem rude but Caleb knew what she was getting at. He briefly looked away from Alma before replying, his face dappled in light and shade as they moved between the whispering trees.

'My mother was human,' he began. This brought up a whole new lot of questions for Alma, but she wisely kept quiet, sensing all would be revealed. After a small pause Caleb went on. 'My father was of the Court of Light. He travelled over to your world, met my mother and they fell in love. When she became pregnant, he asked her to come back here to be with him but something happened, I don't know what exactly and they split up before I was born.

She decided to stay here and raise me but,' his voice grew low, 'I have never known my father.'

'But, I- I don't understand,' said Alma, treading carefully. 'Surely your mother can tell you-'

'She died,' said Caleb, still quiet. 'She died when I was small and so she never did tell me who he was.' His face clenched with anger for a moment. 'I have a set of leather armour from him, but that's all. I don't remember her much really, just an image of long golden hair, a voice singing, warmth.'

'Oh, Caleb,' Alma said, but he shook his head.

'No, it's all a long time ago now. I was brought up in the Court, I've never wanted for anything – it's all fine.'

But Alma wasn't fooled. Gently, she took his arm and linked it with her own, looking into his blue eyes that still carried a shadow of pain. 'My father died before I was born. In an accident. I don't really know much about him either.'

Caleb said nothing, just nodded, squeezing her arm as it threaded through his. Together they walked to the Gate, the sun waning as the day began to end, a cool breeze blowing through the glowing green woodland. Just before they reached the twin oaks, Alma spoke again.

'So you've never wanted to come across to my world?' she asked tentatively, not wanting to offend Caleb. 'You know, meet your mother's family? See where she came from?'

Caleb took a moment to reply. 'No, not really. Not that I'm not interested or anything.' He darted a smiling glance at Alma. 'It's just that the Elders frown on anyone crossing these days. We lost two members of the Court some years ago and so the Council has forbidden anyone from making the journey across to the human world unless it is absolutely necessary.'

'What do you mean, lost them?' asked Alma, intrigued.

'Well, I don't know too much about it,' said Caleb. 'It was a long time ago. One of them went missing around the time I was born, you see. They were brothers, High Lords of Light, both lost under different circumstances. They crossed over to your world and never came back. So the Elders decided that no one else should go.'

'The Elders?'

'Lord Thorion's inner circle of advisors,' Caleb replied. Seeing the questions forming in Alma's eyes he smiled. 'We could stand here all night talking, I'm sure. But I believe you need to get back.' This last was almost a question, as though he didn't want her to go.

'Yeah, you're right, I guess,' said Alma. She felt strangely reluctant to head home, although she was very tired now, her steps dragging as they neared the Gate.

'So shall I come back next weekend?' she asked Caleb, who looked delighted at her question.

'Yes, of course,' he replied, smiling broadly. 'I can meet you here, same time. Just cross over like you did before.'

Like she did before. Alma made a face as she remembered what had caused her to come through the Gate in the first place. She told Caleb, who looked shocked.

'What, they *made* you come through? I thought humans didn't know about us.'

'Well, I don't know how they could have known about it but I felt... herded. And one of the girls pushed me through.' Looking at the Oak Gate she noticed a symbol carved on each tree trunk – one shining with a clear pearlescent light, the other glowing an ominous dark grey, like a thundercloud. 'I hope they're not still there.' She bit her lip.

'By the time you get back, they'll be gone, I'm sure of it.' Caleb tried to reassure her.

'Well, I have to go, either way.'

She moved towards the Gate. Looking up at the huge trees, their branches spreading green above her, she was reminded of the old oak guarding the field gate near her home. But there was something else here, she could feel it. Almost like a thrumming in the earth, moving through the soles of her feet like static electricity. Perhaps she was meant to tap into it somehow. Frowning, she looked back at Caleb. 'So, how do you think it works, this whole bracelet thing? Do I just... focus? Is that right? I think that's what Thorion said.'

Caleb shrugged. 'I don't exactly know, having never done it myself. But I think that's what Thorion meant. Just close your eyes and think of when you'd like it to be.'

'There's no place like home,' murmured Alma. Seeing Caleb's puzzled face she grinned. 'I'll tell you later and... thanks. For everything, I mean.' Still smiling, she turned back to face the Gate and took a deep breath, clasping her hand over her bracelet. Closing her eyes, she pictured the park she hoped was on the other side. No earlier than when she left, Thorion had said. She thought back to the frightening moments before she crossed over – no, that wouldn't do. Instead she thought of the park as she had seen it on so many other evenings, the shadows lengthening under the trees as the sun went down, the lights coming on over the tennis courts and along the pathways. She felt the bracelet become warm under her hand – this must be it. 'See you soon,' she said to Caleb, who had been watching her with interest. Opening her eyes she stepped into the space between the two oaks. With a flash of light, a warping of the air around her, she was gone.

Infinite Possibility

Caleb walked slowly back through the woods in the growing twilight, smiling at the thought of Alma and all her questions. He hadn't wanted to take on the job of waiting for her to cross over from the mortal world, but couldn't turn down a request from the High King. Thorion had sought him out in private, a quiet conversation in the twilit gardens. Caleb came away filled with a mixture of pride and trepidation at the responsibility being laid on him. But now he was glad he had been chosen. It also helped that he thought Alma was the prettiest girl he had ever seen.

Emerging from the forest, he was surprised to see Thorion waiting for him at the edge of the gardens. He picked up his pace and crossed the meadow quickly, bowing his head as he neared the High King.

'Did she make it through safely?' asked Thorion.

'Yes, my Lord, with no trouble. She will be back, I'm sure of it,' replied Caleb, falling into step beside Thorion as he started to walk back to the Palace.

'Did she say anything to you of who she is?' Thorion asked, his face serious.

'She does not know yet,' said Caleb. 'I did not tell her of the Prophecy and, well, how could she know anything? This was her first time here.' Then he stopped, shocked at his presumption in questioning the High King. But Thorion just smiled, laying a companionable hand on Caleb's shoulder as they walked.

'So she knew nothing of this place? You are sure?'

'Nothing,' replied Caleb, his face earnest. 'She was completely confused when she crossed over. But, if you'll forgive me, why do you think she would know anything?' he asked, emboldened by the hand still on his shoulder and the easy manner with which the High King addressed him. Plus, he was curious now. The way Thorion spoke of Alma it was as if she was someone special, not just because of the Prophecy. But Thorion was not to be drawn.

'That,' he said, stopping in the path and turning to face Caleb, 'may be revealed in its own time. But not yet, not here. Alma is special, you can be assured of that – as for the rest, you will just have to wait and see.'

And with that he went on his way, robes flowing behind him as he walked back towards the Palace, leaving Caleb standing on the path, a thoughtful expression on his face. Mysterious Thorion, speaking in riddles again. Still, he agreed with the High King on one thing – Alma was special. He made his way down towards the river, deciding to take a walk and mull things over, see if he could make any sense of Thorion's words.

Alma came stumbling through the Gate, her head spinning. But she had done it – it was definitely the park, the sky not yet fully dark and the same group of boys still playing football. She hailed a passing jogger and asked her the time, astonished to hear it was just over an hour since she had left the house, later than her confrontation with Ellery, but not so late that she'd be in trouble when she got home. Sitting down on her bench she dropped her head into her hands, the shadows growing around her as she considered what had just happened. Then she sat back and laughed out loud – it was all too bizarre. She looked at the Oak Gate, silhouetted against the purpling sky; from where she sat it looked like two trees among a hundred others, nothing special. But to her it was now a doorway to infinite possibility. Really, the only downside was that she couldn't tell a soul.

Getting up, she started for home, running through the darkening fields as her heart pounded in her chest, adrenalin coursing through her as reaction hit her like a ton of bricks. Finally she just lay down in the cold meadow, letting her emotions course through her, refraining with difficulty from screaming out loud. Lying on the cool earth, the scent of grass and leaf mould all around her, Alma calmed down, watching the stars as they came out overhead, still laughing occasionally at the thought of it all. Eventually she sat up and slowly got to her feet, brushing mud and dead leaves off herself as she made her way to the small wooden gate. Stumbling down the street, her legs barely holding her up, she headed for home.

Eleanor stood at the back door, looking at the woods beyond her garden fence, her face creased with worry. Perhaps it was the second sight her mother swore ran in their side of the family, but she felt with growing urgency that the past was about to catch up with her. She thought of Alma's father – how they had loved each other! The pain of losing him was one she would carry until she died. It was a private sorrow, but one that she knew one day she would have to share with her daughter. With their daughter. Alma deserved to know who her father was, where he came from, to understand why she was the way she was. Eleanor had always meant to tell her but had never found the right time. Now she was worried that time had run out – that Alma might discover the truth before she could talk to her. Chewing on her fingernail she stared out into the growing dark, at the beckoning woods, her blue eyes clouded with pain. At least she had given Alma the bracelet, just as her father had wished. Hearing the rattle of the side door she turned, relief flooding through her. She rushed to meet her daughter.

Alma came through the side door to find her mother waiting for her in the hallway, leaning against the wall with arms folded. 'Alma,' Eleanor said, her voice betraying her concern as she took in her daughter's dishevelled state. 'I was starting to get worried about you. Where have you been?'

'At the park, like I told you,' Alma said with a scowl. She did not need this. Pulling an errant grass stalk out of her long hair, she pushed past her mother to get to the kitchen, well and truly coming down from her adrenalin rush of before. 'It's not even eight o'clock,' she said, her voice distant as she rummaged in a cupboard. She was suddenly starving. Eleanor followed her into the kitchen, folding her arms as she leant against the counter and watched Alma.

'I called you,' she said accusingly, 'but there was no answer. What is the point of you even having a phone if you don't keep it turned on?' Alma made a face, realising her mother must have been ringing her while she was in Ambeth. She hastily tried to come up with an excuse, but her mother had already rummaged in her bag and was holding the offending phone up.

'See, you've let the battery run down again,' she said crossly.

'Hey!' protested Alma. She snatched the phone from her mother's hand and stalked out of the kitchen, taking her sandwich with her. 'I'm going to my room,' she said angrily, 'and I'll charge it up, OK? Just give me a break.'

But Eleanor wasn't in the mood. Following Alma upstairs, she positioned herself at the door to her daughter's room and leant against the doorframe, arms folded. 'Alma, where were you tonight?'

Looking hard at her mother, Alma tried to figure out what she was getting at. 'I told you, I was at the park. Alone,' she added, forestalling the next question. Which was the truth, really, as far as she was concerned. She hadn't left the park; she'd simply gone to a... different section. 'Just let me be, will you? I've had a rough day.'

Eleanor raised her eyebrows, then sighed. 'Can I come in?'

'Fine,' huffed Alma, putting her phone on its charger before sitting on the bed, her sandwich on her lap. A yawn slipped out as tiredness threatened to overwhelm her. She knew her mother was just worried about her. She also knew that tone – Eleanor wasn't angry any more, but she did want to talk. Damn. Making a face, she crossed her legs and waited.

'So tell me about it?' Eleanor said, leaning against the chest of drawers.

'Oh, well, there's not much to tell,' muttered Alma, taking a bite of her snack.

'Well, there's obviously something,' said her mother. Alma said nothing, just chewed her sandwich and avoided her mother's gaze, wishing she had never said anything. But Eleanor just waited, her lips folded. Finally Alma sighed, rolling her eyes.

'Fine!' she said. 'I just...I saw this girl from my school, Ellery, at the park and, well, she was kind of – oh, it's nothing, it doesn't matter.' She took another bite of her sandwich. But her mother didn't look like she was going to leave any time soon.

'Ellery was what?' asked Eleanor, concern in her blue eyes. 'Is she causing problems for you?'

'Oh god, Mum, just leave it! It's nothing, don't worry about it.' The last thing she needed was for her mother to get involved. 'Mum,' she went on, taking another mouthful of sandwich, wanting to change the subject. 'I need to ask you about my bracelet.'

'Your bracelet? Why, what do you want to know?' Eleanor's face changed and Alma picked it up immediately. Her mother didn't want to talk about her bracelet. Well, that was just too bad.

'It came from my father, right? From his family?'

Eleanor stared at her a moment before speaking. 'Yes, that's right. He gave it to me when we were... courting.' Alma looked at her mother curiously. An old-fashioned term, courting; it brought to mind chaste walks in the park, stolen kisses and scented letters. While the reality would have been much more intense than that – Alma's existence was proof of it. Pursing her lips, Alma realised just how little she knew about her mother and her life before Alma was born.

'So... is it an heirloom? Do you know where it came from, how he got it?'

'I think, maybe, his father gave it to him. All I know is that it's very old,' Eleanor dissembled, obviously hoping to close the matter. But there was no way Alma was letting it go, not after the day she'd had.

'But, surely you know something more – didn't he tell you anything about it?'

Eleanor closed her eyes for a moment, then she opened them, letting out a sigh. 'Your father gave the bracelet to me not long after we met,' she said quietly. 'He said it would protect me and, well, I humoured him because it was just so romantic, you know, that he wanted me to be safe.' Her voice grew wistful, her blue eyes soft as her thoughts moved back into the past. 'When I was pregnant with you he made me promise I would pass it on to you when you were old enough. It meant a great deal to him; he loved you so much, even though you weren't born yet. So in giving it to you I am honouring his memory, which is why I want you to wear it. You are very like him, you know.' At this Eleanor stopped, tears obvious in her eyes and Alma, her irritation gone, went to hug her mother.

'I wish I knew him,' she said.

'So do I, Alma, more than you can imagine,' said her mother, her voice unsteady. She pulled back to look at Alma and smoothed her long red hair. 'You're so like him.' Her voice choked up and Alma hugged her again, shocked. She'd figured she must look like her dad, but as she'd never seen even a picture of him, it was hard to know. This was already more than her mother had ever told her about him. She let go of Eleanor and looked at her.

'I'm sorry if I worried you, Mum – really I am.'

Smiling through her tears, Eleanor shook her daughter a little. 'I know you are – you just have to ring me, OK? I just need to know you're all right.'

Vanishing Act

'Hey, what's up? Did you hear what I just said?' Sara, sitting on Alma's bed, broke off with a frown and poked Alma in the side. Then she grabbed the controller and turned down the music playing in the background, waiting for Alma to answer her.

'Sorry,' said Alma, who was lying back, gazing at the ceiling. 'I am listening, it's just, last night at the park...' She stopped, tilting her head forward to look at Sara.

'What? Did... something happen to you? You've not really been yourself since I've been here.' Sara made a face. 'And I've been going on about Josh this whole time.'

'Oh no, I mean, it's totally exciting about him,' Alma cut in. She sat up and pushed her hair out of her eyes. 'It's... well... I had another run in with Ellery last night.'

'What!?' shrieked Sara, pushing Alma in the shoulder. 'And you didn't even tell me?'

'Well,' said Alma, rubbing her shoulder, 'you haven't

really given me the chance to - but,' she continued hastily, seeing Sara's hurt look, 'I was going to tell you, I promise. I just wanted to hear your news first.'

'Forget about my news!' cried Sara. 'Tell me what happened. Oh, I can't believe you ran into her again after yesterday. Did she have another go at you?' Sara examined Alma as though she expected to see bruises forming before her very eyes. Alma laughed, gently pushing Sara back. Then her face grew serious.

'She did, and I don't think school's going to be much fun for the next little while, at least while she's around.'

'That bitch!' said Sara. 'Just wait till I see her-'

'There's nothing you can do, Sara,' Alma interrupted. 'She hates me.'

'So, what happened?' asked Sara, her pleasant face creased with worry.

'Well, I had gone to the park just to walk, you know, clear my head...' Alma related the events that led up to her being pushed through the Gate, stopping short at that point. Sara was aghast.

'That absolute cow – who does she think she is? Did... did they hurt you?'

'No, well, that's the weird part. They sort of, um herded me into the woods but then I-' Alma stopped. Hating herself, she decided to lie. There was just no way Sara would believe what had happened next. Rubbing her face with her hands, she went on. 'So, I somehow managed to get away from them and, er, just ran home.'

'Alma, why didn't you ring me! Oh my god, that is just insane!'

Alma shrugged. "Well, my phone had run down and it was late and I was a bit shaken up. I'm sorry.'

'No, no, that's fine,' said Sara, obviously distressed by Alma's story. Her brow furrowed as she considered what might happen next. 'I totally understand. But that's just unbelievable – what is her problem?'

'I know, right? I kind of feel sick about going to school on Monday. What am I going to do?' said Alma.

Flopping back on the bed, Sara looked across at her friend. 'This is not good,' she said. 'But, whatever happens, whatever she does next, we'll face it together, OK?' Alma smiled across at her.

'Thanks,' she replied, 'but I don't want you to-'

'Get involved?' Sara raised her eyebrows. 'I am involved, Alma, and there's no way you're dealing with this alone.'

'Well, thanks,' said Alma. Gratitude and love for her friend mingled with guilt at her secret and she felt awful about not being able to tell her. She poked Sara in the side, causing her to squeal. 'So, tell me more about Josh?'

Alma woke bleary-eyed Monday morning. She barely had time to wash, change and gulp down some breakfast before running out the door - not the best start to what was sure to be a trying day. She met Sara on the front steps of the school, and as the two girls walked in through the large glass doors a pit of dread formed in Alma's stomach.

'It's all right, Alma,' whispered Sara, staying close to her. 'I can't see her anywhere.' She scanned the crowded foyer, teachers and students everywhere. 'Although… that's odd.'

'What's that?' said Alma, instantly on alert. Sara jerked her head. Alma looked across the foyer to see Ellery's two sidekicks standing against the wall, deep in conversation. Nonplussed, Alma looked at Sarah.

'Well, where's Ellery?' Sara said, her expression perplexed. 'They go everywhere together. Maybe she's sick today?'

Alma shrugged. Then, looking again at the two girls, she narrowed her eyes. Grabbing Sara by the arm, she started across the foyer towards them.

'What are you doing Alma?' Sara hissed, frantic. 'Are you seriously going to talk to them?'

'It's two against two,' shot back Alma, 'and besides, what are they going to do here?'

Fronting up to the two girls against the wall, Alma stared at them, arms folded and one eyebrow raised, Sara at her side. The girls' conversation petered out as they turned to look at Alma, clearly irritated at the interruption.

'Yes?' said Dee, her tone dismissive. 'Can we help you with something?'

'Actually, you can,' shot back Alma. 'You can tell me what your problem was in the park on Friday.' She tapped her foot, waiting for an answer.

Dee looked at Nicole who shook her blonde head, looking confused. Dee shrugged, then turned her dark eyes on Alma, who almost laughed. Really, this was some act they were putting on.

'What are you talking about?' said Dee, frowning.

'Yeah, we haven't been to the park in weeks,' put in Nicole, her eyes hard.

'But… you were there. With Ellery. You threatened me!' said Alma, the wind taken from her sails.

'Why would I waste my time threatening you?' Dee asked, her tone scornful. 'And with… Who did you say – Ellery?'

She looked at Nicole as if for assistance but the other girl just shrugged and looked bored. Her black lined eyes lit up for a moment. 'Oh, do you mean that girl who used to go here? Remember, the pretty one – green eyes.' Looking at Alma she said flatly, 'Haven't seen her in weeks.'

'Wait, used to go here?' interjected Sara. 'What the hell are you on about? You were with her on Friday!'

Nicole just stared back at her. 'Are you sure? Cos I don't remember that.' Then she turned back to Dee and they started up their conversation again. Sara, her mouth open in outrage, looked as though she was about to give them a piece of her mind. Alma grabbed her by the arm.

'C'mon' she hissed. 'Forget it. Let's go.'

'But Alma –' protested Sara as she tried to pull away, still glaring at the other girls.

'Let's go!' repeated Alma. 'Talk about it later. Something weird is going on here.'

'Well, obviously,' said Sara, as Alma dragged her away. 'Freak,' she heard Nicole say as they headed to their lockers, Alma's mind working furiously.

'Who do they think they are, just turning their backs on us like that,' Sara said heatedly, slamming her locker closed. 'And,' she went on, leaning on her locker door as Alma finished getting her books, 'why don't they remember Ellery? Now that is weird.'

But things were about to get even weirder. As the week went on, hardly anyone, it seemed, missed or could even remember Ellery. Alma and Sara couldn't understand it – she had been the most beautiful girl at school, despite her obvious personality problems. How could she just disappear like that? But try as they might, they couldn't get anyone they knew to remember her other than vaguely. 'Oh her,' a few people said, 'yeah, I remember her, didn't she move away?' Some thought she had left school, while others were unsure she had ever been there at all. Frustrated, both girls eventually gave up. After all, the important thing was that she wasn't there to bother them any more.

Six Elders of Light and Dark, the most powerful in Ambeth, stood in a ceremonial circle in the Great Hall. Thorion called them to order, marking each of them with his stern blue gaze before moving to the centre of the circle. He waited a moment before speaking, until he had their complete attention.

'I have called you here on a matter of grave importance to both Dark and Light. The child of the Prophecy has been found.' He paused to let his words sink in, let their impact be felt.

Artos spoke first for the Light. He was strong postured despite the silver in his hair, his lined face filled with hope. 'Do you know this to be true, Thorion? Did you see the child yourself?'

'Yes,' replied Thorion, his expression jubilant, 'and I have spoken with her.'

It was the muscled and armoured Denoris who spoke next. The Dark Lord's golden hair shone in the light from the windows as he stood with arms folded. 'So, the child is a girl? When, may I ask, did she make her appearance in Ambeth?'

His voice was deceptively soft and Thorion was immediately on guard. 'She came through the Gate yesterday, venturing into the gardens but no further,' he said, framing his words with care. 'Caleb has been charged with her safekeeping and so will bring her to us once she returns.'

'Caleb,' said Lord Denoris, flatly. 'Ever you favour him with your tasks. Should not some other boy be given the chance to serve you once in a while?'

Thorion regarded Denoris steadily. 'You mean, someone like your son? Caleb was available to assist me in this matter. Deryck, as I recollect, was elsewhere.'

'But this is wonderful news! 'Adara interjected, her soft musical voice ringing like a chime in the vaulted hall. 'Who is she, Thorion? What is she like?'

Thorion favoured the Lady of Light with a smile. 'She is tall, with red hair. About fifteen years old, I think. Somewhat bewildered, as would be expected, but all in all, most promising. She will be back, I'm sure of it.'

'Fifteen? And she had red hair?' asked Lord Artos, suddenly alert.

'Yes.' Thorion paused for a moment, knowing what it would mean to the other Elder, but it had to be faced. 'And she was wearing a talaith bracelet, with a blue stone.'

The older Lord took in a sharp breath, closing his eyes for a moment. Adara placed her hand on his arm, her lovely face sympathetic.

'So it seems, Artos, that all is not lost after all,' said the elegant Lord Cedran, his tone sly. A spasm of grief passed over Artos' noble features and across the circle Meredan glared at Cedran, his dark eyes fierce.

'You know not of what you speak!'

'Oh, does he not?' said Denoris, seeming highly amused by the exchange.

'Enough!' said Thorion in a commanding tone, fixing Cedran and Denoris with a hard stare. 'This is a discussion for another time. What is important is that the girl be allowed to choose of her own free will, that she not be told anything of who she is until the time is right. I believe this is the only way.'

'But Thorion,' exclaimed Artos, 'surely…'

'I am sorry, Lord Artos. These are my wishes on this matter and I would ask all of you,' he looked at each Elder in turn, 'to go along with them. You are all aware that as a Council we decided this long ago – that when the Prophecy was fulfilled it was to be done freely. Meeting the girl has done nothing to change this.' Seeing each of them nod as he looked around the circle, Thorion felt relieved, though his face gave nothing away. He studiously avoided the gaze of Lord Artos; the hurt in his eyes was hard to take, but he must not falter.

'So you believe she is the one who would help to restore the Regalia?' This was Gwenene, splendid in azure brocade, her blue eyes narrowed. 'What guarantee do you have of this?'

'Only that she is here,' replied Thorion, 'in the right place at the right time. If the Dark still followed the skylore you would also know of this.'

His words obviously stung. Gwenene tossed her dark hair and turned to exchange a glance with Lord Denoris, who had tensed beside her. He looked at Thorion, his green eyes hard.

'And does she have a name, this mysterious girl?' he asked.

'Her name is Alma,' replied Thorion. 'And, until she comes to choose, she is under my protection. Please bear this in mind.'

'And if she chooses the Dark?' This was from Cedran, smiling to see Thorion's momentary discomfort at the question.

But the High King rallied. 'Then it will have been her choice to make. But surely, Lord Cedran, you can see the benefits to both sides if the Regalia is returned. Its loss affects us all, do you not agree?' Thorion remained outwardly civil, though inside his anger was growing. 'And,' he went on, turning to include all the Elders, 'I trust I can count on your discretion in this matter, until the time comes for the girl to be named as part of the Prophecy.'

'And when will that be, Thorion?' asked Meredan in his deep voice, white teeth flashing in his dark face.

'Why, in the coming week, I expect. When she returns to us.'

'If she returns, don't you mean?' interjected Denoris, his expression annoyed. 'You have no assurance she will come back here, other than her word. If I had been the one to meet her at the Gate, I would have bound her to our cause there and then!'

'Then it is fortunate for us all that you did not meet her!' shot back Thorion. 'We all know your binding methods are not always... gentle, do we not, Lord Denoris?'

'But you cannot deny that I get results, Thorion.' This last was said with a half smile, while Cedran laughed out loud, earning a glare from Lord Artos. Thorion called the circle back to order – so much power in one place meant that their meetings often degenerated into shouting matches, neither side willing to cede. Still, he was adamant that no one was to interfere with Alma's right to choose.

Later that evening, sitting in his private chambers, Thorion heard a soft knock at the door. He had dismissed his servant, wanting to have time alone; now he wondered who it was had come to disturb him. 'Enter,' he called softly, and the door slowly swung open to admit the graceful figure of Adara, still in her council robes. She carefully latched the door behind her before moving towards him, her steps light on the fine soft rug. The flickering firelight played on the sumptuous fabric of her gown and her delicate cheekbones. Rising from his chair Thorion kissed her in greeting. He offered her a seat before pouring her a drink from the silver flagon on the nearby table. Cool droplets misting the shining metal hinted at the rich wine within.

'Welcome, my dear,' he said, handing her the goblet. 'It is a pleasure as always to see you.'

'Thorion,' she said, her musical voice low. 'I am sorry to disturb you at this late hour.'

'It is of no concern – I was still awake, as you can see,' he said as he sat down, regarding her fondly. He could see, by the slight furrow in her brow, that something was on her mind, and as she sat down she sighed as though letting out a breath long held. They had been friends for many years, had shared many late nights talking and drinking, though it had gone no further. Sometimes Thorion wondered why; he also wondered if Adara thought the same. Smiling a little at the thought, the High King returned his focus to the woman sitting opposite, relaxed now in her velvet chair and sipping her wine appreciatively.

'I can always trust you to have the finest vintage on hand, Thorion,' she smiled, raising her goblet to him.

'Well, what use is being High King if I cannot?' He grinned at her, then his expression grew more serious.

'But you did not come here to discuss wine with me, dear heart. What is it that troubles you?'

Adara looked thoughtful for a moment. Shadows danced around the chamber, cast by fire and lanterns. 'What was she like? I mean, was she...?'

'She was very like him,' Thorion said softly, his face half in shadow. 'And her energy shone clear. If she chooses to help us, I think we will succeed.'

Adara nodded, her face pensive in the golden firelight. 'And if she chooses the Dark?'

'Why would she do such a thing?'

'Denoris is up to something, I know it. You saw him today, him and that cat Gwenene. I am worried they will try to take the girl.'

'Oh, I think they have already tried,' replied Thorion, seeing Adara's golden eyes widen at his words. 'But now that I have brought Alma to the attention of the Council and placed her under my protection, they cannot move against her without moving against me. They will not take that risk, even to get control of the Regalia.'

'Then you know this is what they want?'

'Of course, my dear. They have wanted it for years, for all their talk of co-operation. That's why it is so important this is done properly.' Thorion drained his goblet then refilled it, offering Adara the jug as well. She declined, which made him smile. 'You would not have done so some years ago,' he said, placing the jug back on the small wooden table. Adara laughed a little, tucking an errant curl behind one ear, her eyes bright.

'Nor would I still, but I fear it will just make me sad.'

Her lovely face became contemplative as she looked at the High King. 'I am not quite myself, Thorion. I can feel things starting to move – change is upon us, and I can only hope it is for good this time.'

Thorion leaned forward, taking her hand in his own. 'Linked as we are to the Balance, change is the only constant for us – you know this,' he said. 'Not until our souls travel to the Realms of Light will we know true peace, my dear. But you are right – I too can feel it. It will happen and soon - with Alma, I think, as the catalyst.'

Adara nodded, releasing his hand to lean back once more into the comfort of her chair. Resting her chin in her hand, she smiled at him. 'Clever of you to send Caleb to meet her.'

'Yes,' replied Thorion, his face softening as he thought of the boy. 'I don't think I could have given her a better companion to help her as she came through the Gate. Plus, it gave me the chance to stop Deryck, of course.'

Adara's eyes widened. 'So he was on his way-'

'To the Gate? Of course he was. He could barely restrain himself while I was asking him about the festival.' Thorion chuckled at the memory but Adara wasn't amused.

'Do not underestimate him, Thorion. He is his father's son.'

'But not yet come into his power. He spends his days chasing girls and playing at fighting – no, I do not think him a threat as yet.'

'But the potential is there. He cannot help who he is.'

'No, he cannot,' mused Thorion, sitting back, his blue

eyes contemplative. 'Still, he may yet surprise us. He has his father's intelligence – let us hope he will temper it with common sense at some point.'

The fire crackled in the grate as they sat together. Adara finished the last of her wine and placed the goblet down. Leaning her head back, she closed her eyes and stretched a little, taking in a deep breath that she let out slowly. 'I must go, I think. I am finally becoming sleepy.'

'I am glad to know my company excites you so,' laughed Thorion. Adara laughed too, looking fondly at him. Then she stood and walked over to him, bending to kiss him on the cheek.

'You are as exciting as ever, my dear,' she murmured. 'Don't worry, I can let myself out. Sleep well.' Then, in a rustle of silk and satin she was gone, the door closing softly behind her, her perfume lingering in the air. Thorion shook his head, smiling ruefully. Few knew of his closeness with Adara and he preferred it that way. Her friendship was special to him, a bright thread in the weaving of his life and something he chose to keep close to his heart. He extinguished the lanterns, the glow of the fire the only light remaining.

Once in his bedchamber he opened the shutters to the starry night, pausing to watch the tiny flecks of light as they wheeled across the heavens. Lying alone in the glimmering dark some time later he thought again of what Adara had said, that things were starting to move. Offering up a small prayer he thought, 'May they move for the Light, this time.'

Deryck sat in his father's study, watching as he paced back and forth in front of the fire. Sprawled in a leather armchair, he sipped his wine, wondering what his father wanted with him. Finally, Denoris stopped pacing and fixed his son with a glare. Deryck tensed and sat up. He opened his mouth to speak but his father got there first.

'Tell me again,' Denoris snarled, his green eyes fierce 'how it is you managed to miss making the intercept.' He loomed over his son, furious, as he spat the words. 'Tell me again how you spoilt our one chance to gain control of the Regalia!' Walking back to the fireplace he slammed his fist on the mantelpiece, causing the ornaments there to jump and rattle.

Deryck's face darkened. 'I told you, sir,' he emphasized the word as he leapt to his feet and strode over to the fireplace, catching his father's full attention. 'I was stopped. Stopped by Thorion! What was I supposed to do?'

'You were supposed to make the intercept! No matter what!' The pair stood nose to nose, both of a similar height and colouring, both equally angry. 'Why I left this to you, why I did not give the task to your sister I do not know! Now Thorion has claimed the girl – she is under his protection and so we cannot move against her.'

'So the information was correct? The Child is a female?' asked Deryck, intrigued despite his anger.

Denoris' eyes narrowed as he looked calculatingly at

his handsome son, his mouth lifting in a half smile that was almost a snarl. 'Yes, just as we were told – a girl, from the Human Realms. Thorion has spoken with her already.'

'And did you find out any more about her?' asked Deryck, his indignation starting to subside. Moving away from his father he picked up his goblet again, taking another sip of the fine wine within.

'She has a talaith bracelet,' said Denoris, glancing at Deryck, who raised his eyebrows.

'Really? But where would a human get such a thing?'

'Maybe she found it, maybe she stole it, I don't know,' replied Denoris, waving a hand dismissively. 'Other than that, no more than we already knew. Thorion was not forthcoming with too many new details, other than the fact that he has charged Caleb with her care.' Deryck curled his lip and Denoris nodded, his face taut. 'He wants her to choose, if and when she returns.'

'To choose?'

'A side. Whether to work with Dark or Light. I do not need to tell you that it is imperative we bring her across to our side.'

'Hmmm.' Deryck looked across at his father, who merely looked back at him, waiting. 'I have been told,' he said, raising one golden eyebrow, 'that I can be fairly persuasive at times. When is she coming back?'

Denoris looked briefly amused, but his eyes still glinted fire – Deryck was not fooled that his father's mood had changed so quickly. 'Soon,' he said. 'Thorion did not know when exactly. Why he did not bind her when he saw her I do not know! Ever he seeks to be seen as fair and wise.' Denoris' voice rose again and Deryck sighed inwardly. When his father was in one of his famous tempers there was no sense to be had from him. Taking another sip of wine, he sat back down as his father raged, nodding occasionally in response to some point, his mind elsewhere. A girl, he mused. Perhaps he could still use his talents after all.

The Circle of Elders

Alma stood in front of the Oak Gate, looking around nervously. She rubbed her arms and bobbed from foot to foot, as though warming up for a race. Anticipating the warm air and sunlight she hoped was on the other side she unzipped her fleece top and tied it round her waist. Then she picked up her backpack and shrugged it on. How different this crossing was from her previous one, when she had been so frightened, not knowing what was happening to her. This time she was full of nervous excitement, though a part of her still wasn't sure whether she had imagined the whole thing.

Looking around one last time to make sure she wasn't being watched, Alma took a deep breath. 'Here goes nothing,' she said quietly, closing her eyes and placing her other hand over the stone in her bracelet. Breathing in and out, she tried to access the power she had felt in the woods. Energy started to pulse through the soles of her feet and the stone on her wrist warmed in response. It was happening! Alma squeaked and opened her eyes for a moment. But in doing so she lost the thread of power. 'Damn!' she whispered. She tried again. This time, as she felt the power build and the stone turn warm under her hand she opened her eyes and, keeping her focus, stepped between the trees.

Light flared around her and she staggered. Dizziness took over and her vision went dark. Then it cleared and she found herself in a different world.

She breathed in the warm golden air and laughed out loud, spinning around with arms wide, glorying both in her success and the beauty of the woods around her. Hearing an answering laugh she turned to see Caleb coming up the path towards her, a wide grin on his face. Running to meet him, she grabbed his arm in excitement.

'I did it! I did it!' she laughed, giddy with the sense of achievement. Caught up in the moment, Caleb grabbed her hand and twirled her around.

'I'm glad to see you too.'

Back in her own world it was autumn, where leaves fell from branches that stood stark against a cloudy sky, the winds cold and the days shorter. But here in Ambeth the blossoms were only just starting to fade and the air was pleasantly warm. Alma, still finding it hard to believe that she'd made it through, was bursting with questions for Caleb.

'So, what do you want to know?' he asked, his tone teasing. 'I mean, we only have a few hours so...'

Alma punched him lightly in the arm. 'Hey, that's unfair,' she grinned, 'I mean, there's so much I don't know yet.'

'Well, ask away,' smiled Caleb, rubbing his arm and making a face in mock pain. 'Just don't hurt me anymore, OK?'

Alma shook her head and smiled as she fell into step beside Caleb. She thought hard. What did she want to know about first? She decided to start with something basic. 'So what do the symbols on the Gate trees mean?' she asked. 'I mean, the pearly one must represent the Light, while the thundery one looks to be for the Dark, but do they actually mean anything?'

Caleb smiled at her, charmed by her obvious interest in his world. 'Well, I don't know much more than that myself,' he replied. 'Thorion told me once that they are very old and in a language that few can read or understand any more. Other than that I cannot tell you, except that wherever you see them there stands a Gate between Ambeth and your world.'

'And the Elders?' she went on. 'Who are they? Are they all very old?' At this Caleb laughed, his blonde head going back as the sun danced through the leaves onto them both. 'Hey, what's so funny?' she said, making a face at him. Climbing over a fallen tree, Caleb offered his hand to Alma. Still scowling, she took it and clambered across, letting go as they started walking again. 'So?' she said, nudging him.

'Nothing, I'm sorry,' he said, his blue eyes full of merriment. 'It's just, you have a new way of looking at things, I suppose. The Elders aren't old people. That is, they don't appear old. I suppose to humans they would be very old indeed.' Alma looked at him, slightly shocked.

'So, th-they aren't human?' Her voice went up at the end of the question to almost a squeak.

'Well, no,' said Caleb, giving her a quizzical look. 'You remember, I told you I was only half-human the last time you were here. Those who bear the full blood of either Light or Dark are very long lived – a century passing in your world would be but a few years to them.' Steering Alma around a boulder that jutted from the high bank next to them he went on, warming to the topic. 'Thorion is High King over all and the Elders are drawn from the Dark and Light to form his Council, acting as advisors. There are about twenty in all at any given time, with a smaller number of the highest ranking Lords forming his inner circle.'

Alma was silent for a moment, thinking it over. Thorion had seemed quite young to her - no more than thirty, she would have said, and yet here was Caleb saying he was hundreds, possibly a thousand years old. She remembered Caleb describing himself as half-human but hadn't stopped to consider what that meant.

'But, what about you? I mean, if you are half of the Light, does that mean you'll live longer as well?' she asked.

Caleb shook his head. 'I may live a little longer than the average human,' he said, 'but not much longer – it is just the way of things. The human blood in me, I suppose.'

A shadow seemed to pass over them for a moment as the sun went behind a cloud. Alma shivered. 'Are you cold?' asked Caleb, concerned. 'Here, have my cloak.'

He started to unfasten the neckties but Alma stopped him. She pulled her hoodie from around her waist and shrugged it on over her t-shirt. 'See, problem solved. But thanks for the offer anyway.'

As they resumed their walk, Caleb took her arm to link with his. She glanced at him, unsure and he looked taken aback. 'You don't mind, do you? I mean, we did the other day-'

'No, no, it's fine,' said Alma hastily, smiling at him, It was fine - in fact she liked it. She just wasn't used to it. There was an awkward silence before Caleb spoke again.

'So, how was the crossing?'

'Well, it was fine, I guess,' replied Alma. 'I mean, I just did the same thing as last time and it seemed to work. I'm here, anyway.'

'It's good that you're wearing your bracelet again,' went on Caleb. 'Do you know it will also protect you from being trapped here too long?'

Alma looked at him, surprised. 'You mean, I could get stuck here if I wasn't wearing it?' That didn't sound good – she had better make sure she was wearing it every day from now on. Caleb looked serious.

'Well, it has happened – some humans have crossed over by accident and not been able to get back. There is a village on the other side of the meadow which is mostly humans – those who have come across and chosen to make their life here, others who have come over and not been able to get back for one reason or another.'

'Really?' said Alma, amazed. She didn't remember noticing a village last time but then there had been so much going on it wasn't surprising. As they came through the low bushes into the meadow, Caleb stopped and pointed.

'See?' he said. Alma looked to where he was pointing and saw a small huddle of stone houses at the far end of the field, some with smoke coming from their chimneys. Their small gardens were bright with flowers and greenery. It looked pretty and peaceful, a perfect small village. But if what Caleb said was true...

'But how awful,' she said, glancing again at the village as they started across the field, 'to be trapped here! I mean, I wonder what their families think?'

She looked at Caleb, her face creased in concern and he nodded, although he looked unsure as to why she was so worried. 'I believe they all look after each other, you know, regularly checking the Gates just in case. Newcomers are welcomed into the community and looked after very well, by all accounts. It's not so bad a place, you know,' he added, smiling again.

'Well, no, I guess not,' said Alma, a little shocked at Caleb's casual attitude. They had reached the gardens and went to sit down on a cushioned bench in the shade of a giant eucalypt, silver green leaves scenting the air. She tried to get Caleb to understand. 'But... What about their lives in the human world? I mean, can they ever get home, if they want to?'

Caleb sighed, looking at her with eyes blue as the sea, his expression gentle. 'Well, for those who wish to return to their homes, there are some members of the Light who will take them back across, if petitioned. The problem lies in how much time may have passed since they crossed through.'

'So, they might have been gone only a few days here,' asked Alma, struggling to understand, 'but they could get back and find-'

'-that much more time has passed in their world.' Caleb finished. 'So you can see, it's not always the best solution.'

'Wow,' said Alma. 'That is... a lot to think about. I mean, there are stories in my world of people who spend a night in fairyland only to come back the next morning and find a hundred years have passed. I just thought they were fairy tales, but now...' She was silent for a moment, her hand to her mouth. 'So how is it that I'm able to cross through in normal time? Is it the bracelet?'

'I guess,' said Caleb. 'At least, that's how I understand it.' He ran a hand through his hair, making it even more unruly than before. 'The best person to ask would be Thorion, I suppose. He knows far more about these things than I do.'

'I-I will,' said Alma, a little distracted at the thought of the handsome High King. Her face lit up. 'So, will I get to see him again?'

Caleb smiled at her obvious eagerness. 'Yes, in fact he's waiting for you right now,' he said. 'They all are.'

'They?' said Alma.

'Yes, he has assembled the Court, both Light and Dark. To see you.'

'So, what are they like, the High Court, I mean,' puffed Alma, as they hurried along the paths to the Great Hall.

'Oh, you'll see,' said Caleb enigmatically.

'But – oh, just slow down a moment, will you,' Alma said crossly. Seeing Caleb's face as he stopped and looked at her, she apologised quickly. 'Sorry.'

Caleb shook his head, coming back to Alma and linking his arm through hers. 'No, you're right, I was being unfair,' he said as they resumed their path through the gardens, but at a more sedate pace. 'I always get nervous when the Court assembles. It's just, seeing them all together, the High Lords of Light and Dark, well, it makes me remember just how ordinary I am.'

'How do you mean?' Alma was more curious than ever. 'D'you mean, like, they are mystical creatures and-'

'No, no,' Caleb replied, laughing. 'Nothing like that. No, I mean I just *look* ordinary, that's all.'

Alma considered Caleb as he walked beside her. He was a little taller than she was and nicely made, with straw blonde hair above a freckled, smiling face. His eyes were beautiful, she decided. A shifting blue-grey like the sea, they were fringed with dark lashes and, as they stared into hers, she realised she had been looking at him without saying anything for far too long.

'Oh!' she exclaimed, blushing. 'That was so rude of me, I'm so sorry,' she went on, apologising for the second time in as many minutes. 'I didn't mean to stare, I was just trying to figure out what you meant... I mean, I don't think you look ordinary at all. You look... nice,' she concluded, which brought a broad smile to Caleb's face.

'Thank you,' he said. 'So do you – in fact, I think you'll fit in quite well.'

They arrived at the Hall and Alma had no more time to wonder what Caleb meant as they approached the large wooden doors. They were wondrously crafted, with hinges made from intricately shaped and figured metal that curled across the carved wood like living things, flanked by stern guards in dark blue livery. One of the guards smiled slightly and stepped forward to open one of the massive doors for them. They stepped into the foyer and Alma gasped in amazement, hanging on to Caleb's arm as she took in the magnificent space. Pale pillars of carved stone supported a painted timber ceiling and a large glass dome let in light to flood the mosaic floor, where tiled vines twisted and curled around mystical creatures. The walls were made of the same pale stone blocks as the pillars, their mellow sheen and soft edges speaking of time beyond imagining, hinting at how long ago the Palace had been built. Doors and passageways led off between the pillars. Alma could have stayed there all day just looking around, but Caleb pulled her gently forward to the next set of carved wood and metal doors. These were even more beautiful than the last and manned by another set of stern guards. Once again, the doors were opened for Alma and Caleb to pass through, and once again Alma gasped once she was on the other side. But she really couldn't help it, not this time. It wasn't just the room, the glorious stained glass windows drenching the space with coloured light, the mosaic floor and high arched ceiling of timber and stone. No, it was the company within that had amazed her so. For every single person in that room, regardless of age, colouring or gender, was utterly, heartbreakingly gorgeous.

At one end of the Great Hall, almost hidden behind a tall column, stood Deryck, bored as usual by the assembled Court. Nearby, a small group of young women sighed and giggled at the sight of him, but he had no time for their silliness today. He had answered Thorion's summons only because he had no other excuse, and because his father had insisted he come along. Still, he felt it a waste of a beautiful day.

Then the doors opened and Caleb came in. Deryck's eyes widened and he straightened up, hardly able to believe what he was seeing. For, walking beside Caleb, looking bewildered and nervous, was the strange girl he had seen a week ago in the gardens – what was she doing here? Deryck smiled, moving further back behind the column. All at once the day had become much more interesting.

Despite their overwhelming looks, there was something strange about the assembled Court, an aura of otherness that felt alien to Alma. Each and every one of them was just too perfect, their unblemished beauty looking as though it had been digitally enhanced, making them appear not quite human. Which of course, they were not. And all their eyes were on her. She cast a panicked glance at Caleb, who stood to attention at her side. Catching her eye, he cleared his throat and bowed.

'My Lords and Ladies, may I present the Lady Alma of the Human Realm.'

Alma blushed, her fair skin giving away her discomfort, but she didn't have to worry for long. Stepping out of the glittering throng with his arms outstretched in greeting came Thorion, the High King. Alma bobbed her head and Caleb bowed again, Thorion smiling on them both.

'Welcome to our Court, Alma – it is a glad day that we see you here again. And thank you, Caleb, for bringing her to us.'

Caleb nodded, bowing once more before stepping to the side. Thorion took Alma's hand and tucked it into his bent arm, leading her towards the assembled Court. Hardly knowing where to look, Alma walked beside him, conscious of how close he was to her as the crowd parted to let them through. Her bracelet stone burned hot and she flinched. Thorion shot her a brief look of concern. She smiled back, though it was more of a grimace, moving her hand to try and get some respite from the pain. What was happening? She hoped she wasn't going to be pulled back to her own world.

Then the last of the crowd moved aside and she forgot all about it. Ahead were two thrones on an ornate timber dais, framed by richly embroidered hangings. Beyond the thrones was an alcove with a smooth shelf set into the wall, richly carved with the twisting vines that seemed to be everywhere and a small five-pointed star at the apex. Above it were words etched into the stone and picked out in gold. But the alcove was empty. Nothing lay on the shelf of stone, but Alma could see a sort of spiralling, like a presence within the cavity, shining with its own pale silver light. The weird thing was that she could feel it inside her, twisting and turning, almost painful as it drew her forwards. She let go of Thorion's arm almost without realising, moving between the thrones to stand mesmerised by the shimmering shapes, the strange heat from her bracelet gone as quickly as it came. A murmur ran through the assembled crowd and she realised that Thorion had come to stand beside her.

'Can you see it?' His voice was soft, but the acoustics of the place were such that his words carried through the Hall.

'Y-yes,' replied Alma, 'if by "it" you mean that strange sort of twisting – yes, I can see it. But… what is it?'

At her words, another murmur ran through the watching crowd. Thorion smiled at Alma, his blue-grey eyes shining. Her heart skipped a beat at how close he stood to her, and she tried to control her feelings as she waited for his response. Emotions moved across

Thorion's glorious face – joy, relief and then, hardest to understand, sorrow. Finally, he spoke. 'It is loss, Alma. Loss of the greatest treasures of our kind. And the fact that you can see it is of great significance.'

At the other end of the Hall, Caleb strained to see over the heads of the assembly. He had heard Thorion speak to Alma, but had been unable to hear her answer. However, by the murmur of the crowd he knew it to be important and, as they parted again to let Thorion bring Alma into their midst, he knew. Closing his eyes for a moment, he tried to decide whether he was happy or sad for his new friend, for he now knew she would have to make a difficult choice. Once the Prophecy was read, once she realised her part in it, the decision would be hers as to whether she wanted to help, taking on all the risk that went with it. For finding the lost Regalia would not be easy – the assembled powers of all the Light and Dark had not been able to do it. Well, thought Caleb, at least he would be there to help her, if she wanted him. His face serious, he watched as Alma was brought to stand at the centre of them all.

Alma was dazzled by the beautiful faces that thronged about her, all coming close to have a look, but at what she wasn't exactly sure. Every member of the Court was beautifully dressed in richly embroidered gowns and tunics, making her realise how completely underdressed she was for the occasion. Still, what was she supposed to do? Going to the Armorial Park in formal wear would raise so many questions it wasn't worth even considering. Her bracelet burned hot then cooled as the court moved around her – what the hell was wrong with it? At least it didn't seem like she was going anywhere. But the pain was so bad she tucked the cuff of her sweatshirt underneath the stone to try to get some relief, revealing it to the crowd. Immediately a gasp went up from those closest to her.

'Thorion, she is wearing a talaith bracelet,' said one woman, her red-gold hair bound in braids off her flawless face. Others said much the same, the words swirling around Alma until she could take no more and closed her eyes, trying to shut them out. Thorion, seeing this, raised a hand for silence.

'Enough, my Lords,' he said, though with a note of amusement in his voice. 'Let her breathe.'

The crowd around Alma stepped back, releasing her. Somewhat shaken and definitely confused, she glanced at Caleb, who smiled back reassuringly. It didn't help, really – the day had just become way too weird. Thorion clapped his hands, calling for the Court's attention.

'Three are required,' he said, his voice ringing through the room. 'Three to bear witness to what has happened here. That Alma has been able to see our loss and, as such, is part of us now. That she lies under my protection and may well be the saving of us all.'

Shocked, Alma looked at Thorion who, to her total surprise, winked at her as though they were participating in some huge joke. Maybe they were, she thought. Maybe this whole thing was a giant set up, some outrageous prank show and at any moment TV cameras would appear with a smiling host to tell her how she had been duped. But as quickly as the thought came she dismissed it. Too much that was unexplained had happened for it to be anything else. No, whatever was happening to her was real, and, she felt, about to take an even more surreal turn.

'Now I know how Alice felt,' she whispered to Caleb, who had come to stand next to her.

'Alice who?' he whispered back, but she had no time to answer. Three figures stepped out of the crowd and presented themselves to Thorion. The first was an extremely attractive blonde man, clad in leather armour and a billowing black cape. His green eyes were unfriendly. Alma looked away, quickly, to the next one. This was a woman, tall and slender, with sherry brown eyes in a golden-skinned face, her delicate cheekbones offset with curling honey coloured hair. She smiled at Alma in a friendly fashion as she approached, her russet gown swirling about her. The third was an older man, tall in posture with golden hair turning to silver and blue eyes in a lined yet handsome face. Clad in sea green, he had an unmistakeable air of authority, though his face bore the stamp of some past sorrow. He spoke first, his voice rich.

'I bear witness, Lord Thorion, High King.'

He was followed by the other two, each repeating the

same phrase which had the ring of ritual to it. The woman had a silvery, laughing voice and Alma liked her immediately. The blonde lord had a deep, powerful voice and was undeniably handsome, but something about him set Alma on edge. Thorion had moved to stand on the other side of Alma, and now took her hand, raising it with his own to shoulder height.

'So witness has been borne, by Lord Artos, Lady Adara and Lord Denoris. Let the assembled court see that the Lady Alma is now under my protection, and is to be afforded all the freedoms of our realm.'

The three witnesses all bowed deeply at these words, while the remaining assembly burst into applause. Alma glanced at Thorion, aware that something significant had taken place but not sure exactly what it was. Still, it seemed she was under Thorion's protection now, which couldn't be a bad thing, right? Once the noise died down, Thorion spoke again. He had let go of Alma's hand, to her regret.

'I will now ask your indulgence,' he smiled, looking around at the assembled Court. 'It is time for all but the Elders to leave us, for I wish to take council with them. I thank you all for coming here, on such an auspicious occasion. May Light shine on you all.' This last was greeted with applause from most, although there were murmurs of derision as well. Nonetheless, Thorion's voice was authoritative and it was clear that he held the power here. The gathered crowd began to disperse, all colour and beauty, talking amongst themselves and casting glances, not all of them friendly, in Alma's direction as they left.

Caleb also went to leave but was stopped by Thorion.

'No, Caleb, stay with us. It is your right, after all you have done to bring Alma to us this day.'

Caleb's face lit up, his blue eyes wide and shining. 'You want me to stay, my Lord?' It was clear he was thrilled. Alma grinned, pleased for him, and nudged him with her elbow as he came to stand next to her again. 'Thank you, Lord Thorion,' he said, bowing his head.

Deryck passed through the arched gallery, taking care to stay out of view as he made his way from the Hall. He was shocked to realise that the red-haired girl was not Caleb's girlfriend but instead the one he had been meant to intercept –the Child of the Prophecy. Now that Thorion had placed her under his protection it made things more difficult, but not much more. His father would be staying on for the Council – as one of the oldest and most powerful Lords of the Dark, it made sense for Thorion to keep him as part of his inner circle, even though the two rarely saw eye to eye. What was it the humans said? 'Keep your friends close and your enemies closer.' Whatever else he might be, the High King was nothing if not wise. So Deryck left the Hall, knowing his father would update him later. In the meantime, he had his own plans to pursue.

Alma, standing with Thorion and Caleb, was nervous again, a whole host of butterflies fluttering in her stomach. She wasn't sure why she was going to attend a Council of Elders but felt it couldn't be good. She looked at Caleb, concern written on her face and he moved closer to her.

'Don't worry,' he murmured, but she could see he wasn't entirely at ease either, despite his obvious excitement at being included in the proceedings. The Elders had moved to stand in a circle around Alma, Thorion and Caleb. There were about twenty in all, just as Caleb had said and they dazzled the eye with their beauty. Looking up at the stained glass windows, Alma tried to ignore all the eyes on her, hoping she wouldn't have to endure their gaze for long. Thorion moved around the circle, nodding to each Elder as though satisfying himself of something. Once he had completed his circuit he returned to Alma, taking her hands in his and smiling at her, his blue eyes crinkling at the corners.

'Alma, I thank you for your patience. I imagine this has been quite confusing for you.'

Alma looked at him, then at the assembled circle. 'Thank you… but… well, it still is really. Confusing, that is.' At this a ripple of amusement went round the room and she blushed, feeling completely at a loss.

'Then let me try and explain,' said Thorion. Alma sighed inwardly. There had been a lot of explaining lately but she was still in the dark about most things. Maybe this would be different, though she didn't hold much hope of it.

'You have seen our loss, in the alcove,' he said, and

Alma nodded, her eyes drawn back to the eerie twisting presence in the empty niche. She wrenched her gaze away and back to Thorion. 'Did you read the words above?'

Alma shook her head – she had been so mesmerised by the shifting shapes that she had completely ignored the gilded legend, carved beautifully into the stone.

'Caleb, if you would be so kind…' said Thorion, letting go of Alma's hands and gesturing to him. A hiss came from the circle and Thorion looked up sharply, his handsome face fierce as he scanned the room. Once all was silent he nodded again to Caleb, his face softening and the boy stepped forward. Clearing his throat, he straightened his shoulders and started to read the words graven on the wall, looking somehow vulnerable as he stood there in the middle of the circle.

Child of Darkness, Child of Light
Hair of flame shining bright
Gate of oak, stepping through
An ancient line is born anew
Find the Dark, find the Light
Then shall things be set to right
For what is lost will be found
In mist, in stone, underground

Caleb finished reading and turned to Thorion, almost as though seeking approval. Thorion obliged by nodding at him. 'Thank you.' He then turned to Alma, saying, once again, 'Do you see it?'

Alma was nonplussed. She knew what he was getting

at, of course, but didn't want to say it. The prophecy was about her. Child of darkness, child of light – she supposed that was something to do with being a human. Hair of flame – well, she'd always had red hair and the flaming temper to go with it. She'd even come through an oak gate to get here… oh, it was all very neat. But she wasn't having it, not yet. She folded her arms and raised her eyebrows. It wasn't very polite, she knew, but it was how she felt. A laugh came from one of the Elders; she thought it was Lord Artos, the older man who had stood witness as she was placed under Thorion's protection. Why this had made him laugh she had no idea, but it broke the tension in the room, everyone visibly relaxing. Even Lord Denoris smiled, although there was more calculation than amusement in his green gaze. Thorion laughed as well, his handsome face lighting up as he moved to stand in front of Alma, resting his hands gently on her shoulders. He almost took her breath away with his beauty – it was not fair, it really wasn't. Refusing to give in, Alma simply met his blue gaze, though it was difficult. Gently, no longer laughing, he spoke to her.

'Alma, the signs are all in place.'

Alma shook her head. 'And what does that mean?' she asked, her voice shaking slightly. Stepping back from Thorion, arms still folded, she turned to look around the circle. 'Don't I get any choice in the matter? Is that how these things work?' She felt sick, hating the thought of being pushed into something she didn't understand or want to do. It was all very well, being presented and protected in their fancy hall, but now she felt alone and trapped, the fantasy suddenly very real. Standing nearby, Caleb grimaced in sympathy, his fists clenched at his side as though to hold them there.

'Since the first piece of the Regalia was lost, we have been watching the stars,' said Lord Artos, his rich voice ringing in the vaulted space, 'working towards the moment you stepped into these lands. It can only be you who finds it, if you choose to help us.'

'Finds what?' cried Alma, her voice echoing in the chamber. 'You say I've seen your loss, but I still don't know what's missing!'

'Our sacred Regalia,' replied Lord Artos, his face serious, his eyes never leaving Alma's face. 'The physical manifestation of the great life force that sustains us all. A cup, a sword and a crown – all unutterably precious, all lost.'

A sigh went around the circle as he spoke and Alma stared at him, drawn in by his melodious voice and the weight and mystery behind his words. She was near to tears, feeling all eyes upon her, her arms wrapped tight around her body as though to protect herself. She desperately wanted a chair, or to leave, or to scream. This was always how these things went in the stories and now here she was, being asked to undertake a quest. Great. Bet it would involve dragons, or bats, or spiders or something she hated. She hadn't even wanted to come here in the first place. She had been forced through the Gate by Ellery, had just ended up here without even knowing where she was. It must be a mistake. But then the rational side of her mind took over. She could see what they meant; she just wasn't able to accept it as yet. But the truth was that there were too many coincidences here – the way Caleb had been there to meet her, the way the prophecy so neatly described her, even the mystery of her bracelet. Unfolding her arms she took a breath. 'OK' she said. 'I'm… not sure about your prophecy, or anything. I just need a minute to think about it. But could you at least please tell me something about this bracelet? I still don't know why I have it, or what it does. And why is it burning me?'

Prophecy's Child

Alma looked around the room, her blue eyes challenging someone, anyone to answer. The Elders' expressions varied from hostile to sympathetic, but no one said anything. They all waited for Thorion.

'The bracelet you wear is special for several reasons, Alma,' he said. 'You already know that it helps your passage through the Gates, as well as allowing you to control the time of your return to the mortal world. If you had come through the Gate without it, you could have been here only an hour but returned to find many years had passed in your own world. Its protection is vital for you, if you are to travel here again.' Alma gulped, her eyes wide, remembering Caleb telling her about the human village.

'So it's sort of... a time travel device?' she asked. There was laughter from the group but Thorion, also smiling, raised his hand and the amusement died down.

'In a way, Alma, that is correct,' he said, 'as it allows

you to manipulate time slightly by choosing the hour of your return to your world. However, the longer you remain here, the less leeway you have to return. Just keep that in mind.'

Alma nodded and Thorion reached out, gently taking her wrist in his strong hands, his thumbs moving over the blue bracelet stone and awakening glints of gold radiance that sparked about the room. Looking at Alma, his face grew stern. 'The bracelet's other gift, one perhaps even more important, is that it allows you to distinguish between those of the Light and those of the Dark. For, as you can see-' he gestured with one hand to the group surrounding them, '-you cannot trust your eyes to tell you the truth of the matter.'

Alma scanned the circle of Elders. Every single one of them was completely and utterly captivating, clothed in garments of surpassing richness and elegance of design. She had to admit she would have been hard pressed to pick any one of them as being of the Dark. So much for fairy tales, where evil was usually represented by those who were ugly and twisted. Here, darkness lay beneath the surface, not so easily discerned; perhaps a more realistic way of things. She looked down at her bracelet, her brow furrowed. 'Is it the burning sensation I feel? When one of… them gets close to me?'

The Elder closest to Alma, a vision in crimson velvet, smirked at this, and Thorion nodded, gently releasing her hand. 'That is correct, Alma. The stone heats up in the presence of the Dark, which is why you will feel it burning against your wrist. So it is a powerful gift you carry indeed.'

'Yes,' said Lord Artos, who stood nearby. 'May I?' he asked, before coming forward to lift Alma's wrist gently and examine the bracelet. He smiled kindly at Alma before releasing her and turning to Thorion, his face twisting with strong emotion. 'It is as you said, Thorion, and I-'

'I know,' said Thorion, cutting him off with a warning glance. Alma looked at both of them, wondering what the exchange was about. Artos stared at Thorion for a moment before bowing his head and stepping back to his place in the circle. Thorion returned his attention to Alma.

'As you just saw, Alma, both Artos and I were able to handle your bracelet without any adverse effects. But if any of the Dark were to touch the stone, its power would be lost.'

'My mother told me…' started Alma, perplexed. 'She told me my father gave it to her, that he said it would protect her. Is that why she wanted me to wear it?'

'Your mother is a wise woman, Alma,' said Adara, smiling. Then, intercepting a glance from Thorion, she added, 'She just wants you to be safe, as all mothers do.'

Alma wasn't buying any of this. It was obvious something was going on here. Then another Elder spoke. 'Alma, perhaps it is time we told you the truth about your bracelet.'

Someone, Alma thought it was Adara, gasped, while Thorion snapped, 'Gwenene! This is neither the time or the place!'

Ignoring him, the Elder moved towards Alma and the

stone on her wrist started to burn, so hot she almost cried out. Yet it was hard to believe Gwenene was of the Dark. Beautiful as moonlight on snow, she had long dark hair and a delicate face accentuated with eyes blue as the sky, or as the stone Alma wore on her wrist. Suddenly scared, Alma put one hand over her bracelet, flinching at the heat. The woman laughed.

'I do not wish to touch your bracelet, Alma, despite what you may think. I would not dare to do so… here.' Her voice was lilting, seductive, but the implied threat was clear. Thorion stood rigid, restrained only by Adara's hand on his arm, while Artos had taken a step forward, his face watchful. Alma stood alone in the centre of the floor, mosaic vines and flowers curling beneath her feet as the Dark Elder circled her gracefully. Her words were as sinuous as her movements and the silk of her gown rustled as she moved like some beautiful, dangerous animal prowling around its prey.

'So, Alma, you are wondering how it is that your bracelet made its way from the Eternal Realms to your own sorry land, and how it is that your mother would come to hand it to you.' Her tone was insinuating, inflected with some private humour.

Alma just nodded, her mouth gone dry.

'Well, these talaith bracelets, these so-called treasures of the Light, make their way out of this land so easily, it seems.' Gwenene paused to look accusingly at Thorion, who simply stared back, impassive. She moved behind Alma and trailed her cool hand across her red hair. Alma shivered, though she fought to hide it. This seemed to amuse the woman even more. She moved closer to Alma, brushing her hair aside, almost whispering in her ear. 'You see, when the Light fall in love with one of your humans-' another sideways glance at Thorion '-they wish to protect their loved one and so they give them one of these bracelets, so that not only can their precious one cross over when they wish, but they are also safe from the Dark.' Gwenene laughed, a harsh sound, while across the room, Lord Denoris bared his teeth in response, less a smile than a snarl.

Alma struggled to keep her breath from gasping, her shoulders tight. As the Elder moved away from her again she rubbed her sore wrist and glanced at Caleb, whose usually amiable face was hard with anger. Gwenene continued: 'Not that it would help, not really, if the Dark wanted you.' She smiled again, showing her teeth, obviously amused by the expression on Alma's face, which she was unable to control as her fear took over.

'Enough!' snapped an enraged Lord Artos, but Gwenene was not to be deterred.

'So you see,' she went on in her hissing voice, blue eyes narrowed in her exquisite face. 'Humans who are given these bracelets treasure them, not just because of the powers they bestow, but also because of the precious memories they represent.' This last she said with a slight sneer, which pushed Alma over the edge from fear to anger. She thought of her mother, the pain and tears in her eyes as she spoke of Alma's dead father, and her temper flared. Gritting her teeth, she held up her hand, signalling for Gwenene to pause. This earned a half-smile from

Thorion that he quickly concealed. Summoning her courage she faced the Dark Elder, her chin held high.

'So what you are saying is that someone of the Light loved a member of my father's family and that's how they came to have the bracelet?' she said, challenging Gwenene, unwilling to submit to this woman of the Dark, to her magic and beauty and persuasive tones.

The Elder paused in front of Alma. Lifting one perfect eyebrow, she half smiled then, glancing again at Thorion, nodded her head. 'Yes,' she said, still seeming highly amused. 'Why not? Yes, that's exactly what I mean.'

Laughing, she moved across the room towards Lord Denoris, stopping momentarily in front of Thorion who looked at her for a moment before nodding his head slightly, his face unreadable. Beside him Adara glared at the other Elder, but said only, 'Thank you, Gwenene, for that clarification.'

Alma, alone again in the centre of the circle, was shaking, overcome with a mixture of rage and confusion. She'd had enough. She saw Lord Artos, his face filled with pity and concern, then took in the other Elders, most of whom regarded her expectantly, the combined power of their gaze once again almost too much to bear. Then Artos came closer to her. There was a silence in the room.

'Will you do it, Alma? Will you help us?' His voice was gentle, his lined face kind, and Alma just stared at him. She knew that this was the moment she was supposed to speak out, to say, 'Yes, I will help you,' but found the words wouldn't come.

Then Gwenene said quietly, 'Or you could help me,

pretty Alma.'

Alma's eyes widened. Something about the woman made her feel sick, despite her beauty. She saw Artos glare at Gwenene, his body tensing, and felt caught in the middle, unable to move. Seeing her distress yet another Elder, stepped forward.

'You don't have to help us, Alma,' said this Elder, her voice lilting. She was obviously of the Light, as Alma felt no response from her bracelet. Like all the others, she was beautiful, with long silver hair pulled back from the fine bones of her face, dressed in violet draperies that matched her eyes.

'No,' boomed another voice. 'Nothing is written until it has happened.' This from a tall man, handsome and strongly built, dressed in magnificent gold that shone against skin so dark it seemed to absorb light.

'Yes,' said another voice. 'Lord Meredan is right. You could leave here, after agreeing to help us, and be hit by a bus tomorrow. Sometimes the worst things happen to the nicest people.' Lord Denoris came near, close enough to loom over her. Tall and muscular, his blond hair was swept back from his chiselled face, his mouth smooth and sensual. His eyes were dark green and his smile did not reach them. Alma, filled with a strange mix of fear and attraction, met his green gaze for a moment.

'There is no need to frighten her,' said Thorion sharply. The blonde Elder glowered at him. 'What Denoris means is that there are any number of factors that could change things – you could decide not to help us, or you could, as he so regretfully put it, meet with an accident or some other misfortune that stops you achieving your potential. This is the way of things – we can see so far, but no one can tell what decisions may be made that will change things, whether it is to follow another course of action or simply step into a road at the wrong moment.'

Alma frowned. This was all so confusing! And she tried not to look at Gwenene, who was waiting, blue eyes glinting in the light from the great windows. 'So, you mean I can choose? I'm not, like, locked into this prophecy?'

'No,' said the dark-skinned Lord Meredan. 'You are free to choose, as are all humans. It is your birth right.'

'But I don't understand!' cried Alma, losing her temper. 'All this talk about fate and destiny and prophecy, then you say I can just choose! Is it one or the other?'

The Elders regarded her gravely, but not without sympathy. Finally Adara spoke. 'It is given to none of us to see the full picture,' she said gently. 'At the most we are offered glimpses of a pattern – all we can say is that you must trust yourself. While events have conspired to bring you here to us, the future is still open. We know what might happen, but it can all change in an instant based on your decision. You must search yourself for the answer. It is all we can tell you, with any certainty.'

Frustrated and near tears, Alma gazed at the floor, taking in the swirling patterns of stone. Next to her she could sense Caleb's sympathy, his warm energy. Ugh, this was so frustrating! Just her luck, really, that she would find a magical enchanted land of her very own but then discover she was some sort of long-awaited heroine. It would be so easy to walk away but that would mean she couldn't come here again, at least not in good conscience. Raising her head, she looked at each of the faces around her before her eyes came to rest on Thorion and Caleb. Both regarded her with barely concealed hope. Suddenly, she wanted to do it. When would she ever get the chance to do something like this again, to make such a big difference? The fact that it all felt unreal, as though she was observing from a distance, helped.

Taking a deep breath she spoke, wanting to say it before she changed her mind. 'Okay. Um, I'll do it,' she said, her voice husky. 'I'll help, I guess,' she added. Her hands were shaking and she fought for control, not wanting to let them know how scared she was. Lifting her chin slightly she spoke, louder this time. 'I will help the Light with their quest to restore the Regalia.' There. That sounded a bit more formal, a bit more like something you'd hear in a story, even if she had stumbled a little on the last word. The unreality of her situation hit her again and she swayed. But the reaction to her words was instant.

'Light be praised,' said Thorion, stepping forward to place both hands on Alma's shoulders, his face transformed by joy. Around the circle the relief was apparent for most of those assembled. But not for all. Denoris, Gwenene and another Lord, whose high cheekbones, almond eyes and olive skin put Alma in mind of an ancient warrior, stood together, their faces hard as they looked at Alma.

'My Lords,' said Thorion, his expression triumphant.

'Alma has chosen. Let it be written in our records that the Light is moving, to claim the Regalia and restore the Balance. May it be so.' And, bowing his head for a moment, he closed his eyes, as did the others around the circle. It was a solemn moment, broken only when Caleb grinned at Alma, his pleasure at her decision apparent. Inside, Alma felt a churning fear mixed with excitement. She hadn't the slightest idea where to look for the missing items, despite the Elders' insistence that she was the one from the Prophecy.

Thorion disbanded the Council circle and bade farewell to the assembled Elders, discreetly signalling for Adara, Artos and the golden-clad Meredan to remain. Once the others had left the hall, Alma let out a breath she hadn't realised she was holding. Adara came over to Alma and hugged her impulsively. 'I'm so glad you are here,' she said with a smile. Surprised, Alma returned the hug, not sure what to say.

'Let us adjourn to one of the council chambers,' said Thorion. 'We'll be much more comfortable there.' He summoned one of the waiting servants and ordered refreshments to be brought. All started to move except Caleb, who looked around uncertainly. Noticing his hesitation, Thorion beckoned him.

'Caleb,' he smiled, 'without your help we would not have succeeded today. Please, join us.' Caleb's face lit up as he joined the group and Alma smiled, pleased for him.

'Besides,' laughed Thorion, looking at him affectionately, 'there is not much point keeping you out of this meeting, as I am sure Alma will tell you everything anyway.'

The other Elders laughed, while Alma blushed. Caleb grinned back at her. Huh. Well, Thorion was probably right, she thought to herself. She realised then how much she had been relying on Caleb, his steady presence helping her to cope with her strange reality. She looked at him gratefully as he took her arm.

They followed the Elders through a stone archway into a small wood-panelled chamber furnished with comfortable armchairs. The others were already seated, so Alma chose the vacant chair closest to her, Caleb taking another nearby. She sat back in relief and surveyed the room, struck once again by the combined beauty of the Elders. She didn't know what Caleb had been on about earlier – he looked just as good as the others as far as she was concerned. Smiling to herself at the thought, she took a sip of the drink that had been placed next to her by one of the silent servants. Cool and refreshing, it slipped down her throat, making her realise how thirsty she'd been.

'So, my friends, here we are,' said Thorion, leaning forward as he looked around the group. Smiles greeted his statement.

'Indeed,' agreed Adara, her beautiful face beaming. Alma didn't say anything – she just waited, fear and excitement swirling in her gut as she tried to stay calm.

Artos put down his goblet and looked across at her, his expression sympathetic. 'So, my child, what do you make of all this?'

Alma paused before speaking, not wanting to say the wrong thing, conscious of everyone looking at her. 'I am still a little confused,' she said eventually, her hands twisting in her lap. 'There's so much I don't understand about this. And I really have no idea where to start looking for your… Regalia.' She said the word cautiously, testing it on her tongue.

'I can help you!' burst out Caleb, who'd obviously been waiting for his chance to talk. 'We can research the missing items in the library, try and find out more information. My tutor told me there are documents in there dating back centuries, many of them unread. We just have to start looking and we'll find it, I'm sure!' Then, seeing the combined eyes of the Elders regarding him indulgently, he sat back, suddenly abashed at his temerity in speaking out.

'It is a good thought, Caleb, and I wholeheartedly agree,' said Thorion, bringing a smile to the boy's flushed face. 'But there is more to be considered here. Alma's safety, for one.'

'My what?' said Alma. The fear inside her solidified to a hard ball that banged around inside her stomach. She felt sick and took another sip of her drink, then wished she hadn't.

Thorion turned to Alma. 'You heard me say you were under my protection – do you now see why?'

Alma thought about it before nodding, her face worried. 'It's the Dark – they want me as well, don't they.' It was not a question.

'Yes,' replied Thorion. 'You saw the Prophecy, heard

the description that it held. You cannot deny that it was about you, no matter how much you may wish to.' He regarded her fondly for a moment. His eyes gleamed blue as he smiled at her, then phased to grey. 'But there was no mention in its words of whose side you are on. That is why it is so important that you choose, and that it be done freely. The Regalia is neutral – it represents balance between the Light and the Dark, the necessary existence of both in the world. The Dark may have forgotten much of their knowledge, but not this. They seek the lost pieces just as we do, but for their own purposes.'

'So, I could have chosen to work with the Dark?' said Alma, her eyes wide. 'I… can't imagine doing that. I mean, they just felt wrong to me.'

Artos, smiling proudly, looked at Adara and nodded, as though some long held belief of his had been validated.

'It is always important to trust your instincts, Alma. What did they tell you today?' This was from Lord Meredan, his white teeth flashing in his dark face as he smiled at her.

'That the Dark were not to be trusted. That Gwenene, she was threatening me, I could feel it!' said Alma, her anger rising again at the thought of the Dark Elder. 'She couldn't hurt me there, in front of you all, but-'

'-if you met her somewhere else, somewhere alone,' went on Caleb, his eyes wide, 'she would use her powers, seek to turn you to their side.'

Seeing Alma's frightened face, Adara sought to reassure her. "Alma, you have been presented to the council, placed under Thorion's protection and have chosen for the Light,' she said in her gentle voice. 'This takes a lot of the power to harm you away from the Dark – they cannot move against you in an overt manner now. We tell you this only so you can be on your guard. We will keep you safe, I promise.'

Somewhat comforted, Alma looked across at Caleb, who gave her a friendly look in return. Relaxing, she realised that she could trust everyone in the room. But if she was going to help them she needed more information.

'So, what is the Regalia, exactly?' she asked. 'And why is it so important?'

Standing in the gardens, idly pulling apart a flower, Deryck looked up to see his father coming towards him, his face like thunder.

'So I take it she has chosen?' he said, deciding to jump straight in.

'That she has,' replied his father, his mild tone at odds with his murderous expression. 'For the Light, of course.'

'Did you really expect her to choose any differently?' asked Deryck, smiling a little. He quickly lost the grin as his father looked at him, surprised by the question. Even though he was his son, Deryck took no chances with his notoriously testy father.

'No, not really,' Denoris replied, his jaw clenching as he looked back at the Palace. 'The question is, what do we do now?'

'I have an idea,' said Deryck, smiling again, and this

time letting his father see it. Denoris raised one golden eyebrow, waiting.

'Let me seduce her,' said Deryck.

'And what purpose would that serve?' said Denoris impatiently. 'Other than sating your own desires, of course. I understand you are young and-'

'No,' cut in Deryck. 'It's not like that.' It wasn't, though he couldn't quite explain why. 'I make her fall in love with me. Then, bringing her to our side will be easy.'

Denoris regarded his son for a moment, frowning. 'The idea has merit, I admit. But, have you seen her?'

'I have, and she is pretty enough,' said Deryck, thinking of Alma as he had first seen her, walking with Caleb through the green. 'It will be no hardship for me, don't worry.'

Denoris thought for a moment then broke out into a broad grin. 'I won't,' he replied, slapping his son on the shoulder. 'So, you seduce her, make her fall for you, then you bring her to me? Is that how this will work?'

'Y-yes, I suppose,' said Deryck, the ghost of a frown moving across his face. The fact that he would eventually have to hand the girl over to his father's control troubled him somehow, but it was the only way he could see to make their plan succeed. Recovering his smile, he looked at his father. 'So, I suppose I had better get back to the Great Hall. I need to make a good first impression.'

'I'm sure you'll have no trouble. You're my son, after all.' Denoris looked at Deryck, pursing his lips as though considering. 'Fine, let us try this for a while. And Deryck,' Denoris went on, as his son started to walk away, 'I am impressed. Just make sure it works.'

Deryck grinned – his father so rarely praised him. Now to the hall, and the girl.

'Ah,' said Thorion, settling back into his chair and taking another mouthful of wine. 'That is a story in itself. You already know it has three components – a cup, a sword and a crown.'

'And that they are lost,' interjected Artos in a gloomy tone. Yep, thought Alma, already got that part. The wine, which was excellent, was getting to Artos and Adara discreetly waved away a servant hovering nearby with a full jug. Alma watched the byplay with interest before coming back to the matter at hand.

'But how did you lose them?' she said, trying not to roll her eyes. Her head was starting to hurt. 'I mean, when you lose something, don't you look where you lost it?'

'It is not so easy as that,' said Thorion. 'Our Regalia was part of the great life force that sustains us all, and so when the pieces started to disappear-'

'Wait, sorry, did you say "started to disappear"? You mean, they didn't all vanish at once?' asked Alma, her brow furrowed.

'No,' replied Thorion. 'The first one to go missing was the crown. It was some time ago, over a century ago in your world. One day it was here, the next it had vanished as though it had never been. This was when the Balance started to fail.'

'The Balance?' Alma made a face, concentrating hard as she tried to take it all in.

'Yes, the Balance of good and evil, both in our world and yours,' said Meredan in his deep voice, taking over while Thorion refilled his goblet. 'That is what we are here to preserve, this Balance. Both Light and Dark are necessary, but, with the loss of the Regalia, things have started to tilt alarmingly in favour of the Dark. For, once started, the decline is cumulative.'

'I'm sorry, you've lost me,' said Alma, slumping back in her seat. She massaged her brow as she leaned her head on the velvet upholstery.

'What Meredan means,' said Adara, 'is that bad deeds lead to more bad deeds, hate breeds hate. It has always been so, just as a proliferation of good leads to more good. We are close now to a tipping point, and the Dark is looking to gain the ascendancy once and for all. The Regalia was part of the control - with it gone, it is harder and harder for the Light to retain the Balance.'

'For the Dark has no interest in maintaining it any more,' boomed Lord Artos. 'In times past, we worked together for the common good, but no more. As they have gained in power they have lost their way. This tussle for control has cost us far more than just the Regalia.' He sat back, his mouth tight.

'But, why is the Regalia so important? I mean, they are just things – you are still here, working to maintain the whatchamacallit, the Balance, aren't you?' asked Alma.

'The importance of the Regalia lies in its neutrality – it keeps the worst excesses of the Dark in check yet allows enough pain into our worlds that we are able to appreciate beauty all the more. It also maintains the right to choose with humanity,' said Thorion. 'Humans have always fought – it is in their nature. But there have also been golden ages, times of peace and creativity when mankind has prospered and grown. If the Dark were to gain control of the Regalia then they would use it to force both this world and yours into chaos, removing free will and sending us into a spiral of destruction. This is the way the Dark likes things to be.'

Aghast, Alma stared at him. 'So, if I'd chosen not to help you…'

'The Balance would have failed, eventually. First in your world, then here.'

'But, I mean, how can that happen? Wouldn't people notice?'

Thorion shook his head, smiling gently. 'It would be difficult to notice at first. Small changes happening every day, widespread at first, making it hard to see the pattern of events, of things getting worse. Until it got to the point of no return. And then the Dark would take power and that would be it.'

'Although they wouldn't last long either,' said Meredan. 'We are all part of the same whole, Alma, and if the Balance fails, it is the end of everything. The Dark are short-sighted in this regard.' He sat back, folding his muscular arms, dark eyes sombre.

Alma was horrified. She looked around at them all, the beautiful faces, glad she had chosen to help them yet at the same time feeling more out of her depth than ever.

The end of everything? Great, no pressure then. Swallowing hard, she glanced at Caleb then reached for her drink, taking a sip before speaking again.

'So, um, the Regalia, how does it work? I mean, you both used to maintain it, now you don't. Is there some sort of ritual attached to it…?'

'It simply being here was enough,' said Artos, his lined face sad. 'Golden and glowing in the alcove, rooted deep into the land. Its power kept us all safe, kept the worst of the Dark at bay.'

'So, when did the other pieces disappear?'

'The cup was the next to go,' said Meredan. 'Again it vanished, spirited away one night.'

'Maybe you should be keeping an eye on these things at night,' blurted Alma, then blushed as everyone stared at her.

Meredan started to laugh, as did the others and Alma looked down, feeling silly. Once the hilarity had died down, Meredan nodded, still smiling. 'Yes, you are probably right. But Alma, these things were guarded, in our Great Hall, the centre of our power – we have sentries on watch at all times. We just do not know how it has happened twice.'

'So what happened to the sword? Did that vanish in the middle of the night as well?'

And with that the mood in the room changed. Unsure what she had said, Alma covered her confusion by taking another sip of her drink. Glancing at Lord Artos, she was dismayed to see a look of agony cross the old Lord's face. 'What is it?' she whispered. 'What have I said?'

Artos, unable to answer, looked away, his face working. Instead it was Adara who spoke, her lovely face uncharacteristically sad and shadowed.

'The sword was lost some years ago,' she started, then stopped, seemingly unable to go on.

As Alma looked around at the sombre faces, exhaustion swept over her. She wasn't sure how much more she could take of this. After all, it was well after midnight as far as she was concerned. Seeing this, Thorion gestured subtly to the others. The meeting needed to be brought to a close.

'I think, Alma,' he said gently, 'we have given you enough information for one day. Perhaps you would like some fresh air? I'm sure Caleb would be happy to walk with you in the gardens.' Caleb sat up at this, but Alma shook her head.

'Thank you, I mean, that would be lovely, but I think I just need to go home now,' said Alma, looking apologetically at Caleb. 'I'm just really, really tired.' She yawned then, just to punctuate the point, covering her mouth so as not to offend the assembled company.

'I will take you back to the Gate,' said Caleb, trying to hide his disappointment.

'Thank you Caleb,' said Thorion, looking fondly at them both. 'But I hope we will see you again soon, Alma?'

Standing up, Alma looked around at everyone. 'Yes,' she said, clasping her hands together in front of her as she spoke. 'I'll come back soon, as soon as I can.' She wondered to herself when that would be, then remembered her manners. 'And thank you for your hospitality. I just hope I can help you, that's all.'

Adara rose gracefully and came over to envelop Alma in her scented embrace. 'Just being here is a start,' she murmured, before kissing Alma gently on the cheek. Then she took her leave of the others and left the chamber. Artos and Meredan stood as well, taking their leave of Thorion and pausing to shake Alma's hand on the way out. Artos looked at her for a long moment, his eyes kind.

'I believe you can do this,' he said finally, touching her cheek lightly before he left the room.

Left with only Thorion and Caleb, Alma sagged a little, her mind full of everything she had been through that day. Coming to her side, Caleb put his hand on her shoulder.

'Come on,' he said, 'let's get you home.' Smiling gratefully, Alma let herself be led from the room. As the two of them left, Thorion sat back in his chair, his eyes distant, deep in thought. Could she do this for them? Only time would tell.

Walking out of the great hall, Alma started to feel unwell. 'Caleb,' she said, her voice faint. He looked around in concern, hastening back to her as she swayed.

'Are you all right?' he said, his hand on her arm to steady her, his grey-blue eyes worried.

'I'm OK,' she managed to say, leaning on the closest

pillar. The stone was cool against her hot cheek and she closed her eyes briefly. 'I-I just need a minute.'

Caleb frowned. 'Alma, you're very pale. Perhaps we should sit down.'

'No, it's alright,' she said slowly. 'I can't believe what just happened, I guess,' she went on. 'I mean, I'm supposed to be looking for something but have no idea what it looks like or where to find it, or even where to start looking.'

'I will help you,' Caleb said, his hand still on her arm, and she smiled at him. Turning her head she noticed for the first time the decoration on the pillar, which was carved with the figure of a knight offering a lady a token of some sort. As she leaned there, tracing her fingers over the shapes in the stone, Alma saw the edge of a cloak, deep green, flick around the side of one of the columns opposite – someone was there. Lifting her head she strained to see. Something about the elusive glimpse had caught at her senses, like a piece of music heard once then almost forgotten, drifting at the edge of memory. Her eyes widened as a tall figure emerged from the shadows, walking across the hall towards her and Caleb, illuminated by the glorious light pouring in through the glass dome. Her fatigue forgotten, Alma couldn't take her eyes off him. His walk was sinuous, powerful, smooth muscles working under deep green velvet, his cloak blowing out behind. And his face! Green eyes set above high cheekbones, a strong jaw and smooth moulded lips – it was the face of an angel, framed in golden hair waving back from his brow. She was shocked to feel her bracelet flare into heat against her wrist – surely someone this beautiful could not be of the Dark. But she knew it was possible, had seen earlier in the Great Hall that beauty was no indication of true nature. Yet still she couldn't believe it. All this flashed through her mind as he crossed the hall to stand before them, looking quizzically at Caleb as though expecting him to make the introductions. Which he did, though with a face like thunder.

'Alma,' he muttered, quite unlike his usual amiable self. 'May I present Lord Deryck. Lord Deryck, this is Alma of the Human Realm.'

Alma could not understand Caleb's animosity. Deryck was utterly charming as he bent over her outstretched hand, his lips brushing her knuckle. Her breath caught in her throat as he straightened and looked into her eyes, green meeting blue with an intensity that surprised her and, she thought for a moment, him as well. She cleared her throat and managed to murmur a greeting back to him. Deryck merely smiled and said. 'I hope to see you again soon, Lady Alma.'

'As do I,' she managed to stammer, before, with a swirl of green velvet, he was gone. 'God,' she breathed, gazing after him. 'I mean, wow. He was just...' Caleb looked truly annoyed.

'Don't waste your time with the likes of him,' he said. "He is the son of a Dark Lord and nothing but trouble.'

'But he seemed so... nice,' said Alma lamely. She didn't want to offend Caleb further by gushing over Deryck, but was unable to conceal her feelings completely.

'They all do – that's the trouble,' said Caleb enigmatically. After that he would be drawn no further on the issue.

Deryck smiled as he walked away from the pair. Troublesome Caleb, and... Alma. He had seen the effect he had on her – the flushed skin, the trembling hands - and yet she had affected him also, her blue eyes gleaming clear as they met his own, the flame of her red hair standing out against her dark blue top. She did not realise her own allure and that in itself was fascinating. He shook his head as though to clear it of such distracting thoughts. The plan was in motion again. His father would be pleased.

Friendships Are Tested

Alma and Sara were in the school library, supposedly doing research for a project due in a couple of weeks' time. Instead, Alma was staring into space, twirling a pencil absent-mindedly in her hand as she thought about Ambeth. Well, to be more specific, she was thinking about Deryck. About how he had looked, lit from above as he walked towards her, his eyes meeting hers, his lips on her hand... Sighing, she rested her chin in her hand. Her eyes were half closed against the light shining through the large windows running down one side of the room, the slightly warm dusty smell of books filling the air. She went back to her notes, trying once again to concentrate. Sara, writing furiously on the opposite side of the table, looked up and frowned.

'Have you finished that section yet?' she whispered. Alma, startled back to reality and seeing Sara's annoyed look, felt terrible. Not being able to tell her best friend about Deryck was killing her, but she had no idea how to approach the topic. Looking across at her friend, seeing her familiar and loved face, Alma was overcome with remorse. She reached out across the untidy piles of book and papers and touched Sara's hand.

'I'm really sorry… for everything.'

Sara stared at Alma, incredulous. 'What? Are you kidding me?'

Her voice was sharp and Alma's eyes filled with tears as she looked away, feeling even worse. She hated having to lie to Sara. How the hell was she going to do this?

But Sara's face softened. 'Hey,' she said, reaching out to poke Alma with her pen. 'It's OK. Well, it isn't, but I can see you're going through something you don't want to talk about.' Alma could only nod, while on the inside feeling relieved Sara had finally brought up the issue. Sara, her mouth twisting for a moment, went on quietly. 'But I'm here, you know, if you want to talk about it. I always will be.'

'I really am sorry,' Alma whispered, 'and I wish I could tell you. It's just, I don't even know where to start.'

'I wish you could tell me too,' Sara said. 'I don't like these secrets. I mean, I know something's going on with you, I just don't know what.'

Alma grimaced, her chest feeling tight. It was just too much to keep inside. She needed to talk to Sara, even if she couldn't tell her the whole story. 'Well, there's this guy…'

Instantly, Sara was all ears. 'What? Who? Oh my god, where did you meet him?' Her voice had risen in her excitement and there were several shushes. Lowering her voice, Sara leaned forward over the table and said, 'Tell. Me. Everything.'

Alma thought fast. 'Well, he's from out of town. A-a friend of the family. I haven't seen him in years and, well, I met him again last week and he is, well, he is totally gorgeous.' Wincing slightly, she hoped Sara wouldn't see through the half-lies she was telling. But Sara was agog.

'And…' she breathed, twisting her pen in her hands and wide eyed with anticipation.

Alma shook her head. 'There's not much more to tell. I mean, except I can't stop thinking about him,' she said, blushing furiously.

Sara squealed in excitement. She waved her hand when the shushes came again, as if to say 'Whatever'. 'I knew it!' she hissed, 'I knew it! What does he look like?'

'Tall, blonde, green eyes, gorgeous,' said Alma, smiling as she pictured Deryck walking across the foyer towards her. Hmmm.

'Wow.' Sara sat back, still twirling her pen. Then she frowned. 'But why has this been freaking you out? I mean, why couldn't you tell me about it?'

Seeing Sara's earnest face Alma didn't know what to say. 'I know, I should have told you before but it was all a bit, um, weird, I guess, him being a family friend and all,' she finished weakly. 'I'm really sorry. Plus I'm still a bit freaked out by the whole Ellery thing.'

'I *know*,' said Sara, her eyes wide, forgetting to keep her voice down again. 'It is weird, right? The way no one really remembers her anymore? I still don't get it.'

Alma nodded, standing up and starting to gather her

books together. 'C'mon,' she said, looking around at the indignant faces. 'Let's get out of here and go somewhere we can talk properly. We can do this later.'

'Yes, I need to hear more about this guy!' said Sara, hastily shoving her stuff into the jumble of her bag. The two friends left the library smiling, both relieved that things between them were back to normal.

As she walked up the spiral staircase behind Adara and Caleb, Alma wondered what was going on. Ambeth was still so new to her she was never sure what to expect each time she visited. She had come across as planned to meet Caleb and the Elders but when they reached the Great Hall only Adara was there; the others, she explained, would arrive later. 'In the meantime, though,' she said, looking very pleased with herself, 'Caleb and I have a little surprise for you.'

Intrigued, Alma had followed them out of the Great Hall, through the foyer and behind the great pillars to a stone stair that curved up into one of the towers.

'Where are we going?' she asked finally, amused by all the secrecy and by Caleb, who was obviously bursting with excitement.

'This is one of the towers that house the apartments of the Court,' explained Adara as they continued on up the curving stair. 'On this level-' she gestured with one slender arm as they passed through the first floor and

Alma glimpsed a corridor lined with several timber doors '-our friend Caleb has a room.'

Alma looked quizzically at Caleb – were they going to see his room? But he shook his head and Adara led them up one more level, past a window set into the tower wall through which Alma caught sight of the distant sea. They arrived at the second floor and a similar stone hallway, lined again with several wooden doors. Pausing at one halfway along, Adara, a mischievous smile on her face, produced an ornate golden key.

'Will you do the honours, dear Alma?' she asked, handing her the key. Perplexed, Alma fitted it into the lock and turned it – the latch popped with a click and the door swung open. Caleb and Adara both smiled widely and motioned for her to go in. So she did.

Her eyes opened wide as she looked around. The shape of the room followed the curve of the tower, the stone walls panelled with carved wood to two-thirds of their height. A large fireplace dominated one wall while a bed sat opposite, made up with white linens and a velvet bedspread in shades of green that echoed the twirling vine patterns of the deep rug underfoot, guarding against the chill of the stone floor. The ceiling was vaulted, painted a dark blue with golden stars picked out, just like the night sky. Alma imagined how it would be to lie in that bed gazing up at the stars, cradled in feathers and soft velvet, like lying in a cloud. Another door was to the right of the bed – on further investigation Alma found it opened onto a small bathing chamber.

'What a beautiful room!' she said, turning to Caleb and

Adara, who had been watching Alma as she explored.

Adara winked at Caleb, mouthing 'I knew she would like it.'

Caleb nodded in response, then said simply to Alma, 'It is yours.'

'What!' cried Alma. Mouth agape, she looked at Adara and Caleb, both of whom were now grinning. 'Are you serious? This room is for me?'

Adara nodded. 'It is only right,' she said, golden eyes twinkling, 'that you should have your own space if you are going to be spending time with us. And, you are going to be spending time with us, aren't you?'

'Yes, yes, of course,' said Alma, completely flabbergasted. This room was too much. She spied a wardrobe standing against the wall next to the bed – running over to it, she opened the doors to find it full of gowns.

'A few things I picked out for you to wear, if you want to,' said Adara.

'If I want to…!' Alma pulled one of the gowns from the cupboard and held it against her. It was midnight blue silk, the sleeves and hem edged with silvery ribbon, the neck and waist embroidered with flowers that shimmered a lighter blue than the dress. She twirled a little and laughed out loud, then looked over at Adara and Caleb. Putting the dress on the bed she ran over and hugged them both in turn.

'Thank you so much! This is just too much!'

'It is our pleasure,' laughed Adara, while Caleb looked flustered, but very, very pleased. 'Now, my dear ones, if you will excuse me,' Adara went on, her perfect face looking fondly on them both. 'I must go and meet Thorion and the others. Alma, we will see you in a little while.'

'Oh!' said Alma. 'Yes, of course, I'll be there.'

'See you later, Caleb,' called Adara as she drifted out through the door, lithe in her azure robes.

'Y-yes, my lady,' he stammered, having not yet quite recovered his composure. The door closed softly behind her and Alma and Caleb were left alone in the room. They looked at each other a moment, then Alma, grinning, gestured towards the pair of comfortable chairs set near the fireplace.

'C'mon, let's sit for a while. I don't have to go to the Elders quite yet, do I?'

'So you really like it?' asked Caleb, not moving. Alma eyed him curiously for a moment.

'God, yes, it's fabulous!' she said, sinking down into the velvet chair. 'I mean, this is more than I could have ever imagined. Why, is something wrong?' she asked, realising Caleb still wasn't coming to join her.

Shaking his head, he came over to take the seat opposite Alma. 'No, nothing's wrong,' he said, looking at her intently as he sat down. 'It's just... important to me that you're happy, that's all.'

Alma gazed at him a moment, perturbed. Was Caleb interested in her? She cared about him but she wasn't sure if she felt that way about him. And anyway, her romantic interest was in Deryck, not Caleb. Not wanting to hurt his feelings, however, she reached over, putting a hand on his where it rested on the arm of the chair. 'I really am happy,' she said. 'Thank you so much.' Then, sitting back again, she swung her long legs over one arm of the chair. 'So, what shall we do now?'

Alma came slowly through the door of the council chamber into the Great Hall. She put her hand to her forehead, rubbing between her brows. She felt as though she'd been doing a lot of frowning.

'Alma, hey!' She looked up to see Caleb emerge from a cushioned alcove between two of the pillars. 'You all right?' he asked, coming up to link his arm with hers, his blue eyes concerned.

'Um, yeah. I guess. I mean, I am, I'm just a bit…' She stopped, thinking. 'It was an interesting meeting, let's put it that way.'

'How so?' he asked, pulling her gently towards the alcove. 'Come on, sit down and you can tell me all about it.'

He was so eager Alma couldn't help but grin at him. But it had been an intense morning. Her first meeting with the Elders and already her head was spinning. She sat down on the plush velvet bench, leaning her head back and closing her eyes. She heard Caleb get up, then a moment later he was back, putting something cool in her hand. She opened her eyes to see it was a drink in a silver cup. Perfect.

'Thanks,' she said, taking a long gulp.

'Sooo…' he said, leaning forward with his elbow on his knees, blue eyes bright with interest. Alma made a face at him, then relented.

'Oh, well. It was interesting. I mean, they talked a bit about the history of Ambeth. And the first humans.' She paused, frowning a little. That one had been hard to take in. 'And some stuff about the Balance and why it's so important. So, you know, that's cool.'

'That's it?' Caleb sounded deflated. She grinned at him again.

'Yeah, nosy, that's all. No hidden clues or arcane secrets yet.' Seeing his face fall she reached out and jabbed him in the arm, regretting her sarcastic tone. 'Don't worry, I'll tell you everything, I promise,' she said, conciliatory. 'I'm just a bit tired, that's all.'

'Sure,' said Caleb. She was relieved to see his eyes going back to blue. 'So, shall we eat before we go to the library?'

Alma looked around, realising a long line of tables had been set up on the other side of the Great Hall. Servants were starting to bring in covered dishes and appetising smells were drifting around the room. Her face lit up. 'Ooh, can we?'

'Sure,' Caleb said again, but this time with a smile. 'This lunch is for everyone. Let's dig in.'

Her belly comfortably full, Alma felt revived enough to let Caleb take her to the library after lunch. She was confident her bracelet would get her back in time as long as she didn't stay over, though the thought of spending a night in her starry tower room was very tempting.

'Now, I've already spoken to the Librarian,' Caleb said, as he led Alma along a stone corridor to the right of the Great Hall, 'and she's searching out any reference she can find to the Regalia. So all we have to do is look through them, and hopefully we might find some clues.'

'Well, it's a start,' said Alma, feeling doubtful about the whole thing. Then she squeezed his arm with hers. 'No, that's great. It really is. Thank you.'

They arrived at another large wooden door, this one with a curling latch handle. It was ajar, letting a line of golden light into the stone hallway. Caleb pushed on the door so it opened, and Alma felt her heart leap.

The library was glorious. Large arched windows on three walls let in golden afternoon light, while in between them wooden shelving filled with books reached to the high vaulted ceiling. There were cushioned chairs and wooden desks set in groups around the room and the whole place felt warm and welcoming. Alma immediately wanted to grab a book and settle in one of the comfortable looking chairs for the afternoon.

As they entered a woman got up from a large desk on the other side of the room. Full figured, dressed in a simple dark grey top and skirt, she was quite unlike anyone Alma had seen in Ambeth so far. Her salt and pepper hair was pulled back from her lined, smiling face and, as she came closer, Alma could see embroidery around the sleeves and collar of her top.

'Welcome, welcome, Master Caleb,' she said as she came towards them. 'And this is the Child of the Prophecy?' Alma screwed up her face at this, then remembered herself and smiled as Caleb introduced her.

'Just Alma is fine,' she said, holding out her hand.

'Welcome to you as well, dear Alma,' the woman said, taking Alma's outstretched hand in both of hers and squeezing before letting go. 'I am the Librarian.' The way she spoke it was clear this was more than just a title. 'This way, if you please. I've found quite a few things already that I think will be useful, though I think you may want to start with this.'

As she spoke she started towards the back of the room, where more rows of shelves were weighed down with books and paper scrolls. Alma glanced at Caleb and he winked at her. She grinned, his excitement contagious. They followed the Librarian across the room, Alma's shoes sinking into the rich soft rugs. The Librarian had retrieved a large scroll from one of the shelves, which she presented to Caleb.

'Here it is. I only found it the other day. It's quite old, I think, but very useful.' Her brown eyes twinkled at them both as Caleb took the scroll from her. 'Now, come over here. I've reserved a nice big table for you so you can work in peace.' She shot a glance around the room at the other occupants. Alma looked around too. Several of the desks were occupied by older men, each with a pile of books and a pad of paper. All of them were writing furiously, though one or two lifted their heads to look over. Alma smiled uncertainly, feeling shy under their stares. Meanwhile, the Librarian helped Caleb to unroll the scroll on top of a large wooden table, its surface pitted and marked with years of use. Caleb placed paperweights at the corners and beckoned to Alma. His face was glowing with eagerness.

'Look at this!'

Alma came over and had a look. 'Wow!'

'Well, I'll just leave you to it,' said the Librarian, turning to go. 'Please do ask if you need anything else.'

'Thanks,' said Alma, her attention taken by the images on the scroll in front of her. They were beautifully done, pen and ink drawings touched with light washes of colour. A Sword, a Cup and a Crown.

'Are these…? Is this…?' She reached out to touch the paper gently, her finger lingering on the curving lines of the Cup. Her voice was quiet, reverent and Caleb moved closer to her, his blonde head bent over the page.

'Yes. This is the Regalia. I remember the Sword, at least.'

Alma licked her lips then swallowed as she took in the straight smooth blade, the twisting lines of the hilt. There was an answering twist in her stomach, similar to how she had felt in the Great Hall as she stood before the alcove. It was as if the pieces spoke to her, somehow. She became very conscious of the air around her, the way her feet were on the floor, the warmth of Caleb's arm as he leaned against her. It was as though everything was perfectly poised in that moment, as though she stood at the beginning of something wonderful and terrible, all at the same time.

'Um, so, good.' Her voice was a whisper and she cleared her throat, wanting to break the spell that seemed to be weaving around her. 'I mean, it's good we know what to look for, at least.'

Caleb nodded. He seemed equally mesmerised. 'It's pretty exciting, isn't it? I mean, if we can find them...' His voice was quiet and she looked at him, leaning into him a little.

'Hey, you never know, right?' He turned his head and smiled at her.

'Yeah. You never know.' Realising how close he was to her, Alma wondered at how she'd felt before, the uncomfortable moment in her room where she'd thought he might be interested in her. But, as he leaned forward again to study the document, all she could feel from him was friendship, pure and simple, no trace of awkwardness. Which was fine, she thought. A friend was just what she wanted Caleb to be.

There was writing on the page. Caleb ran his finger along the text under the Sword, reading the words as he went, his voice pitched low:

'A Sword, A Cup, A Crown -
All hearts shall hold them pure.
Heart's love the Sword will lay down,
To rest in blood secure;
Heart betrayed the Cup will take,
Returned to an ancient home;
Cold heart the Crown shall stake,
For death before it is done.'

'It's a Seer's document,' he said when he'd finished, pointing to a small seal at the lower left-hand corner of the page. It was an impression in wax of an island in a wavy sea, three stars above it.

'What does that mean?'

'The Seers live on an island not far off shore,' said Caleb. 'They used to come here quite often, apparently, but the last time was when the Sword was lost. They were the ones who wrote the Prophecy in the Great Hall, you know, the one on the wall?'

Alma's mouth tightened briefly. Yeah, she knew it. The one about her and all the marvellous things she was supposed to do. And here was another load of riddles that she was supposed to solve. Well, they didn't mention red hair, at least.

'So what's this? Another prophecy? Hey, maybe if we keep looking we'll find another one that says someone completely different from me is actually going to find this stuff.' She eyed Caleb hopefully but he frowned at her.

'Alma, it has to be you. You were here on the right day, at the right time, in the right place. Just like the skylore said.'

'The skylore?' Alma folded her arms and glared at Caleb. All at once she was tired. Tired of studying, tired of prophecies and tired in general. But Caleb had turned his attention back to the scroll, missing her pointed stare.

'Yes,' he said, studying the text again. 'The Light watch the stars, read the patterns there. That's how they knew you were coming the other day.'

Ooh. Alma's glare intensified. Then she calmed down,

her mouth twisting. It wasn't Caleb's fault. None of this was. And he was trying so hard to help her. And... she needed him, she realised. She missed him, when she was in her own world. But right now she was so tired she just wanted to go home.

'Hey, Caleb?' He looked up. 'Um, I think I need to go home now.' His lips pressed together for a second, then he nodded, his eyes sliding towards grey. 'I'm sorry-' Alma started, but he stopped her.

'No, it's fine. I get it.' He smiled at her, and she could see he was trying to understand. He was so lovely. In some ways she wished she could like him as more than a friend.

'I'm just so tired, you know. It's already late for me when I come here, and then after this morning and now all this I just... think I need to go. Go home and think about it all.' She stopped, frowning. The way his shoulders had dropped it was obvious he was still disappointed, so she added. 'I'll be back tomorrow, I promise.'

His face lit up at her last statement, his eyes returning to blue. 'Really? Because I can look at some more of this stuff, then we can come back here.'

'Or we could go for a walk and you could show me more of the gardens,' she countered, challenging him. He laughed.

'You're right. I suppose it doesn't have to be study all the time. But can I just-'

'Yes, you can. Tell me all. While we're in the gardens tomorrow. Preferably relaxing somewhere.' She gave him a mischievous grin and he mock groaned at her.

'Fine. Relaxing tomorrow. I'll just put this back.' Carefully he rolled the scroll, going to put it back on its shelf, then came back and took Alma's arm. 'Come on, let's go to the Gate, sleepyhead.'

'Hey! Unfair,' said Alma, but she let him lead her towards the door, glad to be back to their usual teasing ways. He called to the Librarian as they left, 'I'll be back soon!' She looked up and nodded, waving her pen at them both in farewell.

Sara checked her phone for what felt like the hundredth time that day. Where was Alma? They were supposed to be meeting up to go out, so when her mother said she had gone to the park instead, Sara decided to go look for her there. But now she was sitting alone in one of the cafes, a half eaten bowl of fries growing cold on the table in front of her, wondering what to do next. The autumn nights were closing in and it was starting to get dark. Sara wondered what on earth Alma was doing here. Was she meeting that mysterious boy? Sitting bolt upright at the thought, Sara decided to do one more circuit. She picked up her bag and left the café, pulling her jacket around her against the chill air as she headed across the park towards Alma's favourite bench. Up ahead, she saw what looked like a familiar figure stumble out from the trees. Starting to run, she shouted her friend's name, seeing the long red hair as she got closer.

'Alma!' she shouted again, and this time the figure

turned its head. Out of breath, Sara finally caught up to Alma, who staggered a little as she drew near. 'Are you all right?' puffed Sara, concerned as she reached out to steady her friend.

'Wha-what?' faltered Alma, who was still recovering from passing through the Gate. She bent forward, hands on her knees as she fought to regain her balance. Sara regarded Alma curiously, frowning as she took in her shortness of breath and slightly dishevelled appearance.

'What on earth have you been doing?'

Alma just looked at her for a moment, completely at a loss. Straightening up, she took a deep breath and said the first thing that came to her. 'Running. Erm, I've been running. In the woods, you know,' she said, waving her hand at the mass of trees, still breathing hard.

'Why would you do that?' said Sara, mystified. 'And don't you have your phone? I've been trying to get you for ages.'

Reaching into her pocket, Alma bought out her phone, which was starting to beep with all the delayed texts and messages from Sara. Blowing out a breath, she looked back at her friend, hating herself for lying to her again.

'Well, I had it turned off. Didn't want to be disturbed. I've only just turned it back on again. Sorry…' she trailed off lamely.

Sara looked at her, a suspicious expression on her face. 'Were you with that guy?' she said, her tone mildly accusing.

'Wh-what guy?' said Alma, taken aback for a moment. Seeing Sara's face she realised what she meant and rapidly recovered. 'Oh, you mean the guy I-'

'Yeah,' said Sara, her eyes narrowed. 'The guy you like? The family friend you won't talk about and haven't introduced me to? Is that who you were with?' Sara folded her arms, starting to look angry.

Alma hung her head, shamefaced. 'Yes,' she said finally, her blue eyes meeting Sara's brown ones, registering the hurt in them. 'Yes, I was with him and I'm sorry. It's just, he likes to spend time with me alone, that's all.'

'Running?' said Sara, highly sceptical, her eyebrows raised.

Alma decided her only chance was to go along with the lie. 'Well, you know, and other stuff,' she said, blushing a little. For once her propensity to redden at any moment was actually useful. Sara's eyes widened.

'Like what?' she said, her expression softening. Anything to do with the opposite sex was exciting to Sara and Alma hated herself for playing on that fact. Still, what could she do? She couldn't exactly say where she had been.

'Well, come over to mine now, and I'll tell you more, I promise,' she said, looking hopefully at Sara.

'But it's Saturday night,' she said. 'Aren't we going out still?'

Alma's face fell. She just wanted to go home, put on her pyjamas and curl up in front of the TV. However, the look on Sara's face and the fact she was wearing her new jacket meant that was obviously not an option. Sighing a little, Alma summoned up what was left of her energy, feigning an excitement she didn't feel.

'Well, sure,' she said, 'there's that new pizza place. We could go there, I guess. I just need to go home and get changed first.'

'Oh, and I hear the waiters are cute,' said Sara, suddenly excited. Linking her arm in Alma's, she said, 'Let's go then, running girl. And, you can start by telling me this mysterious guy's name.'

Alma smiled weakly as she fell into step beside her friend, her mind working frantically. Dreading the night ahead, she smiled brightly at Sara nonetheless. 'OK,' she said, 'let's go. And, it's, um, De-David,' she said, making a face at yet another lie. 'His name is David.'

All Hearts

Friday afternoon and Alma was finally home from school. She ran in and headed through to the kitchen at the back of the house, almost colliding with Aidan on her way through the door. 'Hey!' he said, very nearly spilling his milk.

But Alma ignored him, dropping her bag and opening cupboards, searching for something to eat. Eleanor, sitting at the table, watched with amusement as she whirled around the kitchen.

'Do you want tea, Mum?' asked Alma, buzzing with excitement. The weekend was here, and that meant another trip to Ambeth. She could hardly wait to bolt down her snack and head to the park. She sliced two pieces of bread and poured the boiling water into her cup, narrowly avoiding knocking over the sugar in her haste.

'No thank you, Alma, I've just had one,' smiled Eleanor, watching her daughter bustle around. 'So, what's the big rush?'

'Oh!' Alma stopped stirring her tea and turned to her mother. 'Oh, nothing, really,' she said, trying to look innocent. 'I mean, I'm going out later with Sara but first I'm going to the park, you know, before dinner?' She turned back to her sandwich, spreading the bread with mayo before loading it with cheese and salad and slicing it in two.

'What, again?' said Eleanor, mystified. 'That's the third time in a week. What's so special about the park these days?'

'Mmmph, nothing,' said Alma, around a mouthful of sandwich, trying to avoid her mother's eye. 'You know, I'm just doing more exercise these days, I guess.'

'Really?' said Eleanor, one eyebrow arched. Alma had never been a sporty type, so this sudden interest in exercise was unusual, to say the least. Then she realised. Of course, it had to be a boy. Smiling, she looked at her daughter, red hair in disarray as she munched her sandwich between gulps of tea.

'Well, take it easy,' she said, 'you'll get indigestion if you eat like that.'

Alma rolled her eyes. 'Fine, Mum,' she said, finishing the last of her sandwich. 'Just going to get changed.' She left the room, taking her tea with her, and a moment later Eleanor heard the thump of her feet on the stairs and the creaking of the floorboards overhead. She smiled again. It was about time, she supposed. Getting up, she drained the last of her tea and rinsed the cup before starting to tidy the mess Alma had left behind.

Caleb walked over to the shelf full of scrolls, carefully lifting one and bringing it back to the table. He blew a fine layer of dust from it and Alma waved her hand in front of her, crinkling her nose as she tried not to sneeze.

'What's that?' she asked.

'A map of Ambeth. You know, these are some of the oldest records we have.' He sounded so interested Alma couldn't help but smile despite her itchy nose. As Caleb gently unrolled the map across the scored and marked surface of the ancient wooden table she took in a breath.

'Wow.'

The map was a thing of beauty, drawn in ink and richly coloured, with gold leaf picking out places of interest. The sunlight coming through the tall arched windows made the gold leaf shimmer, dust motes dancing in the air. Placing paperweights at the corners, Alma studied the map carefully. Small golden stars along the far left border and at other places on the map marked what Alma thought must be Gates to the human world, with one just where the Oak Gate would be, at the end of the path through the wood. Blue sea shimmered to the right, dotted with small islands in greens and purples. Tall mountains spread to the top of the page, castle-shaped dwellings carefully drawn at intervals through the rolling valleys and ridges, while woods ran down the left of the page and across the bottom. Looking closer, she spotted the Palace, beautifully rendered in gold and pearly white, the gardens spreading all around. There was the Long Walk and the winding path across the meadow, while the human village was represented with a tiny cluster of stone dwellings, complete down to the miniature roses on their pale walls.

A large building to the rear of the Hall caught her attention – she had noticed it on one of her last visits but had thought it an extension to the vast stable blocks. However, it was clear from the map that it was separate. Pointing to it, careful not to touch the delicate paint with her finger, she said, 'What is that place?'

Caleb looked where she was pointing. 'That's where many of the Court keep their apartments. You know, to stay in when they are here.'

'So, they don't all live in the Palace?' asked Alma, surprised. She had just assumed, seeing the row of doors near her own room, that they all had apartments there.

'No,' said Caleb, smiling a little. 'Many of them keep estates in the hills and valleys beyond, both Dark and Light. It's where much of our food comes from.' He indicated the castle-like structures dotted through the top portion of the map. 'They spend most of their time there, just coming here for special occasions and when Thorion calls Council together. So this building was made for them to have somewhere to stay, there being not enough room here to accommodate them and their entourages.'

'Entourages?' asked Alma, raising an eyebrow. This all sounded a bit fancy.

Caleb laughed. 'Yes, you know, servants, messengers, grooms and so on – some of the Lords are very particular about who looks after them.'

'And these servants are usually…'

'Human,' said Caleb. 'Yes, mostly from the village.' Seeing Alma screw up her face, he asked, 'What's wrong?'

'Oh, well, it all seems a bit… separate from all this talk of high purpose and guarding the great life force. I mean, what did they do before humans came along?'

'Er, I don't know,' said Caleb. 'I guess it's been this way for so long we don't even think about it anymore.'

'Huh,' said Alma. 'Guess your great Lords are more like humans than they think.' She smiled then, not wanting to give offence, but she could see Caleb was perplexed. Changing the subject, she pointed to the gleaming islands dotting the blue seas. 'And what about these islands?' she asked. 'Does anyone live there?'

'There are rumours,' Caleb began, his blue eyes bright as he looked at Alma, 'of people dwelling on those islands, but no one has ventured to see them for many years. I believe one of them is home to some sort of spiritual order, an off-shoot of your own world. And of course there is the Island of the Seers,' he went on, pointing to a small island just offshore. 'You remember I told you about them, the other day. But as to the rest of them, I don't really know.'

'Okay.' Alma nodded, her hand tracing the small shapes on the map without touching the paper. 'And is there anything further out? Say, beyond the sea? Or the forest, even? I mean, it can't be the end of your world.'

Caleb shook his head, looking perplexed. 'I suppose,' he said. 'I've never really thought about it. It would be a good question to-'

'Ask Thorion?' said Alma, grinning and giving him a nudge. She knew Caleb was in awe of the High King. 'So, the Regalia could be out there somewhere for all we know.'

Caleb's expression changed from thoughtful to surprised. 'Well, I suppose that's true.'

Sighing, Alma twisted her mouth as she looked at the map. 'Basically, we have no idea where to look,' she said. 'I still don't know why I'm the one who's supposed to find it – I keep waiting for some sort of revelation, some piece of information that will lead us to one of the pieces, but instead all we seem to be coming up with is more questions.'

Caleb looked at her, his own face serious for a moment. Then he brightened. 'Well, there's some more scrolls we can look through. The librarian sorted them out for us the other day. You never know, the clue could be in there.' Then, seeing the doubt in Alma's face, he said, 'I believe in you, Alma. I believe you are the one to do this for us.'

His expression was so earnest that Alma couldn't bring herself to say anything to burst his bubble, though the thought of poring over musty old scrolls for the next few hours really didn't appeal to her. So she just smiled at Caleb. 'Thank you – that means a lot.'

Gently removing the paperweights from the map, she rolled it up carefully and placed it to one side. 'So, let's get started,' she said. 'But will you promise me something?'

'Anything,' said Caleb.

Alma smiled at his suddenly nervous expression. 'Can we do something fun later, please?'

After meeting with the Elders Alma left the Great Hall to find Caleb waiting for her in the Foyer, a mysterious bundle in his hands. She was about to ask him what it was but he shushed her. 'No questions please, Lady Alma. Fun awaits, as promised.'

Grinning widely, Alma followed him out through the double doors into bright sunshine, saying with a flourish, 'Lead on, Sir Caleb.'

Caleb smiled broadly, slinging the bundle onto his back, and headed towards the Long Walk. But instead of turning towards the woods he went the other way, the sea glimmering blue ahead.

'Are we going to the beach?' Alma asked, falling into step beside him.

Caleb looked at her. 'No questions please – ow!' Alma mock-punched him in the arm. Laughing, he put his hands up as though to defend himself. 'Okay, okay, yes, we are going to the beach.'

'Yay!' said Alma, dancing with excitement. As they neared the end of the Long Walk she saw rolling green meadows stretching to the edge of a low cliff. Colourful wildflowers bobbed in the fresh breeze that blew towards them, bringing with it the smell of the sea. They made their way carefully through the pastures, avoiding the sheep that baaed as they approached the edge of the cliff.

'Be careful here,' said Caleb, as they reached the rocky incline. 'It can be a bit steep.'

'Oh really?' said Alma, already moving past him, sure-footed as a goat, holding the skirt of her dress away from her sneaker-clad feet. She had been negotiating steep cliff paths like this since she was small – they were often the only way to get to the beaches near her grandmother's house in Wales.

'Hey!' he said, laughing as he picked up the pace, the two of them slipping and sliding on the rough path, each one trying to be the first to get to the golden sands below. Finally they reached the beach, Alma shouting in triumph as she jumped down to the soft sand.

'Not fair,' he puffed, landing a moment after she did. 'I was carrying a pack.'

But Alma just laughed, sitting down to take off her shoes, enjoying the rough feel of warm sand against her bare feet, the taste of salt on her lips and the ceaseless shushing of the waves as they met the shore. Getting up, she brushed the sand from her skirt and went over to Caleb, who was removing his boots. Offering her hand, she pulled him to his feet and he smiled down at her, she beaming back at him, both of them pleased to be free of the confines of the library.

'C'mon,' she said, 'leave the pack here. Let's go for a walk.'

Alma darted along the sands, jumping and splashing at the water's edge. She squealed a little as the cool waves splashed around her ankles, holding her skirts high. Caleb followed a little more slowly. He didn't spend much time at the beach, preferring the shady reaches of the wide river that flowed, smooth and strong, to meet the sea a little further down the coast. A day's fishing, dreaming under overhanging branches as he floated on clear water, was his idea of heaven. But Alma was really enjoying herself and he soon found himself caught up in her mood, especially when she bent down and, flicking her hands through the water, splashed him from head to toe. Roaring in mock outrage, he ran after her, splashing her until she collapsed, heaving with giggles, onto the dry sand near the water's edge.

'Oh Caleb, thank you for this. It's just what I needed.'

Caleb lowered himself to sit beside her, picking up a delicate ivory shell and looking at it for a moment before passing it to Alma. She smiled her thanks and leaned back on one elbow to study the gift. Caleb fought to control his pounding heart as he looked at her, splashed and sandy, reclining on the sand. He was finding it harder and harder to conceal his feelings. Alma looked over at him and he saw her expression change, becoming more guarded. She leaned over, handing the shell back and he smiled at her, knowing he needed to, that his feelings were too apparent. She smiled back cautiously and he could see her thinking, wanting to change the mood.

'Caleb,' she asked. 'Will you tell me about the Lords? The ones that went missing in my world, I mean. Please?'

Well, that would do it. He frowned and slowly sat up, hooking his hands around his bent legs and staring out at the crashing waves, his eyes becoming distant. Sea birds cried their haunting song as they wheeled above them, the smell of salt and seaweed in the air. 'It's… not a happy story, Alma. Are you sure you want to hear it today?' he asked, looking back at her, unsure.

'Yes, I do,' said Alma. She sat up and crossed her legs, arranging her long skirt around her and trying to brush off some of the sand. She nodded, encouraging him. Her eyes, blue like the sky, held his as he began the tale.

'They were brothers, the two that went missing, and their names were Galen and Gwion. They were both Elders in the Court of Light and very powerful.' Caleb stopped then, looking at Alma, his face troubled. 'I don't know the whole story, only bits and pieces I've heard here and there, but the gist of it seems to be that the younger one, called Galen, was the first to be lost. Apparently he was killed in an accident in your world, I don't know for sure. He and his brother spent a lot of time over there but one day Galen crossed and did not return.'

'Oh, that's awful,' said Alma, her face mirroring her genuine sympathy. 'How sad.' She frowned, tracing patterns in the sand with her finger, red hair blowing in the breeze. 'So, what happened to the other brother? To… Gwion, was it you said?'

'Ah, well, that's another mystery. He was sent on some sort of errand to the human realm, I'm not sure what exactly, and he just disappeared. It was a few years after Galen died… I remember it being a big deal, actually. That was when the Elders set the decree that crossing over was forbidden. They had already wanted to stop it when Galen went missing and there was a lot of arguing about it. I think they had already banned humans from being brought across at the time, you know, if they fell in love with a member of the Court, but it wasn't until Gwion's disappearance that they put a total ban on crossing through the Gates.'

'But, that's really weird,' said Alma. 'Why on earth would they close off the access? Why wouldn't they want to search for Gwion? I mean, he could have needed their help.'

'I don't really know. Perhaps they knew it was hopeless.'

'But, I wonder what he was doing? What his errand was?' asked Alma, sounding intrigued.

Caleb shrugged, his gaze distant. 'Who knows?' he said. 'Perhaps it was something to do with his brother? I guess we'll never know.'

'Maybe we'll find the answer in one of those dusty old scrolls you keep putting in front of me,' said Alma, her tone teasing.

Caleb half-smiled. 'Hey, those scrolls are important,' he said softly, glancing at her through slanted eyes.

'I know,' she said, and he saw her mouth twist a little. 'And I really appreciate all the help you're giving me.' Reaching out, she laid her hand on his arm for a moment. 'I couldn't do this without you.' She met his eyes, her hand lingering on his arm, warm from the sun. 'And thanks, for telling me the story.'

Something passed between them and Caleb opened his mouth to speak but, before he could say anything, Alma's stomach growled loudly and she blushed. Caleb looked at her in amazement before laughing out loud. 'Never have I seen someone eat as much as you.'

Alma shot him a challenging look. 'Well, I enjoy food. What of it?'

'Enjoy it?' scoffed Caleb. 'I don't know where you put it all. You should be twice the size you are.'

'Hey!' said Alma, pushing him in the shoulder. Then her stomach growled again and she burst out laughing, as did Caleb. Getting to his feet, he offered her his hand.

'Let's go,' he said. 'We can sit up on the cliff and eat our picnic, if you like.'

Alma's face lit up. 'You brought food?'

'Well, yeah,' said Caleb, turning and starting to run. 'I do know you, after all,' he called over his shoulder as she squealed in outrage and ran after him.

Late afternoon found Caleb and Alma relaxing in a sun-drenched meadow overlooking a golden curve of sand. Bees buzzed in the wildflowers and Caleb idly chewed a piece of long grass while Alma lay back with her eyes closed, enjoying the sun's warmth on her face, her thoughts drifting. The story about the lost lords came back to her, the whole thing mixing in with the missing Regalia. She still had no idea where to look for the Sword or any of the Regalia, despite Caleb's confidence in her abilities. As she lay there listening to the sea pounding the shore, the words from the scroll came back into her mind, pulsing with the waves.

'*Heart's love the Sword will lay down... Heart betrayed the Cup will take; Cold heart the Crown shall stake...*' Well. None of it really made sense. The Seers seemed to enjoy a riddle. Then she realised something.

'Caleb.'

'Hmmm?'

She opened her eyes to see him looking at her, blue eyes creased against the sun. 'The riddles, you know, from the Seers. That's an old document, right?'

He took the grass from his mouth before answering. 'Yes, I think so. A few centuries at least.'

'So, they knew the Regalia was going to go missing?'

'What?'

She rolled over onto her side, resting her head on her bent arm as she looked up at him. 'Well, that's what it says, right? That the pieces will be taken away. By all the different... hearts?'

Caleb thought for a moment, his amiable face screwed up as he concentrated. Then he stared at her. 'You're right.'

'So then why, if they knew about it, haven't any of the Elders contacted them? To see if they know where it is?'

'Well, they did. Remember? The Prophecy in the Great Hall?'

Alma raised her eyebrows. 'That's it? That's all they could come up with?'

'Well, it's pretty good, I think,' said Caleb, frowning at her a little. 'I mean, it describes you perfectly.'

'Oh really?' Alma snorted, then realised she couldn't be bothered arguing about it, not on such a nice day.

Besides, it seemed they might have their first clue after all. After a pause, during which Caleb seemed to be waiting cautiously, she spoke again. 'So could we go and see them?'

Caleb looked relieved and she hid a smile. 'Well, I guess. But I don't know why we'd bother. I don't think they'll come up with anything new.'

'Huh.' Alma rolled over onto her back again and closed her eyes. Then, unbidden, the thought of Deryck came to her and what she might be doing if he were there with her, instead of Caleb. Her cheeks grew hot and she put her hands up to them. Ugh, it was so complicated, that he was Dark! She just knew that Thorion and everyone would be not exactly... thrilled, if she ended up with him. Not that it was likely to happen. Not that he cared about her anyway. At least, she didn't think so.

'So we need to figure out who these "hearts" are then,' said Caleb, cutting into her thoughts.

'Um, yeah,' she said, opening her eyes and shading them against the sun. 'I guess we do.'

There was silence for a minute, Alma closing her eyes again and thinking of hearts. But that just brought her mind around to Deryck again. And then to a question she didn't really want to ask.

'So, how do we know the Dark just didn't take the Regalia? You know, because they want it too, right?' Caleb didn't answer straight away and she opened her eyes to see him looking at her with a shocked expression. 'What?'

'There's no way,' he replied emphatically. 'I mean, I

don't like the Dark, for a lot of reasons-' his face grew troubled '-but, it's one of our greatest taboos. Everyone knows the Regalia is what keeps us going. No-one would dare to steal it, at least none of the Elders, anyway.'

'Well, at least that's somewhere we don't have to look.' Alma, feeling obscurely relieved, waved away a persistent fly buzzing around her face. Then she noticed how far the sun had dropped and sat up reluctantly, realising it was nearly time for her to go. Caleb's face fell as he realised what she was about to say. Raising a hand, he forestalled her.

'Don't go yet, Alma. Stay for a while longer, have some supper. You don't always have to rush off, do you?'

'Well,' Alma started, then realised he was right. Thorion had said her bracelet's power to get her back on time would lessen the longer she stayed in Ambeth, but so far she'd had no problems. She really didn't want to go – perhaps she could stay a little longer, test it out. 'OK, you're on,' she said, grinning at him. 'So, what shall we do?'

Caleb's face lit up with excitement. 'Really?' he said, his eyes bright. 'You'll stay? Well, we could go back to the Hall. There is always something going on of an evening. Music or dancing, or both. Then we can have supper – I know you're still hungry.' Alma made a face at him and he grinned back. 'What's the use of having that nice room if you don't use it for anything except getting changed?'

Alma had to smile at this. She loved her tower room and went there every time she crossed over, choosing a gown from the selection in the wardrobe, leaving her human world persona behind. Today's choice was red, with autumn leaves embroidered around the hem and ribbons at her waist.

'Music sounds nice,' she said, looking at him affectionately. But not too affectionately. She didn't want to give him any ideas. 'I'm not sure about the dancing, though. And definitely we should have supper. But then I must go back, OK?'

'I will make sure you get back to the Gate,' Caleb said, hand on heart and looking solemn. Then he beamed. 'I can't believe you're going to stay.'

Alma smiled back, happy to see him happy. 'So, shall we get going? I guess I'll have to get changed again,' she said ruefully, looking down at her skirt, which was covered with sand, salt and grass stains. 'This gown is pretty wrecked. Adara won't be happy with me.'

'Ah, you look fine,' said Caleb, hauling her to her feet. Alma screwed up her face and Caleb surveyed her again, taking in her dishevelled state. He reached out and gently picked a strand of seaweed off her sleeve. 'Well, maybe getting changed isn't a bad idea, after all,' he said, frowning a little. 'I should probably do the same.'

Alma was curled up in her chair, her head pillowed on her arm and snoring softly. Caleb stood up quietly, not wanting to disturb her. They had spent a pleasant hour in the Great Hall, listening to harp and drum music. Alma's eyes were bright in the lantern-lit space and her expression rapt as she listened to the songs, moving to the beat. Caleb had almost burst with pride to be sitting with her, seeing the glances from the others, some of his friends coming over to greet them and to be introduced. Supper had been in Alma's room, an enjoyable meal shared by the fire, their conversation gradually dwindling to a companionable silence until Caleb realised that Alma had fallen asleep. He sighed regretfully, a corner of his mouth lifting in a smile – he had hoped things might have gone differently, even though he knew she only thought of him as a friend. Leaning over he stoked the fire, coaxing it to burn a little more before retrieving a blanket from Alma's bed to lay gently over her. She half-smiled in her sleep, sighing a little, and Caleb had to restrain himself from touching her cheek. She would be fine, he thought – he would wake early and come get her, making sure she got back to the Gate on time. He left the room, quietly latching the door behind him.

Alma stretched and groaned – she'd been having the best dream. She had been with Caleb in the Great Hall, listening to music and eating a delicious meal before falling asleep under a starry sky. She wriggled, wondering why her bed felt so strange and uncomfortable. The blanket slipped off her and she reached for it, her eyes finally coming open. The shock was profound. Fully awake and in a complete panic, Alma gazed around her tower room. She felt sick with horror – she had slept here! It had been no dream, the night before; she must have fallen asleep in her chair after supper. She had to leave, and fast.

Jumping up she ran her fingers through her tangled hair and hastily got changed into her normal clothes. Her shaking hands made the process harder than usual as she struggled with the fastenings on her dress. She threw it on the bed – there wasn't time to tidy things up. She was going to kill Caleb, absolutely kill him!

Once dressed she grabbed her bag, flung the door open and ran headlong down the hall and curving stairs, taking them two at a time. Two startled courtiers coming the other way saw that she wasn't going to stop for anyone and pressed themselves up against the wall to let her pass. Gaining the foyer, Alma sprinted for the main doors. Bursting through, she stopped for a moment to catch her breath and get her bearings, ignoring the concerned looks from the guards. She was near to tears, her vision blurring against the bright morning light. The Long Walk – that was the fastest way she knew to get through the gardens. Shouldering her pack she started to run again.

About half way down the Long Walk, enjoying the early morning solitude, sat Thorion, the first rays of the sun warming his face. Then a whirlwind rushed past him. A whirlwind with red hair.

'Alma?' he said, standing up. 'Alma!' he called, louder

now. She stopped a little way along from him, turning to face him with a panicked expression. 'Alma, what is it?' he said, hastening towards her.

'Oh, Thorion,' gasped Alma, obviously out of breath and near tears. 'I fell asleep. I don't know what time it is and I need to get back. Caleb left me-'

She stopped abruptly, choking back a sob and Thorion pulled her into a gentle hug, feeling her shaking against him. 'It's all right,' he said, though worry grew within him at the mention of Caleb. 'Whatever it is, I can help you.' Releasing her he took her hand, leading her to sit on the stone bench. She protested at first but he insisted, and finally she acquiesced. A few tears had escaped – hastily she wiped them from her cheek.

'Alma, explain to me what has happened.' Holding her hand in his and stroking it gently, Thorion spoke quietly, not wanting to upset her further. 'You fell asleep, you say – when was this?'

'Last night,' said Alma, her voice shaking. 'Oh, I'm in so much trouble, I just know it!'

Thorion looked at her, puzzled. 'But, Alma, do you not remember what I told you about your bracelet? Haven't you been using it to cross back over?'

'Well, yes,' said Alma, 'but you said that the longer I am here, the less time it gives me and I have been here all night.' The last part was almost a wail and Thorion, seeing her real distress, sought to comfort her.

'It will not matter, Alma,' he said, keeping his voice gentle. 'The bracelet will still help you to cross back to a time of your choosing. It would only be if you stayed here for a couple of days that you would have less of a window to choose from. So do not despair, dear one. You can still get home.'

'Really?' said Alma, an expression of hope dawning on her face.

'Really,' smiled Thorion, feeling a pang as he looked at her. Her red hair gleamed gold in the morning sun and her blue eyes shone. She let out a deep breath then smiled.

'Thank you,' she said, her voice calmer. 'So much. For everything.' Then, to his surprise, she gave him a hug before jumping to her feet and starting to run again.

'Wait!' called Thorion, stopping her in her tracks. 'The quickest way to the Gate is through here.' He pointed to a path stretching off to her right.

'Thank you… again!' she called. She turned down the path, waving as she went.

Thorion, smiling, sat back on his bench and considered the future in all its potential. Alma's arrival had given them all hope, and it was obvious Caleb thought the world of her. Offering a silent prayer of thanks he got to his feet and started to walk, his thoughts filled with Light.

Alma slowed her pace, huffing and puffing, her hand to her side as she tried to regain her breath. She wouldn't kill Caleb after all, she decided – she would just make him suffer for a while instead. Slowing to a walk, she jumped in alarm as a tall elegant figure stepped into her path. 'Oh!' she said, completely flustered to see Deryck. He bowed, extending a strong hand to her in greeting.

'Lady Alma, we meet again.'

Alma took the extended hand and Deryck let her hold it a moment before retrieving it, smiling to himself.

'Lord Deryck,' said Alma. 'It-it is a pleasure to see you again.' Inside she was dying. She had no idea what to say to him, plus she really, really needed to get back to the Gate. But she couldn't pass up this chance to speak to him again. If only she could think of something to say.

'The pleasure is mine,' said Deryck, his green eyes meeting hers. 'And where do you go in such a hurry this fine morning?'

'Well, I am going home, actually,' she said. 'In fact, I'm sorry, but I'm a bit late.' She was moving from foot to foot in her agitation – realising this, she forced herself to stand still, focusing on Deryck. He was clad in brown trousers and tunic with leather armour pieces tied on over the top, outlining his well-made form.

'Did you stay here last night?' asked Deryck, sounding surprised, his tone less formal. 'Do you stay over often? It's just, I did not see you in the Great Hall, to my regret.' He smiled at her and she almost stopped breathing. Then, realising he was waiting for an answer, she tried to put her thoughts in order.

'Um, no, I mean, I've never stayed here before, overnight, that is. It was... kind of an accident.' Deryck raised his eyebrows but said nothing and Alma ploughed on. 'You see, we were at the Hall for a little while, listening to the music, but then we decided to have supper in my room and I fell asleep in my chair and then woke up this morning. So you can see, I really need to get back home.'

Deryck, who had been listening with a smile, suddenly narrowed his eyes. 'We?'

'Oh, well, Caleb and I,' Alma said, unsure why this would matter so much to him, although by the frown on his face it obviously did. 'We spend a lot of time together here – he's helping me with my research, you see.'

Moving closer to Alma, Deryck looked at her, one corner of his mouth lifted in a smile. 'And does research with Caleb usually involve supper in your room?'

Alma swallowed. Was Deryck... jealous? She dismissed the idea as ridiculous – she hardly knew him, and had no idea why he would be worried about anything she did. She smiled at Deryck, her mouth trembling a little. 'No, not at all. I mean, we're just friends.' All at once it was very important that she let Deryck know this. 'And when he suggested it, it sounded like a nice thing to do, that's all.'

'Oh, so Caleb suggested it, did he?' asked Deryck, his smile becoming broader and reaching his eyes, changing his face completely. 'Well, I would keep an eye on friend Caleb, if I were you,' he went on, his tone teasing. Alma blushed. She didn't know where to look. Desperately wanting to change the subject, she cast around for something to ask Deryck. Anything.

'So why are you up so early this morning?' she asked, braving his smiling green gaze. The effect he was having on her! She needed to calm down.

'Arms practice,' he replied. 'As you can see, I am still

147

wearing my armour.' He spun around to give her the full effect and Alma's blush deepened. Desperately trying to be cool, she nodded her head.

'Impressive,' she said, then mentally kicked herself. But Deryck seemed pleased by her response.

'Well, it's a bit battered,' he said, indicating the scratches and scrapes across the supple leather, 'but it does the trick. I have another set for tournaments.'

'Oh, OK,' said Alma, not really sure what else to say. Deryck seemed momentarily at a loss as well. He broke a twig from the hedge next to him and twirled it around in his hands.

'So, well, I suppose I should keep going,' ventured Alma. The sun was becoming warm and she undid her hoodie and took it off, tying it around her waist. Was it her imagination or had Deryck's eyes widened a little?

'Er, yes, Lady Alma. Forgive me if I have delayed you,' he said, formal again. Then, his voice slipping back to its normal tones, he asked, 'Do you know the way from here?'

'Yes, I'll be fine from here,' replied Alma without thinking, then could have bitten out her tongue. A prime opportunity for him to escort her to the Gate and she had thrown it away – she was just no good at this kind of thing. She looked at him as he stood there, a smile playing on his well-moulded lips. Oh well. She stuck out her hand. 'Um, it was nice talking to you.'

Deryck took her offered hand, kissing it gently as he bowed. She tried not to gasp. Straightening, he held her gaze for a moment. 'Yes, it was nice. Safe travels, Lady

Alma – may we meet again soon.'

Stepping aside, he let her continue down the path to her destination, watching her as she went.

Thorion moved down the Long Walk on his way to meet Adara. Still amused by his conversation with Alma, he inclined his head as he passed the turning where he had sent her, wondering if he could still see her. He could – standing in the pathway, talking to Deryck. Thorion's eyes widened and he drew back, not wanting to be seen. But Deryck's focus was all on Alma and Alma's, Thorion could see as she scuffed her toe in the gravel and tilted her head in response to what he was saying, was all on Deryck. Breathing hard for a moment, his mouth tight, he stood in the shadow of the tall hedge and took stock, trying to calm down. Even though he knew it didn't have to mean anything, words spoken in a firelit room echoed through his mind. Adara could see what others could not – was she right in her concern about Denoris' son? He knew he could not bind Alma any further than he already had, that he would not permit it. Her choice to work for the Light had to be made freely or not at all. But he could not deny the small tendril of worry that had started to grow in his mind. He needed to talk to Adara.

Do You Always Talk To Birds?

Caleb woke with a start, knowing there was something he was supposed to be doing. He sat up slowly, rubbing his hands over his face, trying to recall what it was. Then he remembered – Alma! It was like a shock of cold water. He jumped out of bed, pulling on the clothes nearest to hand and running his hand through his hair in a vain effort to make it presentable. He hoped she hadn't woken yet – oh, why of all days had he chosen today to oversleep! Leaving the door wide open he ran out of his room and raced up the stairs. But when he got to her room he found the door unlatched, her dress from the night before thrown across the bed and no Alma.

He sank down into one of the chairs by the fireplace. Noticing Alma's blanket on the floor, he reached over and picked it up, draping it over the chair opposite. Then he leaned forward, his head in his hands and let out a groan. He had failed her. Leaning back, he blew out a breath, considering his options. Perhaps she was still here?

Maybe if he ran he could catch up with her and apologise. As soon as the thought entered his mind he was on his feet and running out the door for the stairs. When he reached the foyer below he ran out the main doors then stopped, blinking in the bright sunshine. The guards! They would have seen her. Turning, he spoke to the nearest one, who was looking at him with barely concealed concern at his dishevelled state.

'Have you seen the Lady Alma this morning?' he said abruptly, too worried to bother with pleasantries.

'Yes, Caleb – she passed by some time ago. Seemed in a hurry, if you don't mind my saying, sir,' replied the guard.

'Which way did she go?' asked Caleb, crestfallen. He had no hope of catching her now, but he could still try.

'To the Long Walk, sir,' said the other. Caleb whirled and ran, calling his thanks over his shoulder as he did so.

Thorion saw Adara before she saw him, her lithe form clothed in green, her hair shining in the sun as she bent to smell an early blooming rose. Smiling, he moved quietly towards her, hoping to take her by surprise.

'Good morning, my lady,' he said, laughing a little as she jumped.

'Oh, Thorion,' she said, laughing back at him, 'I didn't hear you coming. Look,' she went on, 'it is one of the first roses. Is it not beautiful?'

Thorion looked at her tenderly. 'It is not the only thing

of beauty in these gardens,' he replied, and had the pleasure of seeing her blush, her long lashes lowering to hide her golden eyes. He took her arm, twining it through his. 'Come my dear, let us go. I am in need of open space and fresh air this day.'

Adara lifted her eyes to his, a questioning look in them as she fell into step beside him. 'There is something troubling you, is there not?' she asked, leaning close to the High King. 'And on such a fine morning too.'

Thorion looked at her. 'Ever you see to the heart of me, Adara. I would take your counsel, if you please, for I confess I am worried about Alma.'

A furrow appeared in Adara's smooth brow and she waved her hand in front of her face, discouraging a buzzing insect. 'But – she is working hard with Caleb, is she not? I get no sense that she is anything but committed to our cause.'

Thorion frowned, looking ahead as they strolled along a well-kept gravel path. 'You are right, of course – there should be no cause for concern except…'

'Except?'

'This morning, I saw her in the gardens. She was terribly distressed, had slept here accidentally and was worried she could not get back in time. I had to calm her down, remind her that the bracelet she bears will get her back to her own world.'

'So, is she all right?' asked Adara, her lovely face worried. 'The poor thing! And it will not go well for Caleb if he has let her oversleep.' She chuckled a little at the thought and looked at Thorion, expecting a similar response, but his expression was serious. 'What is it, Thorion, what has happened?' she asked, placing her other hand on his arm as they stopped for a moment in the shade of a tall tree.

'It is Deryck. I think you may have been right to be worried about him,' he replied, his blue eyes shifting to grey.

'But, what has he done? Surely... he has not tried to take her?' said Adara, sounding shocked.

'I do not think he will have to try, Adara,' said Thorion sadly. 'A moment after I sent Alma on her way I saw her talking to him, all her urgency forgotten. And he seemed as taken with her as she was with him,' he went on, his face becoming thoughtful.

Adara frowned and shook her head slowly, light and shade moving across her face as the tree above them swayed in the gentle breeze. 'Perhaps it is just that, Thorion, an attraction between them unrelated to who Alma is. Perhaps they just like each other. Stranger things have happened, you know. Though it is a shame for Caleb.'

'But he is Denoris' son,' he said quietly. 'And you know what that means.'

'It doesn't have to mean anything!' said Adara. 'The boy is his father's son, yes, but he is not his father. And if they want each other we cannot do anything to stop them. You know this to be true!' Her voice became more emphatic as she spoke, her golden eyes wide. 'If you forbid her to him, or him to her, you will only make things worse, for what may be a momentary infatuation will become something more intense. There is nothing more exciting than forbidden fruit.'

Thorion breathed deeply, exhaling through his nose. His face relaxed as he looked at Adara, his hand reaching to tuck a loose curl behind her ear. 'You are right, of course,' he said, smiling affectionately at her, though a shadow of worry still lay behind his eyes. 'There is nothing we can do but watch over her and hope she chooses to stay on the path. I will not bind her any further. And I agree,' he went on, a wry smile on his face, his eyes sliding back to blue. Adara looked at him quizzically. 'It is a shame for Caleb.'

Running down the Long Walk, Caleb quickened his pace, even though he knew he was too late. His arms pumped and his chest heaved as he darted past two elegant figures walking slowly along the path. 'What ho, Caleb,' one of them called. Caleb slowed immediately, recognising the voice of the High King. He hastily tried to fix his tousled appearance, then turned to bow to Thorion and Adara.

'What is it about this morning?' asked Thorion, laughter in his voice. 'First Alma, then you, racing down the Long Walk as though wolves were after you both.'

Caleb's face lit up. 'So you have seen her, my lord?'

'I have, Caleb,' said Thorion, looking kindly at him. Caleb became more aware than ever of his state of disarray and tugged at his tunic, trying to straighten it. 'But she will be long gone, I'm afraid. I sent her to the

Gate an hour or more ago.'

'Then she is all right? She will be able to get home?' He still couldn't believe he had let her down. Adara took his arm and gently led him to a bench to sit. As she offered him a drink from the slim silver flask she wore at her waist, her perfume wafted all around him, the soft floral scent calming him slightly.

'Peace, Caleb,' she said. 'Alma is fine, and she will not be late home.'

'Though she may not be too pleased with you the next time you see her,' smiled Thorion.

Caleb hung his head, running a hand through his hair and making it even messier than before. 'I know,' he said. 'I-I meant to wake on time, but...'

'Done is done, Caleb,' said Adara, darting an amused glance at Thorion. 'Alma is fine and no harm will come to her. Do not worry now. Save it for when she returns.'

She smiled mischievously at Caleb, who stood up and wiped the top of the flask on his tunic before replacing the lid and returning it to Adara with a bow. 'Thank you, my lady,' he said. 'And my lord,' he continued, turning back to Thorion.

'So, what will you do now, Caleb?' asked the High King. 'The day awaits, and it is lovely.'

'Well,' said Caleb, somewhat shamefacedly, 'I thought actually I might go back to bed.' Bowing again, he took his leave of Thorion and Adara, hearing their combined laughter behind him as he made his way slowly back to the Palace. At least she got home, he thought. Maybe, if she wasn't too angry with him, she would stay over again.

Deryck stood on the path, still twisting the small twig in his fingers, so deep in thought he had stripped it of bark and leaves. His armour was beginning to chafe and he really needed to get back to his rooms and bathe, but he wasn't ready. Not yet. He could not stop thinking about Alma. It had been a stroke of luck to run into her this morning and, he had to admit, she intrigued him more than ever. How well she had looked, her cheeks flushed, eyes sparkling, tousled red hair gleaming in the morning sun. Used to seeing women in their long gowns, her tight jeans and fitted t-shirt were fascinating to him, the way they outlined her body. He had tried to hide his reaction from her, but wasn't sure he had succeeded.

He had been with many girls before, beautiful girls, but there was something different about Alma. He liked hearing her voice and would have been happy to stand there talking all morning had she not needed to leave so urgently. And then there was the issue of Caleb. The surge of jealousy that moved through him when he heard Alma name him as her supper companion was unlike anything he had experienced before. Ever Caleb sought to be at the front of things, to impress Thorion! And now he had wormed his way into Alma's quest, into her research, into her rooms.

Deryck clenched his jaw in anger – he needed to make his move, and fast. He was sure Alma was interested in him; Deryck knew he was interested in her. The question was, how to remove Caleb from the picture without upsetting Alma? He fought to control his feelings, knowing it was vital he kept his focus and remembered what was important. He could not fail his father again, not like he had at the Gate. Finally letting the tortured twig fall to earth, Deryck started to make his way back to his rooms, rubbing his shoulder as the aches and pains from his practice became more apparent. His thoughts turned to Alma again, and he smiled.

Alma blinked, fighting to regain her vision after the disorientation of the crossing and the move from sunlit forest to twilit park. For she had done it. It was definitely the park, and it was definitely evening. She just needed to find out what day it was. Taking off her pack, she rummaged in the pockets for her phone, praying the battery had not gone dead. Finding it, she held down the power button and waited. The screen icons appeared and she flicked through to find the calendar. Seeing it, she let out a sigh of relief. The day still read 'Friday' – she had been in Ambeth for less than 24 hours and was wearing her bracelet, so there was no way it was next Friday. She really, really had done it! Sinking down to sit cross-legged on the cold ground, she thought what that meant. She could stay overnight in Ambeth now, spend more time with Caleb, sleep in her beautiful room and, hopefully, see more of Deryck. She even felt rested, a change from her normal state after crossing over. This was perfect, she thought, hugging herself with excitement. Getting up she made her way home, noticing the glow of the television in the front room as she let herself in quietly through the side door. Sticking her head around the door she found her mother watching a movie, a half-eaten bowl of popcorn on the low table in front of her.

'Hi, Mum,' said Alma, her mood still buoyant after the success of her crossing. 'What're you watching?'

'Oh, hello Alma,' said Eleanor, looking around. 'I didn't hear you come in. How was the park?' she said, her blue eyes momentarily concerned.

'Fine,' said Alma, 'but I'm starving. See you in a sec.' Pulling her head back she made for the kitchen, hungrier than usual, having had no time for breakfast in her mad dash from Ambeth. She made herself a sandwich and added a bowl of crisps and a large glass of mineral water, making her slow way back down the passage to the front room.

'Where's Dad?' she asked, depositing her food on the table before sitting down next to her mother, exhaling a sigh of relief.

'He's working late again. Alma, don't eat all that in here,' Eleanor protested, but Alma cut her off with a look, pointedly indicating the popcorn on the table.

'Mum, I'm fifteen, not five,' she said, frowning. 'And you eat in here all the time.'

Eleanor looked at Alma and her face softened. Smiling, she conceded. 'Fine, but don't spill anything.' Leaning forward, she stole a crisp from Alma's bowl and winked at her daughter. Alma rolled her eyes before picking up her sandwich, her mouth watering. Tuna salad, made with mayonnaise, celery and spring onions; one of her favourites. Opening the bread, Alma placed a few crisps on top of the filling, to her mother's amusement.

'Hungry, are we?' she said as Alma took a huge bite of her sandwich, closing her eyes for a moment in contentment as she chewed.

She glanced sideways at her mother, swallowing her mouthful. 'Oh, not you too.'

'Not me too what?' countered her mother, intrigued.

'Oh. Well.' Realising what she had just said, Alma took a moment to think of her answer. 'It's just, some of my friends give me a hard time about how much I eat, that's all,' she answered, taking another bite.

'Really?' said Eleanor, making a face. 'Why would they do that? You have a healthy appetite, there's nothing wrong with that.'

'That's what I say,' said Alma through a mouthful of sandwich, and Eleanor laughed.

'So, what's on?' asked Alma, once she could talk again.

'Oh, it's an old film,' said Eleanor. 'I started to watch the news but it was too depressing, so I put this on instead. Nothing like a bit of make-believe to make you feel better.'

'Looks good,' said Alma, reaching for her bowl of crisps and sitting back, a contented expression on her face.

Eleanor reached over and patted her daughter on the leg, 'It's nice to have you here,' she said. Alma said nothing, just smiled at her mother and Eleanor caught her breath – it was almost, for a moment, as if Alma's father was sitting there. Then Alma reached forward for her drink and the moment passed. Together they sat, mother and daughter, the flickering light from the TV on their faces as they immersed themselves in the fantasy playing out on screen.

It was Saturday, a bright cold day and Alma and Sara were slowly working their way through a rack of vintage dresses, each with several items over their arms already. The new store Sara had heard about was even better than they'd thought it would be. Hidden in a small arcade, it was lit with fairy lights and painted in swirling colours, the scent of fresh flowers on the counter fighting with the slightly musty smell of the old clothes crammed onto racks lining the walls. The proprietor, a young woman with unnaturally red hair worn like a 1940s pinup, sported an extraordinary array of items, from a Victorian lace chemise to a pair of shiny 60s go-go boots. Her smile as the girls came through the door was welcoming. She obviously loved her work.

'So, what's on for tonight?' asked Alma as she moved hangers along, checking out each piece for wow potential.

'Not much,' said Sara. 'Want to see a movie? We could get something to eat beforehand.'

'Yeah, that would be fine,' said Alma, only half-listening, taken with a velvet dress she had just found on the rack. Deep green, it had embroidered ribbons in cream and green that crisscrossed over the bodice and around the waist, the full skirt flaring out. It was an Ambeth dress if ever she saw one. She pulled it out and turned it around. It looked to be from the 1960s, a wild party dress from a wild era, but she knew it would be perfect in the Great Hall. Maybe Deryck would even…

'Where on earth would you wear that?' asked Sara, cutting in on her thoughts.

'Oh! Well, I don't know,' said Alma, her face going red as she surveyed the dress. 'I just like it, that's all. But yeah, you're probably right,' she said, putting it back on the rack reluctantly.

'Oh, try it on,' said Sara, sounding amused.

'Really?' Alma ran her hand over the soft velvet, her mouth curved into a half smile. 'Do you think so?'

'Oh Alma, when do you ever listen to me anyway?' said Sara, laughing, 'Yes, try it on, the colour would really suit you, actually.'

Alma slung the dress over her arm with the rest of her goodies. Moving over to a nearby rack of skirts, she glanced at Sara, who was still concentrating on the dresses.

'Are you doing anything tomorrow?' she asked.

'What, Sunday?' said Sara, seeming a little distracted. She held up two different frocks as she tried to decide which one she liked better.

'Yes,' said Alma, 'and I think you should try both of them.'

Sara looked surprised, then smiled. 'Yeah, you're right. Um, tomorrow…' Her expression grew guarded. 'Well, actually I'm spending the day with Colleen and Anna. We're going to that artist's market, you know, the new one?'

'Oh,' said Alma, 'right.' She didn't say anything else. Her long red hair fell forward as she rummaged through the rack, hiding her expression from Sara.

'Alma, I'm sorry I didn't ask you,' she began, 'it's just-'

'No, it's OK,' said Alma, swinging her hair back to look at Sara, trying to hide her hurt. But Sara wasn't fooled.

'I would have invited you,' she said, looking guilty, 'but you're never around on Sundays any more, at least not for the whole day. You always have to rush off to see David. And then you're tired the rest of the time.'

Alma looked at Sara, her face perturbed. 'Really, it's OK,' she said. 'I understand. I know I haven't been around as much lately. Don't worry about it.'

'Really?' said Sara, sounding relieved. 'I mean, I wish you were coming, you know? You still can, if you want.'

Alma shook her head, smiling. 'No, you go,' she said. 'I'll hear about it when you get back.'

'Definitely,' said Sara, smiling back. 'Now, which of these do you think suits me best?'

Alma came through the Oak Gate, her bracelet warm on her wrist. The stars spinning across her vision slowly cleared to reveal Caleb waiting apprehensively. The woods were cool and breezy, the sunlight coming and going as white clouds scudded across the blue sky above the feathery treetops. Alma hid her smile, affecting a serious expression.

'Alma, I'm-I'm so sorry,' he began, his face anguished.

Alma looked at him sternly, shaking her head, but then could keep up the façade no longer. She broke into a broad grin that grew even wider as she saw his expression change from pained to hopeful. 'It's all right,' she said, trying not to laugh. 'Really. I mean, I wasn't happy at the time, but it's all worked out perfectly.'

'How do you mean?' asked Caleb, starting to smile as well.

'Well, now I know I can stay over, it means I can be here for longer,' she said, linking her arm with his as they started to walk through the woods. 'So really, I have to be grateful to you. Even though I wasn't at first,' she went on, glaring at him for a moment then laughing at his shocked expression. In her bag was the green dress she had found in the vintage store. It had fit almost perfectly, needing only a few minor alterations and Alma had not been able to resist it, spending almost all of her money on it.

'So you will stay? Tonight?' asked Caleb, his pleasure apparent.

'Yes,' smiled Alma. 'I even have a new dress for the occasion.' Laughing, the pair made their way arm in arm through the whispering green woods to the field beyond.

Another meeting with the Elders, another lesson about Ambeth and the importance of the Balance that made her head hurt. She'd been starting to enjoy the meetings, fascinated by the rich history of Ambeth but today she was just too caught up in her own thoughts. As she made her way slowly to the library to meet Caleb, Alma couldn't stop thinking of another library, and the concern on Sara's face that she had tried so hard to hide. Concern that Alma was slipping away from her, distracted by something she wasn't able to share.

Pushing open the heavy wooden door she saw Caleb, head down, studying from the pile of ancient texts next to him. If she had wanted to do homework, thought Alma wryly, she could have stayed at home. Still, Caleb was convinced that the clues they needed to find the Regalia were hidden here somewhere, and that Alma was the one to find them. The least she could do was humour him for now. 'Hello, Caleb,' she said as she neared the table, her tone subdued.

He lifted his head, looking pleased to see her. 'Hello Alma – was it a tough session with the Elders today?'

Alma frowned at him. 'No. Yes. I don't know. Why do you ask?' She sat down at the table opposite him and pulled the nearest pile of papers towards her, picking up the top one with a sigh.

'Well, you just seem a bit... not yourself. A bit sad,' he said, regarding her with a worried expression.

'Oh,' said Alma. She bit her lip, looking at Caleb, so obviously concerned about her. 'No, sorry, you're right. I am a bit down.'

'Do you want to talk about it?' he said, closing his notebook. 'These notes can wait for another day, if you like. Let's go for a walk instead.'

'Really?' Alma's face lit up, and she pushed her chair away from the table. Caleb regarded her with a droll expression.

'I didn't realise you disliked doing research so much,' he said, his eyes twinkling as he came around the table to offer Alma his arm.

'Oh, well, no, I mean, normally it's fine,' replied Alma, flustered, not wanting to hurt his feelings. 'So, have you found anything new?' she asked, feigning enthusiasm.

'Well, there is an old scroll that mentions the sword,' began Caleb as they left the library, walking along the echoing stone corridor towards the foyer. 'It says...' He stopped abruptly, noticing Alma wasn't listening any more. 'Hey,' he said, his voice gentle, 'are you all right?'

'Sorry,' she said. 'It's just, I was thinking about my friend.'

Caleb looked puzzled.

'My best friend,' Alma said. 'In the Human Realm,' she hastily added, seeing Caleb's face cloud over. 'Her name is Sara. I've never told you about her, I know, but lately, well, I miss her.' Caleb nodded, his expression making it obvious he was trying to understand, and Alma loved him for it. Smiling at him she went on, saying, 'I just wish I could share this with her, you know?' Caleb looked at her quizzically. 'All this,' said Alma, indicating the magnificent Foyer as they walked through. 'The magic of being here. I would love you to meet her, and I know she would love it here.'

'So, why not tell her, bring her with you next time?' asked Caleb, standing back to allow Alma to step through the doorway first. They linked arms and continued onto the Long Walk, squinting a little in the bright sunlight.

'Apart from the fact that she'd think I was crazy, I'd love to tell her,' replied Alma. 'But I can't take the risk. I mean, I know my bracelet protects me, lets me cross over when I wish, but there is no guarantee it would do the same for her. Imagine if I brought her here and then she couldn't get back, or when she did get back fifty years had passed.' Worried, she looked at Caleb, who was trying not to notice what the sun was doing to her hair and skin, or how good she looked in her new green gown.

Clearing his throat, he sought to comfort her. 'But you spend time with her in your world, do you not?' He looked thoughtful for a moment. 'I've never really asked you, have I, about your life through the Gate?'

Alma shook her head. 'It's just never come up, I suppose. When I'm here, I really don't think about it at all. Ambeth feels like home to me, as much as my own home.' She realised she hadn't really answered Caleb. 'Yes, I do spend time with her, of course I do,' she went on, 'but not as much as I used to, and I guess that's the problem. I feel guilty about it, but I can't stop coming here, not now.'

Caleb looked at her aghast then hastily coughed, going red. 'You wouldn't, I mean, you can't stop coming here,' he said, his face so upset Alma felt it in her own heart. She reached out to console him.

'No, no, never Caleb. How could I?' she said, squeezing his arm and leaning her head on his shoulder for a moment as they walked. 'I would miss you too much,' she went on, pleased to see the distress leave his face, while at the same time sad she didn't feel for him the way he obviously did for her.

'Well, good,' he replied, his voice gruff, not looking at Alma. 'I mean, I can't look for the Regalia by myself, can I?'

'Well, exactly,' said Alma, playing along. 'But, let's take a break from it for today, shall we?' She led him through to one of the gardens she knew, a small dell furnished with cushions, the perfect place to relax and take a nap on a sunny afternoon.

'Sit down,' she ordered, indicating one of the big striped cushions. Caleb did as he was told and Alma plopped down next to him on another pillow, making herself comfortable. 'Now, relax,' she went on, 'and, if you like, I'll tell you about my life in the Human Realm.'

'Hmm, I think I'd like that,' said Caleb, lying back and closing his eyes against the warm sun, content.

The Great Hall was lit with flickering warmth from fire and lanterns. Alma sipped her drink as she looked around, enjoying the music being played by the trio near the dais. She smiled as she caught Caleb's eye – he was at the buffet, loading up their plates with more food. Then she realised that someone had come to stand next to her.

Looking up she was shocked to see Deryck, dressed in grey tunic and breeches, his golden hair falling forward as he smiled down at her.

'Lady Alma,' he murmured. 'Such a pleasure to see you here, and looking so well, if I might add. Are you enjoying the music?'

She stared up at him thunderstruck, her cheeks aflame as she rubbed her suddenly clammy palms on the soft green velvet of her skirt. Across the room, a group of girls shot her dirty looks and, noticing this, she frowned. Deryck, momentarily confused, followed her gaze and let out a chuckle before turning his attention back to Alma, who had recovered enough to stammer, 'Y-yes, they are very good.'

'Do you think?' He smiled at her, the interest in his face genuine. 'I enjoy them as well. It is nice to meet someone who seems to appreciate music as I do. Perhaps some time – ah.' He stopped as Caleb joined them, the expression on his face making it clear that Deryck was not welcome.

'Lord Deryck,' he said courteously, though without smiling.

'Caleb,' replied Deryck, his face expressionless as he inclined his head. Turning to Alma, the image of courtesy, he held out his hand and she took it. Bowing, he kissed her hand gently. 'I hope we can talk again soon,' he said softly as he released her hand with a warm smile. She felt breathless all of a sudden.

'Yes,' she said, managing to smile back at him. 'That would be lovely.'

She could feel Caleb bristling with anger beside her. As Deryck turned to leave he bent over, hissing, 'What did he want?' into her ear.

'Nothing, just to talk, I guess,' snapped Alma.

'Hmmph!' said Caleb, watching the Dark Prince as he crossed the room. He sat down next to Alma and tried to catch her eye, but she was still watching Deryck. She took the plate of food Caleb gave her with thanks, but her appetite was gone. Across the room, Deryck caught her eye and winked. Her eyes widened in response, but then a group of dancers moved across the room and the contact was broken.

It was Friday evening, a week later and Alma was sitting on the kitchen sofa, fidgeting in her seat as she looked out onto the darkening garden. Eleanor, busy preparing dinner, glanced at her in amusement.

'Off to the park again tonight?' she asked, as she deftly peeled potatoes and dropped them into a pot.

'What? Um, oh yeah, I guess so,' said Alma, squirming in her seat. 'Um, so, how long til dinner?'

'Maybe an hour,' replied Eleanor, her lips twitching. 'So, why don't you go now, you know, before it gets too late. I imagine you're seeing Sara later?'

'Oh, right,' said Alma. 'Well, yeah, maybe that would be good…' She trailed off, thinking hard. Then her face lit up and she looked at Eleanor. 'Really?'

'Just go,' smiled her mother. 'But don't be late back,' she called. But Alma had already dashed out the side door, which banged shut behind her.

She ran through the cold December dark to the Armorial Park, her stomach burbling with excitement. Reaching the Gate she stood and caught her breath as she looked up at the silent trees, their bare branches black against the purple sky. Then she began to focus, feeling the familiar flare of warmth under her palm as she stepped through the Gate. Ooh. She staggered out into wet and cold woodland, raindrops hitting her head and face as she tried to regain her balance. Once she could stand she dug in her backpack to find her waterproof, hastily shrugging it on over her long-sleeved top. But where was Caleb? Alma looked around, realising with surprise that he was not there as usual to meet her. All around her were green and dripping branches, but nowhere could she see Caleb in his habitual brown and green attire.

A blackbird hopped past, its shiny black eyes regarding her quizzically. It shook its feathers to clear them of the crystal raindrops weighing them down. She smiled - the Narnia books had been favourites of hers when she was younger, especially the bits about the talking animals. Now she had her own enchanted place, she still didn't know what was going to happen next – maybe the blackbird would speak to her. The thought made her laugh out loud and, smiling at her fancy, she greeted the little bird with a cheery 'Hello'. But there was no answering chirrup – instead, he flew off, no doubt looking to shelter from the rain. With a sigh, Alma decided to start on the path that led out of the woods and find Caleb. Turning, she let out a squeak of shock, which, red-faced, she tried to cover with a cough. Deryck, clad in grey and holding a large umbrella, was standing on the path, an amused expression on his face.

'Do you always talk to birds?' he asked, smiling in a way that made her blush even more. She wished the ground would swallow her up, but no such luck.

'N-no, it was just, I was... Oh, it's a long story. But no, I don't usually talk to birds, I just thought maybe...' She trailed off, realising by the expression on his face that he was teasing her. What on earth...? And *where* was Caleb?

'Come on,' said Deryck. 'Let's not stand in the rain all day.' Strolling up to her he offered his arm, holding the umbrella over them both. Alma pulled her hood back, her dampened hair clinging in tendrils to her flushed cheeks as she looked at Deryck, confused.

'Sorry... What are you doing here? Where's Caleb?' she asked, her heart pounding to feel Deryck's warm arm twined through her own.

Deryck gazed down at her with those dreamy green eyes, lips parted as though he was about to say something. Then he seemed to pull himself together.

'He was detained, so I decided to come and meet you instead.'

'Detained?' said Alma, worried. 'Is he all right?' Deryck looked briefly annoyed.

'He is fine,' he said curtly, his tone harsh. Alma, taken aback, didn't reply. She didn't understand what was happening at all.

They walked on through the dripping damp trees

towards the field without saying another word, though Deryck was painfully aware of her, close as they were. He knew he should say something, had planned to invite her to meet his father, but found himself uncharacteristically tongue-tied. He could feel her tension as they moved through the trees and knew the effect he was having on her. What was surprising was the effect she was having on him. He wanted nothing more than to pull her into his arms, taking advantage of the intimacy of the umbrella, but knew he had to play it cool. And he was jealous. Again. Of Caleb. This would not do at all.

Alma, meanwhile, was lost for words. She could hardly believe what was happening. Wet gravel crunched underfoot as they reached the gardens. Trees and bushes hung heavy with raindrops, the sky above grey and cloudy. The distant hills were shrouded with mist and Alma shivered a little under her light waterproof. Deryck glanced at her then gently pulled her closer as they walked. Alma looked up at him, taking in the perfect profile, the golden hair brushed back from his brow. She could barely breathe; her head was spinning, her bracelet burning uncomfortably hot against her wrist. She didn't mind, though – for Deryck, she would endure it. Despite the fact that it was raining, that she could think of nothing to say, that her feet were damp and her hands were cold, she wanted this walk to last forever.

All too soon they reached the Great Hall. Deryck released her arm as they arrived at the double doors, flanked as usual by the guards, impassive in the rain. He kept her sheltered under the umbrella as the door was opened but did not enter, bowing instead as he said quietly, 'I will see you again later, I hope.' His green eyes met Alma's one last time before he turned to go, leaving her standing open-mouthed in the rain, too stunned to go inside. Then she heard a shout and turned to see Caleb running from the opposite direction, under his own blue umbrella.

'Alma!' he said. 'I'm so sorry! Quick, come inside, you're getting soaked.' He ushered Alma inside, shaking out his umbrella as he came in behind her and nodding his thanks to the guards as they closed the heavy wooden doors, leaving them in the relative warmth and dryness of the Foyer.

Alma found herself inexpressibly glad to see Caleb, his calming presence the perfect antidote to the whirling emotions that Deryck inspired in her. She shook herself, scattering raindrops everywhere, glad to be inside. Peeling off her waterproof, she rolled it into a ball under her arm and gave him a smile. 'Come on, then, we haven't got all day.'

He grinned back. 'You don't fool me. I know you're not that keen on getting to the library.'

'No, but it's good to see you,' replied Alma, meaning it. Together they went towards the tower stair leading to Alma's room and started to ascend.

'I'm so sorry I was late,' said Caleb, 'though I'm glad to see you got here all right. I suppose you know your way through the woods well enough at this point.'

'But, I wasn't alone,' said Alma, running her hands through her wet hair and releasing a shower of drops onto the stone steps. Caleb stopped on the stair above, looking at her, confusion on his face.

'What do you mean?' he said, frowning. 'Did Thorion come to meet you?'

'No,' replied Alma, twisting her hair into a long rope, wondering why Caleb had stopped. 'It was Deryck. Didn't you know he was coming to meet me? He said-' Alma stopped, realising Deryck hadn't said anything about Caleb.

'Deryck?! That sly dog!' said Caleb, his expression outraged. 'And where did he say I was?'

'Well, he said you'd been detained… I'm sorry, is something wrong? I mean, I thought it was a bit strange he was there and everything, but the walk here was fine,' said Alma, mystified as to the source of Caleb's anger.

'Oh yes, I was detained,' he continued hotly. 'Detained by his father, doing his dirty work. I should have known…'

'Known what? What are you talking about?' said Alma, but she was starting to guess. Deryck had obviously fixed things so that Caleb wouldn't be able to meet her today, so that he, Deryck, could be there in his place. She wasn't sure how she felt about that. To be honest, it was almost too much to think about. Not for the first time she wished Sara could be there with her, for there was absolutely no way she could discuss this with Caleb. He was furious, and with some reason.

'Deryck gave me a message that his father required my assistance – I knew I had to meet you but couldn't refuse. It's part of the protocol of the court. I never dreamed it was a set-up – how could they have known when you were coming across?'

Obviously furious, Caleb looked as though he was ready to run back downstairs and confront both Deryck and Denoris. Alma hastily sought to placate him, in fear of what he might do. 'Caleb, it's OK. I'm fine, nothing happened.'

This was the wrong choice of words.

'*Nothing happened?* Did you want something to happen?' snapped Caleb. Regret crossed his face and she looked away, not wanting him to see her reaction, but she knew. Of course she wanted something to happen with Deryck. And Caleb knew it too.

Her heart hurt from it all and she sagged against the wall, damp hair falling forward as she struggled to find an answer. But Caleb beat her to it. Reaching out, he put his hand on her shoulder, trying to look into her face with his best puppy dog eyes. Alma laughed, unable to help herself. The tension broken, they resumed their passage up the curving stairs until they reached the door to Alma's room. Caleb remained silent, though Alma could sense his heartache and knew there was nothing she could do about it. She couldn't bear the idea of hurting Caleb. He was so dear to her, but she also knew that, given the chance, she would be with Deryck. Which would hurt Caleb. So she was stuck, whatever she did.

Temptation, Frustration

Opening the door with her key, Alma entered her bedroom, feeling better as she took in the calm, cosy space. The stars glistened in the vaulted ceiling and the shutters were closed against the damp, while a fire glowed in the fireplace. Her soft feather bed had been freshly made. Caleb must have arranged this, knowing she was coming across today. He stood resting one arm on the mantelpiece, staring into space, his jaw tight, obviously still upset. Dear Caleb – what a good friend he was to her. She wished so much he could be more, that she could feel for him what she felt for Deryck, for she knew it would make him happy. But what about her own feelings? Putting down her bag, she went over to him.

'C'mon,' she cajoled, trying to shake him out of his dark mood. 'Let's go study. You never know, today could be the day we figure out who those 'hearts' are.'

At this Caleb brightened somewhat. 'OK,' he said, managing a half-smile as he looked at Alma. 'Let's go. We can research until lunchtime, then you have to meet with the Elders again.' Alma sighed. 'Is that all right?' asked Caleb, his expression perturbed. 'I mean, maybe we can do something else later...'

'No, it's fine,' said Alma, shaking out her waterproof and hanging it on a hook on the wall near the fire. Then she turned to face Caleb. 'It's just, I mean, I love meeting with the Elders, I'm learning so much, you know? Even though it's confusing at times, it's still really cool.' Sitting down in one of the chairs, she rubbed her hands over her face before continuing. 'I can just feel how much they expect of me and...'

She trailed off, looking at Caleb and he came to sit opposite her, watching her as she shook out her hair to dry by the fire. 'They can be a bit overwhelming, can't they,' he said sympathetically, watching the play of red and gold light on her hair as she combed her fingers through it. 'I don't envy you.'

'Yes!' said Alma, relieved he seemed to understand. Encouraged, she went on, warming to her topic. 'That's just it. It's fascinating hearing about the history of this place, but I don't know why it's so important to them that I learn so much about it. And then when they start asking about the Regalia...'

She twisted her mouth, feeling uncomfortable as she realised Caleb was staring at her. Tucking her hair behind her ears she stood up. 'Well, I suppose we should get going, hey?'

177

'This is interesting.'

'What's that?' Alma looked up, smiling at Caleb. He waved the paper he was holding at her.

'It's about the Cup.'

'Ooh, does it tell us where it is?' Caleb made a face at her and she stuck her tongue out at him. He laughed. The tension between them was gone and Alma felt gladness down to her toes that they were back to their usual laughing, teasing relationship. 'Well, it would make things easier,' she said. Caleb just gave her a look. 'Oh, okay, let me see,' she went on, holding out her hand. Caleb passed her the paper. It was torn at the top, remnants of what looked like printed black letters at the ragged edge. Alma stared at them but couldn't figure out what they might say, so she concentrated on the straggly writing instead, screwing up her face as she tried to figure out what it said.

'*She has left me again,*' she read, puzzling out the words. '*I know she has gone to him. But I can't care. Not as long as I can look upon the Cup. She is my heart's desire.*' She looked at Caleb.

'Sounds a bit odd,' she said. 'Like, I'm not sure if it's the woman or the Cup he desires. What do you think?'

'Well, I was thinking maybe it was something to do with one of our hearts.'

'Because he's… upset? I mean, I guess it's a he.' She looked at the paper again, reading on.

'*Her eyes gleam like jewels in the private heat of our bed, her skin like silk under my hands. I see the marks he leaves on her and I know she cannot leave him. But I love her more than anyone or anything and I cannot leave her either.'*

'Bleurgh,' said Alma, her cheeks going red. 'Um, that's a bit… um…'

'Yeah,' said Caleb. He coughed, his own cheeks a bit pink as he looked away. 'So, a candidate for our "heart betrayed," d'you think?'

'Well, I guess,' said Alma, turning the paper over to see if anything else was written on it. Her face was starting to cool but the intimacy of the words coupled with her own troubled feelings had left her feeling shaken, to say the least. 'Are there any more of these?'

'Nope. It was just loose in a pile of stuff.'

'So, no idea who he is or was or why he was so into the Cup.' She shrugged, putting the paper down. 'I mean, maybe. But without any more information, we can't say for sure.'

Caleb nodded. 'Guess we'll have to keep looking.'

'Maybe we can ask Thorion?'

'Er, I'm not asking Thorion about that,' said Caleb, going red again. 'No way. You can, if you want to.'

Alma thought about reading the words in the presence of the handsome High King and blushed again. Um, no. Caleb was right. 'Hey, maybe you should come to the meeting with me?'

He looked up, one eyebrow raised, a half smile on his face. 'Why's that?'

'Well, I've been thinking about it and I think you should. I mean, we're both doing this, so you should get to come to the meetings as well.'

'I thought you didn't talk much about the Regalia,' he said, though his face had lit up. Alma smiled at him. Dear Caleb.

'Well, I just let them know what we've found. So, maybe you could do that today. Um, except for... you know.' She blushed again. Damn! What was up with her at the moment? But she knew what was up with her. She also knew she wanted to make it up to Caleb, that it was important he wasn't upset. Plus, it was right he should come along – he did most of the work anyway.

'But-'

'Thorion won't mind, I'm sure of it. C'mon, come with me. You know you want to.' She shot him a teasing look and he grinned.

'Okay, I'll come.'

Alma smiled back then looked up at the clock on the wall. 'Looks like it's time for me to get changed,' she said. 'So, I'll meet you there?'

'Sounds good,' said Caleb. 'In the meantime, I'll carry on with this.'

'Really?' But Alma could see how pleased he was. Getting up from the table she bade him farewell. Then she left, heading for her tower room.

Deryck stood in the comfortable surrounds of his father's apartment, deep in thought. The panelled study was furnished in rich woods and leathers in deep browns and reds, the fire in the fireplace reflecting gold light onto the fine carving and intricately woven carpet. An inherently masculine room, it was a place both Deryck and his father used often, his mother choosing to remain on their country estate. Deryck suspected that had more to do with not seeing his father than anything else, but beyond that didn't give it much thought. He was alone, Lord Denoris being occupied with business elsewhere for the day. This left Deryck at a loose end, which was normally not a problem for him. He could find a friend to practice swordplay or archery with, or a girl with whom to while away the afternoon. There were books to read, the gardens to wander or he could take his horse, a fine black steed called Thetis, for a run through the woods and beyond. For the noble son of a high-ranking Lord there were no end of pursuits, which made his current situation even more untenable.

Walking across the soft carpet to the bookcases that lined one wall, Deryck ran his hands through his hair, torn by indecision. Alma. He could not get her out of his head, the way she had looked at him as they walked together through the rain. Her mouth as she talked... He groaned, sitting down in a richly upholstered leather chair with his head in his hands. He needed to see her again. Deryck knew where her room was in the Great Hall, had made it his business to find out as soon as it was assigned to her. It had been an easy matter, bribing one of the chambermaids with a kiss and a promise of more. At the time his purpose had seemed so clear, his plan so simple. Seduce Alma, bring her across to the Dark and, at the same time, score a point against Caleb. But now things were more complicated. She had wormed her way into his head, and thoughts of her came to him at the most inopportune moments – although he had only seen and spoken with her a handful of times, she had made an impression on him like no other girl. Standing, Deryck chose a book from the leather-bound selection in the carved timber cabinets, then made his way out of the apartment towards the Great Hall. The rain had stopped and the gardens smelled fresh and green, a watery sun starting to break through the clouds. Coming to the heavy double doors, Deryck paused to be admitted, then made his way to the tower stair. He would talk to her, that's all, he thought. Just see her again.

Alma looked around her room with pleasure as she got changed, selecting a long burgundy gown in place of her usual sweatshirt and jeans. Twirling a little and laughing at herself, she crossed to the window, its wooden shutters open wide to the sun which had finally broken through the rain clouds. Leaning on the sill, breathing in the sweet cool air, Alma took in the view. The gardens spread out below her and she watched the small figures of the Court as they walked the pathways, the patterns they made as they moved on errands unknown. To one side was the green field leading to the forest with its Gates and mystery, while beyond the gardens the land stretched away to distant hills, green in the spring sunshine, the shadows from drifting clouds above causing an endless play of light and shade across their rolling peaks.

Filled with the joy of the day, Alma moved reluctantly away from the window, realising it was time to meet Caleb – she had lingered long enough. She carefully latched the door behind her and set out along the narrow stone hallway, trailing her hand along the carved panels and admiring the pierced metal lanterns that lit the way. Not paying attention, she was almost upon the figure sitting in the window alcove before she noticed him.

It was Deryck. He was reading a book, his golden hair falling forward and catching the light and Alma was so startled that she stopped dead. She had only just recovered from their encounter this morning – twice in one day might be too much for her to bear. Her heart started pounding as it usually did when she saw him, her bracelet burning against her wrist. Hearing her step, Deryck looked up and smiled. He closed his book, got up and came towards Alma, who stood as though rooted to the spot.

'Oh!' she gasped. 'I'm sorry, I-I didn't mean to disturb you.'

'You didn't,' he replied, still smiling in a way that made her feel weak at the knees. 'I was only reading while I waited.'

'While you waited... for me?' said Alma, confused then shocked at her own boldness. Why on earth had she said that?

'Well, yes, actually,' said Deryck, surprising her again. 'I wanted to talk to you – alone.'

Alma stared at him, dumbfounded. With what seemed

to be the last rational piece of her mind she remembered that Deryck, for all his beauty, was of the Dark and that she was not a favourite of the Dark. At all. Which made his attention all the more confusing. Still, she had to say something.

'What is it that I can help you with, Lord Deryck?' she said, wincing inwardly at her formal tone. But it was her only defence against his charms. A defence that, she now saw, was useless. Deryck moved towards her, backing her up until she was almost against the wall. He was standing far closer to her than he needed to.

'Why so formal with me, Alma?' he murmured, his green eyes warm and smiling as they gazed into her own. 'Do you not like me, a little? I thought maybe, in the woods-'

'W-well, yes, of course,' stammered Alma, totally thrown. 'B-but, I don't understand, wh-what-'

Deryck, seeming to realise the effect he was having on her, smiled, his expression teasing. Alma didn't know where to look. She tried not to gasp for breath. 'Alma, my father is aware that you are searching for the Regalia, and so would like to offer you the use of the libraries of the Dark for your research. He asked me to tell you, and so here I am.'

'Oh.' Alma swallowed then licked her lips, her blue eyes on his. 'Um, so, you needed to speak to me... alone?'

Deryck moved even closer, one hand coming to rest on the wall beside Alma's head. 'We-ell,' he smiled, arching one perfect blond eyebrow, 'not really, I suppose. I just thought it might be nice, that's all. Do you not think this is nice? After all, we didn't talk much earlier today.' Reaching out, he lifted a strand of red hair that had fallen across her eyes, his touch feather light. Alma could hardly breathe. Her head whirling, she fought for control. Moving slightly to one side, she tried to increase the distance between them. Then she smiled back at Deryck, her lips trembling despite her efforts to hold them steady. She could feel the rough stone of the wall against her back, the soft folds of her gown around her legs. It was all she could do to stay standing. It was infuriating, the effect he was having on her! The sudden burst of rage cleared her head enough so she could respond.

'It is very nice, I suppose,' she said, trying, but not really succeeding, to sound cool. 'But why would the Dark want to help me with this? Not that I don't appreciate the offer, of course,' she went on, belatedly remembering her manners.

'Oh, we have our reasons,' said Deryck, moving closer again. At the edge of the stairs, her back against the wall, Alma had nowhere left to move. As his face moved closer to hers, she held her breath, lips parting as her eyes started to close. She was not sure what she would have done next if Caleb hadn't come up the stairs at that very moment, looking for her.

'Alma,' he exclaimed, looking from her flushed face to Deryck, who still stood unnecessarily close, his hand resting on the wall next to her head. 'Are you all right? The Elders sent me to fetch you – they are waiting.'

But it was Deryck who, a frown marring his handsome

face, turned his attention away from Alma to address Caleb. 'And why would she not be all right?' he enquired, his tone icy. 'I would not harm her.'

'No, I'm sure you would not, Lord Deryck,' said Caleb. His words were polite but his tone and expression made it perfectly clear that he did not, in fact, agree.

Deryck stiffened and was about to reply when Alma intervened, laying a hand on his arm. She turned to Caleb and with a smile said, 'Of course I'm all right, Caleb.' Her eyes pleaded with him not to take things any further; she knew he was still upset by the day's earlier events. Turning back to Deryck, her hand still resting lightly on his arm, she added, 'Please thank your father for his generous offer. I will let you know.'

Finally Deryck stepped back. He made a small bow. 'Be sure that you do,' he said curtly then, with a glare at Caleb, he reclaimed his book and walked swiftly away down the passage.

'What was going on here?' asked Caleb, and, though his tone was more gentle than accusatory, it still annoyed Alma. She was totally shaken, both by the closeness of her encounter with Deryck and the abruptness with which it had ended. This did not make her feel charitable towards Caleb, despite his obvious good intentions.

'Nothing!' she snapped. 'He was just waiting for me, as I left my room. I don't know why,' she continued crossly, seeing the query in Caleb's face. 'He said he needed to speak with me alone, had an offer from his father for me to use the libraries of the Dark.'

'What?!' Caleb blurted. Alma clenched her fists, her

mouth tight as she watched Caleb fighting with his own emotions. She did not need this. He looked away, then back at her. 'No matter,' he said, his tone mild. 'You can tell Thorion when you see him, see what he thinks.'

Though Alma knew he meant well, his words only infuriated her even more and she lashed out. 'Why should I tell him anything? Surely this is my business!'

Seeing Caleb recoil, a look of shock on his usually amiable face, she was immediately contrite. She felt tired and irritated, her good mood of earlier destroyed by the awkward tension of meeting with Deryck. The last thing she wanted to do was upset her closest friend.

'I'm sorry,' she muttered, not looking at Caleb. 'It's just, he, well-'

'I know,' said Caleb resignedly. He looked away for a moment, blowing out a breath. 'It's just, Alma, you need to be careful. With… him.'

'Oh Caleb,' Alma whispered, her eyes starting to well up. This was too much.

'Come on,' he said, gently taking her arm and leading her to the window seat where Deryck had been resting just minutes before. 'Let's sit for a moment. Here, have some of this,' he continued, offering her a drink from the same heavy silver bottle he had on the day he met her.

Alma wiped her eyes and looked gratefully at Caleb as she took the drink, taking a long swallow before wiping the top and passing it back to him. 'Thank you,' she said. 'What would I do without you, dear Caleb, to find me seats and offer me drinks when I need them?'

Caleb took a breath, his longing clear to her for a

moment, his blue eyes ocean deep. Then he looked down, huffing out a laugh. 'Well, you'd be tired and thirsty for a start,' he teased, nudging her with his elbow.

Grinning, she nudged him back, relieved to see him smiling again. 'I really am sorry,' she said. 'I didn't mean to snap at you.'

'It's forgotten,' said Caleb. He stood and offered his hand to Alma. She took it and they linked arms as they walked down the stairs to meet with the Elders, good humour restored once more.

Further along the hall, around the curve where the tower ascended to its highest level, stood Deryck, still seething. Caleb! Always Caleb! A thorn in his side, the boy constantly irritated him just by existing. Deryck didn't know why he disliked Caleb so much but he did, had for as long as he could remember. His closeness to Alma was just another layer of irritation. Deryck wanted Alma; there was no doubt in his mind now. Not just for the Dark, but for himself. He thought back to their encounter, how she had looked in the soft velvet gown, wine dark against her pale skin, the way she had trembled as she stood with her back to the wall, fighting for self-control. He'd had to work to control his own feelings, for he found he wanted nothing more than to kiss her, to be close to her. He had almost had her, but then Caleb had come along to spoil things. Furious, he threw his book to the ground, then, ashamed at such a childish gesture, bent to pick it up. He knew she would come to him eventually – he just had to find the right moment. Then she would be his.

Sitting in the small circle of Elders, Alma framed her questions carefully, not wanting to reveal her longing for Deryck. But she couldn't believe that the boy who stirred her so was of the Dark, that his beauty and charm were not of the Light. She wanted to understand their nature for her own reasons, for all that she firmly told herself it was just part of her learning here.

'But what is the difference?' she asked, looking around at the group. Adara and Thorion exchanged glances, Adara hiding a smile while Thorion answered. Caleb, sitting to one side, folded his arms and looked away.

'On the surface it appears that we are the same. As you know, it is impossible to tell simply by looking at us whether we are of the Light or the Dark – however the reality is that we are quite different. Those of the Light believe in truth, beauty and love as they happen: truth in our undertakings, in being honest with ourselves as well as with others; beauty found in all things, from the love of a mother for her child to the play of light on a single drop of water, and love for yourself as well as others – loving yourself enough to choose what is right for you, to become the best person you can be, but also to care for others as you care for yourself. Balance in all things is very important to us. That is why the Light have always been guardians of the Regalia.'

'And why we are shamed that it has been lost,' boomed another voice, that of a stately and dignified older lord, his wavy hair and full beard silvered with age.

'And also why the Dark has ever been seeking to take this control from us,' continued Thorion, his blue eyes stern. 'To them, our loss is their gain. For the Dark also believe in truth, beauty and love. But truth only as it appears to them, not how it is in reality, beauty in its most superficial aspect, that of the physical, regardless of the nature that lies within, and love in its most selfish form – the love of self and of one's own aims at the expense of all others. This is what makes them so dangerous. With their physical beauty and seductive tones they can easily confuse others into believing their lies; in fact, over the centuries they have crossed over into your world to do just that, whispering their ideas into receptive ears, fanning the flames of hatred and fear, simply to bring about the chaos and disorder in which they delight. It is their meddling that has led us to this tipping point and caused the Regalia to be lost.'

'So the stone you carry is a precious gift indeed,' said Adara with a smile. 'Shame, though, that you do not seem to be using it,' she added slyly, her golden eyes bright in her mischievous face.

Alma blushed to the roots of her hair. She didn't dare look at Caleb. She had thought her infatuation with Deryck was a secret but now, listening to the soft laughter of the Elders, realised her feelings had been clear for everyone to see.

Walking along the stone corridor with Caleb, Alma was deep in thought. She needed to go home, she decided. Forget about staying the night here – if she ran into Deryck again she wasn't sure what she would do. What she really wanted was normal things around her, like Sara and her mother and her room and even her brothers, annoying as they were. She just needed a break from all the magic and confusion of Ambeth. Caleb was quiet as he walked next to her, seeming to be deep in thought. Then, as they reached the foyer, he nudged her with his elbow.

'Are you all right?' he said. 'Shall we go for a walk? I thought maybe later we could-'

'I'm sorry, Caleb,' said Alma, looking at him with stricken eyes. She hated hurting his feelings. 'But I think I need to go home now.'

'What?'

'I'm sorry,' she said again. 'Come on, I need to get changed and grab my stuff. Will you walk me to the Gate, please?'

Caleb looked at her for a moment, saying nothing. Alma could see how disappointed he was. Then he pulled himself together, managing a half smile.

'Okay,' he said. 'Let's go.' Resignedly he followed her up the stairs, waiting while she got changed and collected her bag. Then they walked together in silence through the trees towards the Gate, the occasional splat of raindrops from above and the rustle of their passage the only sounds. Finally, after huffing out a breath, Caleb spoke.

'So, what do you see in him?' He sounded belligerent, unlike his usual self. Alma stopped and looked at him, frowning.

'What are you on about?' she said, though she knew. Caleb had been in a bad mood all day despite her best efforts and she knew it was because of Deryck. Well, it wasn't her fault! Her temper rising, she looked at Caleb with her mouth tight, her eyes challenging him.

'You know who I mean,' said Caleb, meeting her stare with his own as he folded his arms. 'The Prince of Darkness.' Alma had to laugh at this, a short sharp yelp that surprised her almost as much as it did Caleb.

'Oh, come on,' she said, then stopped. Caleb deserved better than this. Her anger subsided. 'He's not bad, you know. He can't help who his father is.'

'He cannot change it either, Alma. Nor can he change what he is.'

'And what is he, Caleb?'

'He is Dark,' the boy replied. 'And no matter what he does, or tells you, that is what he will always be, what his nature will be.'

Alma looked down, biting her lip. She knew all this, of course she did, but it didn't change how Deryck made her feel. Or how she seemed to make him feel. Lifting her head, she brushed her red hair out of her eyes. She wanted to make Caleb understand. 'He likes me, I think,' she said hesitantly. Seeing the pained look on Caleb's face that he quickly tried to hide, she wished she hadn't.

'Oh Alma,' he said, before stopping, unable to go on.

Alma felt it like a physical pain in her chest – hurting Caleb was the last thing she ever wanted to do.

'Caleb, I'm… sorry,' she said quietly. Sorry for what though – for liking Deryck? She couldn't be sorry for that. For not loving Caleb the way he did her? Perhaps, but she couldn't change the way she felt. 'I wouldn't hurt you for all the world.'

He came closer, putting his hands gently on her arms, looking at her with eyes that shifted from blue to grey. He opened his mouth as if to say something, then closed it again and Alma met his gaze, not wanting to look away, wanting him to see how much he meant to her. Finally, he spoke. 'I will always be here for you, whatever you choose to do. I will always look out for you.'

Alma felt close to tears. Blinking in a vain effort to contain them, she wiped her cheek with her hand, her heart full. 'I'll be here for you too, Caleb – you couldn't be a better friend.'

Again he looked as though he was about to say something, then thought better of it. Instead, he pulled her into a hug, sliding his arms around her back, his hands gentle on her hair. After a moment's hesitation she hugged him back, gently breaking his hold a moment later. They stood close together in the damp woods, a few errant rays of sun coming through the trees, and as Caleb looked at Alma one corner of his mouth lifted in a half-smile.

'So, see you here on Friday as usual?'

Alma smiled back at him and nodded her head. 'Yes, I'll be here,' she said. Stepping away from Caleb towards the Gate, she placed her hand on her bracelet and started to focus, then stopped. She ran back to him, impulsively kissing him on the cheek. His face broke into a delighted grin, as did hers. Moving back to the Gate she began to focus again, still smiling. The bracelet's magic started to work and Alma stepped through, back to her world and her normal life, just as she had wished.

Heart's Love

Humming along to Christmas songs playing on the radio in the kitchen, Alma licked the spoon she was holding, savouring the mingled flavours of raisins and spices. This was her favourite time of year. She was making mince pies, something she had done each Christmas since she was small, first as a helper then taking over the job once she was old enough. Her mother and the rest of the family wisely stayed clear of the kitchen when Alma was cooking, not wanting to be in the firing line if something went wrong. Still, Eleanor liked to check on Alma every so often and did so at just that moment, sticking her head around the door.

'How are they coming along?' she asked, smiling she took in the dab of flour on her cheek and the spread of utensils, pastry and raisins across the scrubbed pine table. Outside it was cold and dreary, but the kitchen was a cosy haven, light gleaming off the golden wood and soft sofa and the oven pumping out heat, making the room even warmer.

'Oh fine,' said Alma, smiling in return. Holding out the spoon, she offered her mother a taste of the mince mixture. Eleanor shook her head.

'Oh, I shouldn't,' she began, but then gave in as Alma gave her what she liked to call 'The Look.' An expression somewhere between love and exasperation, she had done it since she was small whenever she thought her mother was being silly. It reminded Eleanor so much of Alma's father that she always gave in, though with good humour.

'Oh, all right then,' she said, coming over to take the spoon. 'Mmmm!' she exclaimed, tasting the mixture. 'What have you done differently? This is delicious!'

'I marinated the raisins with orange and lemon zest before adding the spices,' Alma said, pleased. Each year she challenged herself to try something new and creative when she made the mince pies – it didn't always work out but when it did, the results were always appreciated. She was happy they'd turned out well this year, as she planned to take some for Caleb when she next crossed over.

'So, any plans over the holidays?' asked Eleanor, settling herself down in one of the chairs and looking expectantly at her daughter.

Alma looked at her, raising an eyebrow. 'What – other than the whole Christmas and New Year's thing?'

'Well, of course I know you're going to be celebrating with us,' said Eleanor, giving her daughter a look of her own. 'But what about the other days? Are you going to see Sara?'

'Oh, yeah,' said Alma, turning her pastry dough out onto the floured surface of the table. She took a moment to round it and sprinkle it with yet more flour before starting to roll it out using the old wooden rolling pin that had been her grandmother's. 'Yes, we've got some stuff planned, parties and things. And we're going out shopping tomorrow.' Getting the pastry to the thickness she desired, Alma took the little circular cutter and started to cut out the tops and bases for her pies. 'I think tonight though,' she said casually, glancing at her mother, 'I might just go for a walk.'

'In this?' said her mother, gesturing out to the cold garden, the light already fading even though it was not yet four o'clock.

'Yes,' said Alma, starting to put the circles of pastry into the baking tray so they made little cups. Once she had done that, she started spooning in the spiced raisin mixture. 'I don't mind this weather, you know? And I want some fresh air after being in the kitchen all day.' She darted a smile at her mother with that comment, knowing how much time Eleanor spent in her beloved kitchen.

Her mother smiled back at her, shaking her head. 'Well, just make sure you wrap up warm, OK?'

'OK, mum,' said Alma in a mocking tone, though she softened it with another smile. How old did her mother think she was? Still, she got it - the love behind her words. Gently she brushed the edge of the pastry cups with some milk before placing the little circles of pastry on top, completing her pies. After pricking each with a fork she stood back, wiping her hands on her apron with a look of satisfaction on her face. 'All finished,' she said. 'Now, time to put them in the oven.'

'And then clean up,' said her mother, an amused look on her face as she surveyed the general devastation.

'Hmmm, yeah,' said Alma, as if noticing the mess for the first time. 'A messy cook's a good cook, right?' she said hopefully.

'Well then, your mince pies should be especially tasty this year, Alma,' said Eleanor, getting up. 'Good luck!' she said as she exited the kitchen. Alma could hear her chuckling as she went down the hall to the front room.

Letting out a sigh, Alma placed her pies carefully in the oven, before starting, slowly, to clean up.

Though the night was dark and cold, the park was still populated with die-hard exercise enthusiasts and dog walkers. Alma threaded her way through them on her way to the Oak Gate which waited, dark and imposing even without its crown of leaves. She had dressed in layers, looking forward to the warmer weather of Ambeth and feeling the sun on her skin. In her backpack were half a dozen of her mince pies, carefully wrapped as a gift for Caleb. She wasn't sure whether he even celebrated Christmas but he meant too much to her to let the season pass without marking it in some way.

Stopping at the Gate, Alma closed her eyes, reaching within for the focus that helped her to cross at her chosen time. Hearing the slap of feet on the path coming nearer, she opened her eyes and stepped back to let two joggers go past, one of whom gave her a curious look. She smiled back innocently, though she went cold at the thought of how close she had come to being seen. Once they had passed and she had made sure there was no one else nearby, she tried again. Closing one hand over her bracelet, she breathed deeply, waiting for the answering warmth in the stone that would let her know she could pass through safely. Feeling it flare under her palm, she opened her eyes and, checking once more that no one was there to see her, stepped through.

This time she stepped into early summer, the forest glossy and green, the blossoms almost gone. The rich smells of earth and foliage filled her nostrils, birds sang in the trees and small forest creatures rustled in the undergrowth. Unzipping her fleece she stuffed it into her pack, enjoying the warm sunshine as it filtered through the green canopy above. Caleb was waiting in his usual spot, a smile lighting his face as he saw her.

'Alma,' he called out. She ran to meet him, matching his smile with one of her own, squashing down her mild disappointment that it wasn't Deryck waiting for her.

'I made it!'

'You always do,' laughed Caleb. 'Took your time though, I didn't think you were coming.'

'Why, am I late?' asked Alma. 'I'm still working on getting the timing right – I thought I had it this time, although I had to wait for a couple of joggers to pass before I could step through the Gate.'

They fell into into step together, taking the well-worn path through the woodland to the open green and gardens beyond. Alma's face was full of joy as she took in the familiar view and Caleb grinned at her obvious delight, purposely bumping into her and making her giggle. He laughed as well, his eyes full of affection for her.

'Hey,' Alma said, stepping out of Caleb's way as he tried to bump her again, stopping on the path. 'Be careful! I have something for you and I don't want it to get squashed.' She smiled at him, shading her eyes from the sun.

'Really?' said Caleb, his face lighting up.' Because… I have something for you as well.'

It was Alma's turn to be amazed. 'I didn't know you celebrated Christmas!'

'Oh, we don't,' said Caleb, 'but we do mark Midwinter in your world, regardless of the season here. It is a Feast day for us… anyway,' he went on, blushing slightly. 'This is for you.' He held out a package wrapped in soft green tissue and tied with string. Alma's eyes widened.

'Wow, thanks!' she said, taking it from him. 'Can I open it now?'

'Of course.' He looked down to the side, rubbing his hand through his hair and making it messier than ever as Alma started to pull the string undone. Then she glanced at him and stopped.

'Wait,' she said, 'let me give you your gift as well.' Reaching into her backpack she brought out a small rectangular tin, dark blue and covered with gold stars, a red bow tied around it. Passing it to Caleb, she said, 'Merry Christmas.'

Caleb took it from her, his eyes crinkling as he smiled

at her. 'Thank you,' he said, turning the tin around to look at it before undoing the bow. Opening the lid released the scent of spices and pastry and he inhaled with pleasure, looking at Alma with amazement.

'Oh, I hope they're OK,' said Alma anxiously. 'I made them today, so I hope you like them.'

Caleb, already munching his way through one of the mince pies, nodded his appreciation, his blue eyes bright with enjoyment. Alma, pleased to see him enjoying her gift, turned her attention to her own. Pulling the string off and tucking it in her pocket, she opened the tissue to find a little notebook, bound in green leather with a tree embossed on the front cover and two leather ties to hold it closed.

'Oh Caleb,' she breathed. 'This is beautiful. I love it. Oh, and I only gave you mince pies.'

Caleb swallowed his mouthful of pie and brushed some crumbs from the front of his tunic before answering. 'Are you kidding?' he said. 'You *made* these for me. It's the most thoughtful gift I think I've ever had.'

'Really?' smiled Alma, while at the same time feeling a little sad for Caleb.

'Really,' echoed Caleb. He raised his eyebrows then, his expression teasing. 'In fact, they almost make up for waiting in the woods half the morning for you.'

'Oh, come on,' she laughed. 'Are you serious? I was *that* late?' She placed her little book safely into her pack while Caleb closed his tin and tucked it under his arm, linking his other one with Alma's as they started to walk towards the gardens.

'We-ell' said Caleb, regarding her affectionately as they walked, 'you're actually about an hour late – just a few seconds in your world can make a difference, I guess. Why couldn't you have just stepped through anyway – does it matter if anyone sees you?'

'Yes, actually, it does matter, silly,' said Alma, playfully elbowing Caleb. 'I can't just disappear in front of people – they would have the papers and television there and the next thing you know, half the world would be trying to get through the Gate. Or they would think aliens had taken me, or something. It would be a huge drama.'

'Really?' said Caleb, sounding unconvinced. 'I bet stuff like that happens in your world all the time. Stuff that can't be explained,' he went on as they passed under an archway weighted with clematis, green leaves and feathery seeds trailing all around. 'People just choose not to see it a lot of the time, I think. They explain it away as something else. I've heard the Elders talking about it, how so much Mystery has been lost from your world.' The way he said the word 'mystery', as if it were something with material presence rather than just a simple noun, intrigued Alma.

'What is this Mystery?' she asked. 'Is this what the Elders are always talking about, the force that governs us all? And no, stuff like that doesn't happen all the time. I've never had anything like this happen to me before. Well, except...' Alma stopped talking for a moment, thinking about the strange valley of her childhood.

'No, Mystery is a part of it, that's all, it's-' started

Caleb, before he realised what Alma had said. He looked hard at her and she tried, unsuccessfully, to look innocent, but it was no good. Her expressive face, as always, gave her away.

'Something happened to you!' he exclaimed. 'Something weird, something other than coming here, something in your own world. Come on, you can't hide it from me. Tell me!'

'No, it's nothing,' said Alma, wrinkling her nose and shaking her head. Damn. She knew Caleb wouldn't let this go.

'It is!' cried Caleb. 'I knew it – you must tell me!'

They reached the Long Walk when Caleb suddenly pulled her onto a path twisting off to the left. 'Hey!' she protested, laughing at him and trying to pull away, until she realised where he had taken her. It was a small garden fragrant with herbs. Mint and rosemary scented the air in the sheltered space, where beds were laid out in a complex knot pattern edged by low stone walls. The high hedges blocked out any cool winds. Alma was instantly enchanted. She picked some of the fragrant leaves and held them to her nose, breathing in the mingled heady scents. Meanwhile, Caleb sat down on a bench near the hedge, patting the seat next to him with an expectant expression on his face. Alma smiled at him, shaking her head. 'You're not going to let this go, are you?'

'Nope,' replied Caleb, 'so you might as well start talking.' Realising she had no choice in the matter, Alma gave in and came to sit down next to him, pausing to sniff from her posy of herbs as she gathered her thoughts.

'Well, I was ten years old, at the park near my house,' she began, twirling the herbs in her fingers. 'And, it was the weirdest thing. I mean, I know the park so well, but that day I found a valley.'

'A valley?' Caleb sounded intrigued and she half smiled at him before continuing.

'Yeah. I mean, it shouldn't have been there. It *couldn't* have been there.' She brought the herbs to her nose again, breathing their scent, her eyes distant as she thought about the strange events of the day.

'What do you mean?'

'Well, where I live, it's all houses. And then the city. And the park is surrounded on all sides, so there was no way... It was just so strange. But it was exciting, you know?' Caleb nodded. 'So anyway, the valley was all pines, mist under the trees and a track running through the middle of the wood. I was about to run along it when I heard the scream.'

'The scream?' Caleb was agog as she went on, describing the atmosphere of menace, the piercing shriek that had so frightened her and the silver light she had seen beneath the trees that had sent her running away in panic. 'Huh,' he said, once she had finished. His eyebrows were raised and he leaned forwards, his hands clasped in front of him. 'That is weird.' He looked at Alma, his face bright with interest. 'So, did you ever go back there? Find out what it was that screamed?

'No,' said Alma, shivering a little. Thinking about the valley always did that to her, made her feel a mix of fear and sadness, though she couldn't really say why. 'I mean,

I went back later, when I felt ready, but, that was the strangest thing of all. *It wasn't there any more.* No matter how I looked for it, I could never find it again.'

'Really?' Caleb's face lit up with interest. 'I *told* you things like that happen over there.' His brow furrowed as he considered what she had told him. 'Perhaps you should-'

'-ask Thorion about it?' smiled Alma, leaning on him for a moment as she finished the sentence for him. She felt strangely relieved to have shared her story – she had never told anyone before, not even Sara, but here in this place of magic and dreams she felt she could tell the truth about that day in the valley without fear of ridicule. 'So you believe me?' she went on, feeling relieved. 'I mean, it *was* weird, wasn't it? I kind of talked myself out of it for years, pretended it didn't happen, but it did, didn't it?'

They looked up as Thorion entered the garden. Neither of them had heard him approach and they both stood up hastily, Caleb bowing and Alma nodding her head as usual. The King, clad in armour rather than his customary robes, had a strange expression on his face – a mixture of wonder and excitement, mixed with sorrow.

'Forgive me,' he said. 'I could not help but overhear your conversation. You are correct, Alma – what happened to you was real, very real. What you may not realise is how significant it is. Can you tell me please, how long ago this event took place in your world?'

Alma cast her mind back 'Well, I was ten,' she said, 'so about five years ago?' It had been autumn, the leaves falling and the smell of smoke in the cool air. 'In October,

I think.'

Thorion took in a sharp breath and closed his eyes, while Alma looked at Caleb, mystified by Thorion's interest in her story and his reaction to her words. He shrugged his shoulders, equally confused.

'So it was the Feast Day? Hallows Eve?'

Caleb looked sharply at Thorion. 'My Lord, do you mean?' But Thorion gestured to Caleb to be quiet for the moment, wanting to hear Alma's answer.

'Yes, I suppose it was,' said Alma, thinking back. 'I was supposed to go trick or treating later, but didn't go in the end. Why, wh-what is going on?'

Caleb and Thorion both stared at her, their shocked expressions identical, but it was Thorion who recovered first. Taking Alma's hands, he gently led her to sit back down on the bench.

'Alma I know, thanks to Caleb, that you have heard some of the story of Lord Gwion, who was sent into your lands on a secret errand. Here is the rest of it. He was entrusted with the last piece of the Regalia, the sacred Sword.' Caleb gasped and Thorion glanced at him briefly before continuing. 'He left on a Feast Day, a time of power, hoping it would help in his quest to hide the Sword in your realm until such time as the unrest between Light and Dark was... more balanced. It was our way of trying to preserve the last piece of the Regalia but it sadly backfired. Lord Gwion did not return and his fate, and that of the Sword, remained unknown.'

'Until now,' breathed Caleb, looking at Alma with something like awe.

'Yes,' smiled Thorion, 'until now.'

His blue eyes were warm as he looked at Alma and inwardly she sighed. Thorion was so handsome she found having all his attention focused on her, as it was now, completely distracting. Pulling herself together, she gave Thorion a wary look. 'Do you mean…'

'Yes,' said Thorion. 'I think you may have been witness to the last moments of Gwion, whatever they were, in your land. *And that means that you are the only person in all the realms who can lead us to the Sword.*'

All was silent in the little garden, the high hedges blocking out much of the outside noise, so they seemed to be in a little bubble of their own. Alma and Caleb both gazed at Thorion, their eyes wide, but it was Caleb who spoke first.

'So the prophecy is true!' he said eagerly, looking at Alma. 'You will lead us to the Sword, then find the other pieces of the Regalia and the Balance will be restored!' He sounded so excited, his blue eyes shining as he looked from her to Thorion, Alma didn't have the heart to tell him she still wasn't quite sure about all this. She wasn't even sure where the valley was now. Then she realised something and her temper started to flare.

'Why on earth did no one tell me about this before?' she asked, her voice rising. 'I mean, I've-' she glanced at Caleb and hurriedly amended herself '-we've spent weeks in the library looking for clues about… all this,' she said, waving her hands and trying to stay polite, 'and the whole time you knew the Sword was in my world!'

'Well, no, not exactly,' said Thorion, raising his hands

as though to defend himself against Alma's sudden anger.

'Well, why not exactly?' she asked in an irritated tone. Folding her arms she sat back, eyes narrowed. Caleb gave her a nervous look.

'Alma, when Gwion left here with the Sword he chose his own path through to your world. Not even I was privy to his route, for it was thought to be safest that way. Understand that this was a mission of highest secrecy, the last attempt by the Light to preserve the Sacred Regalia.' Thorion looked at Alma intently and she nodded, glancing at Caleb who was listening to Thorion, his eyes wide. 'From what you have just told Caleb, it seems Gwion chose to cross over using one of the Closed Gates – his powers as one of our highest ranking Elders should have given him sure passage but it sounds, from your story, as though he did not get far.'

'But, didn't anyone look for him? Didn't you wonder?' asked Alma, her brow furrowed.

'Of course we did,' said Thorion, 'but it was some time before we realised he was not going to return and by then the trail was cold. It was a difficult time in our world and we did not wish to risk anyone else on what would most likely have been a fruitless mission to retrieve him.'

'But I still don't understand why no one *said* anything about this before,' said Alma, her arms folded.

Thorion looked troubled for a moment. 'I understand your anger, Alma, and you are right – we should have told you before. I can only say that it is a… painful topic for us still,' he said apologetically. 'I think our hope was that you and Caleb would find some clue amongst the manuscripts, that the other pieces could be retrieved first. However, it now seems that you can lead us to the Sword after all.'

Fear started to curl in Alma's stomach. 'You mean, you want me to go back to that place? I mean, I don't even know where it is…' she trailed off, her heart starting to pound at the thought of the dark valley.

'I do,' said Thorion, his face alight with hope. 'Now that I have heard your description, I know exactly where it is and how to get there. We just need your help, if you will, to find the precise place where the Sword, and Lord Gwion, were lost.' He looked at Alma, his handsome features becoming sympathetic as he took in her disquiet. 'I can see that this is frightening for you, Alma,' he went on, his voice gentle, his eyes holding hers, 'but we will let no harm come to you, I promise. Caleb,' he said, turning to the boy. 'Can I also trust in your help with this?'

As Caleb nodded, Alma realised what Thorion meant and felt her stomach lurch with fear again. *The Dark.* Great. She was already not one of their favourite people. She knew that the Dark had been marking her, but she also knew that they had not yet moved against her because of Thorion's declaration before the Council. But now the game had changed. Once any of their kind found out that she had all the information in hand to find the Sword – well, she didn't fancy her chances of getting back to the Gate in one piece, Thorion's protection notwithstanding.

He was still waiting, courteously, for her to respond and Alma looked at him, then at Caleb, both of them trying so hard not to influence her decision. It didn't help, really – in a way she wanted them to insist, to make her help them. Choosing was a lot harder than it sounded, especially when she felt sick with fear at the thought of going back to the hidden valley and its dark shapes. She just had to trust that they would look after her and she knew, despite her fear, that it was the right thing to do. Summoning her courage, she spoke. 'Okay,' she said, her voice little more than a whisper. 'I'll do it.'

'Thank you, Alma,' replied Thorion, letting out a held breath as though in relief. '*If you will*,' he had said earlier. Alma saw that up until that moment, until she had spoken, the choice truly had been hers. Had she chosen not to co-operate, there was nothing the Light could or would do to make her. The choice had to be made freely or not at all. She was not so sure that the Dark felt the same way. And with thoughts of the Dark, lay thoughts of Deryck. Alma pulled herself away from that line of imagining, back to the present moment and the two who sat with her in the herb garden, their eyes bright with hope.

'Let us go now to the Great Hall, where I will need you to tell your story again, Alma,' said Thorion. 'I will summon certain of the other Elders to join us and we can decide on the best course of action together.'

Alma nodded, then got to her feet. She started to move towards the path but Thorion stopped her, coming to link his arm with hers.

'Caleb,' he said, inclining his head. Caleb immediately stepped ahead of them both onto the path leading out of the knot garden and Alma realised with surprise that he was scouting ahead, making sure none had overheard their conversation and that the route they would take to the Hall was safe. Keeping Alma close, Thorion moved with such haste through the gardens that she had to run to keep up with him. As soon as they reached the Palace he sent guards fanning out through the Foyer, moving between the columns to clear the space and ensure no one was there. Then he turned to Alma and Caleb who stood close together as if for comfort, both a little stunned by the speed of events.

'Please, if you will, wait here a moment while I summon the others. Then shall we go to the Crystal Chamber.'

The Closed Gate

Thorion stepped alone into the Great Hall, multi-coloured light from the long windows moving across him as he strode to the centre of the room, the centre of their world. This was a chance for the Light – he could not let it fail. He needed to tread carefully and, above all, discreetly. He would have to choose wisely from the Circle, for only a few could know of this story before the mission was undertaken to retrieve the Sword. Breathing deeply, tapping into the power built into the stones beneath his feet, Thorion focused his will to one brilliant point. Standing tall, eyes closed, he gathered within himself the names of those he wished to consult. Then, using the energy that surged through him, he sent the summons, breaking contact once the process was complete.

Caleb and Alma stood together in the foyer, trying to act casual, the expressions of the guards around them giving nothing away. Finally Alma, unable to bear the tension any longer, nudged Caleb.

'What's the Crystal Chamber?' she whispered.

'It's the Inner Sanctum of the Light,' Caleb whispered back, eyes wide. 'I've never been in there. I'm not even sure where it is, just that it's somewhere in this building. I can't believe we're going in there.'

He was overheard by Thorion as the King came back into the Foyer. 'Believe it, Master Caleb,' he said, looking kindly on him. 'I have summoned the others so let us go. Follow me if you please.'

With a gesture, Thorion sent the guards back to their posts at the door with instructions to admit only those he had summoned. After satisfying himself once more that the three of them were alone, Thorion passed between two of the pillars lining the Foyer, beckoning Alma and Caleb to follow. He stood in front of the solid stone wall, blank save for a small carving of a five-pointed star, and moved his hands in a complex twisting pattern, murmuring words as he did so. Alma and Caleb gasped as the stones melted away, dissolving like mist to reveal a stone stair going up through the centre of the wall. Light shone down, radiant and golden like afternoon sun. Thorion turned, beckoning to them both.

'Come,' he said. 'Be not alarmed. The others will be along soon.'

Alma and Caleb followed Thorion to the magical stair, exchanging looks of wonder as they started to climb. The stone ceiling arching above them was etched with many small stars, each one picked out in gold. Balustrades carved as twisting vines were set into each side of the wall, so real to look at they almost seemed to tremble. Underfoot the stairs were covered in ancient patterned tiles, worn smooth in the centre by the passage of feet over the centuries. Alma ran a finger over the delicate carvings, marvelling at the craftsmanship as they climbed, while behind her Caleb was unusually silent. After a short ascent they emerged to find themselves standing on the flat top of one of the towers.

'Wow!' breathed Alma, grabbing onto Caleb's arm for support as they both looked around in wonder. A circular table surrounded by upholstered wooden chairs sat at the centre of the tiled floor, but other than that there was nothing to obscure the view of the gardens stretching to the woods and distant rolling hills leading to higher mountains. The sea shone blue below, dotted with tiny whitecaps and, far out near the horizon, Alma could see what looked like a little boat. It was simply magnificent and completely unsettling. Yet, though the trees outside moved in the breeze, no wind blew through to trouble them and Caleb, when he tentatively tried to put his hand through to the outside, encountered what felt like solid stone under his hand, though the view was as clear as ever.

Thorion laughed, answering Alma's unspoken question with a smile. 'From here, we can see all, yet none can see us. From the outside this is just another tower, so do not fear, you are perfectly safe. Please, take a seat.' Alma and

Caleb each took a chair at the table, looking wide-eyed at each other, each glad of the other's presence in the strange room. Caleb ran his hand over the richly inlaid table, which had a small five-pointed star at its centre just like the one on the wall below. Alma was particularly taken with her chair, upholstered in deep purple velvet on which golden lilies bloomed and white doves flew. She gently touched the soft fabric, enjoying the workmanship, until her attention was diverted by the arrival of the first of Thorion's advisors. It was Meredan, magnificent in crimson armour, the golden light shining on his shaven head and muscular bare arms as he entered the chamber. He nodded to Caleb and Alma and went over to greet Thorion.

'What is this, my Lord? Why have we been summoned?' His rich deep voice boomed around the chamber but, before Thorion could answer, a light laughing voice did so for him.

'Patience, my Lord Meredan. No doubt Thorion has his reasons and they will be revealed in due course.'

This was Adara, her perfect face smiling, her supple figure clothed in robes of olive green that brought out the rich colour of her eyes. She winked at Alma and Caleb before taking a seat at the table opposite them both and they smiled back nervously. Meredan also took a seat, his hands tapping on the table's polished surface as he cast an inquiring glance at Thorion.

'There is one more to arrive,' said the High King, his voice amused as he looked at his friend.

'And here I am,' said a last voice, belonging to Lord

Artos. Clad in ivory and brown, he smiled at Caleb and Alma as he pulled up a chair to sit at the table. All eyes then turned expectantly to Thorion who took the tallest chair of all. A carving of a crown over a tree touched with fine gilding marked it as the chair of the High King. Clasping his hands loosely on the table in front of him, Thorion fixed each of them in turn with his blue gaze, as though assessing them all, before he spoke.

'Thank you all for coming on such short notice. I bring you here on a matter of the utmost urgency and importance.' Raising one hand, he forestalled Lord Meredan, who had opened his mouth to speak in impatience. Adara placed her hand lightly on the Elder's muscled forearm, gesturing him to wait, to be patient. The King's face became grave.

'You will all remember the sad fate of Lord Gwion and the loss of the Sword. A dark day it was, for those of the Light.'

'And for those who loved him,' said Adara softly, her lovely face becoming wary. Beside her, Lord Artos placed a gentle hand on hers as it lay on the table, his own expression guarded. Alma glanced their way, interested, as Thorion continued.

'My friends, it seems that Alma may have been witness to the last moments of Lord Gwion as he crossed over to her world. You will all know what this means, and why, therefore, it is so important that we gather here today.'

Thorion leaned back in his chair as the reactions to his statement swirled around the small table, his eyes storm grey. Meredan's face lit up with excitement and a burning desire to know more. Adara half rose from her seat, hand to mouth, unshed tears gleaming in her eyes. And Lord Artos, he of the sea-blue eyes, simply looked at Thorion, sorrow on his noble features. Under the table, Caleb took Alma's hand and gently squeezed it. She looked at him, surprised at the contact but grateful for it. She felt quite out of her depth and the reassuring presence of Caleb at her side was the only thing keeping her from running out of the peculiar room and back to the Gate as quickly as she could.

'Then the prophecy spoke true!' exclaimed Meredan, looking excitedly at Alma. 'You will find the Sword for us, and help us to restore the Regalia!' He sounded so like Caleb that Alma, overwrought with emotion, almost giggled. Catching Caleb's eye, she realised that would be completely inappropriate and folded her lips tight.

'Then it is true, Thorion – he is dead?' This was Adara, the grief in her eyes hinting at another story, another angle to this game of swords and prophecy.

'Yes, I am afraid it looks that way. I am truly sorry, dear heart,' said Thorion, and all at once the desire to laugh was gone from Alma, lost in the face of Adara's obvious sorrow.

'So we have lost both of them, Galen and Gwion, to the land beyond the Gates!' Lord Artos, white with anger, looked at Alma with a strange expression on his face, as though he were assessing her but at the same time was worried for her. Alma met his gaze for a moment before looking down, unable to bear the real pain in his eyes. 'This is why the Gates should be closed, Thorion. I have said this before!'

'Had I closed the Gates when you pressed me to do so, Lord Artos, then Alma would not be here and we would never have learned of Gwion's fate,' returned Thorion, a thread of command in his voice that subdued the older man. Artos leaned back in his chair, his eyes distant as they looked to a tragic past.

Steepling his hands in front of him as he leaned on the table, the High King addressed Alma, his eyes back to gleaming blue. 'Alma, will you be so kind as to tell us your story, just as you did to me earlier.'

So Alma, her voice soft in the golden chamber, told her tale once more, careful not to leave out any detail. When she spoke of the scream cutting through the still autumn air, Adara made a sound of distress, while Artos simply closed his eyes, grimacing for a moment as though in pain. As Alma finished her story, speaking of the strange silver light she had glimpsed beneath the massed pines, a single tear fell onto Adara's perfect cheek. She slumped back in her chair, bowed as though some great hope had gone from her world.

By contrast, Meredan's interest and excitement had increased as the story unfolded. As soon as she finished, he jumped to his feet, slamming one hand onto the table with such force that the whole thing shook. Alma jumped. 'We must go!' he almost shouted. 'Let us retrieve the Sword before it is too late – we cannot tarry! If the Dark gets even a hint of this, the game is over before it has begun.'

'I agree, my excitable friend,' smiled Thorion. 'Speed

is of the essence, but so is Alma's safety.'

All heads turned to look at Alma. She stared back, trying to hide how frightened she was. Caleb gave her hand another reassuring squeeze.

'We will protect you, Alma,' said Meredan, his face eager. 'Trust us to do so. But the sooner we act the better.'

'Then let us go now, just the six of us,' said Lord Artos, sounding resigned. 'It is the Pine Gate, is it not? The Closed Gate of Penwyth Gawr.'

'We must be discreet,' said Adara, her voice shaking slightly. She fought to gather herself, obviously still recovering from the impact of Thorion's news. 'No doubt there will be those who are watching us.'

At this Thorion nodded, while Artos looked across at Alma. 'Fear not, my child. No harm will come to you, I promise.' Alma smiled faintly at him, not wanting to offend the Elder lord, though her heart was pounding. From fear or excitement, she wasn't really sure.

Thorion stood, taking a deep breath. 'So are we agreed?' he said, looking around the table at the assembled company. 'Is this the best course of action?' Alma could feel Caleb trembling beside her and, as she turned to catch his eye he smiled at her so warmly she couldn't help but return it, while under the table he squeezed her hand so hard she nearly yelped out loud.

But it was Adara who had the final word, her voice low and sorrowful. 'Yes, let us go now,' she said. 'Let us see if we can find the Sword, that his death not be in vain.'

Thorion looked at her, sorrow and pity mingled in his gaze. His voice was gentle as he spoke. 'Then it is decided. May the blessing of Light be upon us all.'

With those words, as though it was a signal, the Elders at the table stood and bowed their heads. Caleb and Alma hastily joined them, still holding hands, bewildered by how quickly the day had changed. After a moment Thorion pushed his chair back to step away from the table, beckoning Alma and Caleb to follow. 'Stay close, if you please.'

The other Elders moved aside and Alma let go of Caleb's hand, casting one last glance around the strange chamber before stepping onto the narrow stair and following Thorion's broad straight back as he descended to the foyer below. Standing with Caleb, Alma saw Meredan, the last in their group, come through the opening in the wall. As soon as he had done so the stones were back in place, looking as though they had always been there. Her eyes widened and Meredan gave her a wink, moving on past her to join the group.

'Did you see that?' she whispered to Caleb, who nodded.

'I know,' he whispered back, linking his arm in hers once more. Alma hung onto him as they made their way through the Foyer, grateful he was there with her. She wasn't sure she could do this by herself. The group came out through the double doors, the guards saluting them smartly, and took a sharp left to double back along the side of the Great Hall, towards where the mingled smells of horse and leather indicated the presence of stables. When Alma realised where they were going, she panicked.

'I can't ride a horse!' she whispered to Caleb, her eyes wide.

'Don't worry.' He grinned at her. 'You can ride with me.'

True to his word, when the horses were led out, their hooves clattering in the stone yard, Caleb mounted first before offering a strong arm to Alma who, with a helpful boost from Lord Meredan, managed to get herself seated behind him. Their horse, a gentle grey mare, seemed huge to Alma and she wrapped her arms tightly around Caleb. She had only ridden a horse once before, pony trekking in Wales when she was younger, so was very happy to let Caleb have control in this instance. Thorion, buckling on his sword, smiled at them both as he saw their arrangement, his grim expression softening.

'Keep her safe,' he said, nodding at Caleb.

'I will, my Lord,' he replied, a note of pride in his voice at the responsibility.

Then Thorion mounted his silver grey mare, walking her over to where Meredan sat waiting astride his magnificent chestnut horse. 'You know where we are going?'

'I do, Thorion,' replied the Elder, his handsome face stern.

'Then will you lead us to the woods, my friend?' said the King.

'I will.' Meredan's eyes met Thorion's gaze for a moment. Then, wheeling his horse around, Meredan started from the yard with Thorion close behind. The others followed him.

'Keep close,' the King said as they left the yard, 'and do not be distracted. We must do this as quickly and quietly as possible.' Caleb turned his head to look at Alma with raised eyebrows, but said nothing. She gave him a weak smile, barely managing not to squeal as he spurred his horse on after Thorion.

They were soon on the Long Walk, picking up speed as they reached the edge of the gardens, their horses' hooves thundering on the grassy meadow. Alma clung to Caleb, her hair blowing back from her face. They neared the dark green wall of the looming forest and she ducked her head as they entered the trees. Once in the woods Thorion moved to the front of the pack, turning to ascertain everyone was still there. They lessened their pace slightly and the group began to relax. All except for Alma. She still held tight to Caleb, her eyes closed as they rode between the trees. Noticing this, he laughed out loud.

'What are you doing?' he asked, most unhelpfully, Alma thought, as it was fairly obvious she was trying to avoid being scraped off against the nearest tree.

'Just trying to stay on,' she managed, through gritted teeth.

'But we're not even going that fast!' cried Caleb, laughter in his voice. 'We can't – not in the woods. It would be too dangerous. Come on, open your eyes, you're fine.'

Grimacing, Alma opened her eyes to find she and Caleb were third in the line of riders, Thorion and Meredan in front of them, Adara and Artos bringing up the rear. They were moving quickly, as far as she was concerned, but at a pace she thought she could handle, at least with Caleb. Still, she kept her arms around his waist, just to be sure, the green and fragrant trees flashing past as they rode.

'See, it's not so bad, is it?' said Caleb, as she relaxed her grip slightly. 'A ride through the woods is a nice way to spend the day,' he continued. 'Perhaps we can do it again, some other time when things aren't so...' But he was interrupted by Thorion, who had called the riders to a halt.

'Here,' the High King said tersely, indicating a tangled path to the left of the group. Dark and narrow, it twisted off into the undergrowth. Its entrance was like an open mouth, waiting for them to enter. Alma swallowed. Thorion, his dark hair blowing back from his stern face and looking every inch a king from legend, drew his sword and turned his horse towards the path.

'Follow me,' he called over his shoulder, his deep voice ringing with command. He used his sword to cut through the undergrowth as best he could, framing a path for them all to take, his bright presence the only comfort in the gloom growing steadily around them. In single file they followed the High King, their pace reduced to a slow walk. The mulch underfoot muffled the horses' hooves and the crack and slash of Thorion's blade was the only sound. Clinging to Caleb more for comfort now than anything else, Alma became increasingly nervous as they neared the closed Gate.

'Are you all right, Alma?' said Caleb, his voice quiet, shifting slightly against her arms.

'No,' she said, not wanting to let go of him. Caleb laughed again, but this time he sounded nervous rather than amused.

'Neither am I,' he whispered. 'This was not how I thought we'd be spending the day. Still-' he shifted again, half turning to look at her '-it beats hanging around the library, doesn't it?'

'I guess,' said Alma, sounding unconvinced. At that moment she would have been much happier sitting in that comfortable room, perhaps with a cool drink, searching the ancient volumes for clues. 'I mean, I still can't quite believe all this,' she went on, her voice a murmur in the gloom as they slowly rode along. 'It all just seems like too much of a coincidence, the fact that I knew about this place.'

'Well, I believe it,' replied Caleb, in a whisper, 'and the fact that you knew where the Sword was lost just proves it, as far as I'm concerned.'. But Alma could not agree with him, though she leaned her head on his warm back for a moment, taking comfort in his solid presence. Feeling downcast, she considered that perhaps she was just not ready to believe.

Her glum mood turned to one of abject fear when they came out of the tunnel into a clearing. Green and peaceful, it seemed like any other part of the woods, except for the two tall pine trees that seemed to loom and curve over the company. They had reached the Gate.

Reining in their mounts, they dismounted one by one, Caleb helping Alma who by now was starting to shake. Looking at her with concern, Caleb put both hands on her arms and forced her to meet his gaze, his blue eyes earnest. 'Hey,' he said quietly. 'Nothing's happened yet. And we'll all look after you.'

Alma took a deep breath, trying to calm herself, staying close to Caleb as they neared the trees. Their trunks were carved with the usual symbols of Light and Dark but neither glowed with their own light. They were just shapes carved into the wood, with no power attached to them. Nonetheless, Alma was reminded uncomfortably of the strange valley and realised that in a moment, if things went as planned, she would actually be there again. She felt sick at the thought of it.

'Lord Meredan, if you please,' said Thorion. The armour-clad Elder inclined his head to the High King and stepped forward, dry pine needles crunching underfoot. He stood in front of the Gate with his eyes closed, arms straight and held at an angle in front of him as though feeling for something that couldn't be seen.

'Lord Meredan is a Tracker,' whispered Caleb to Alma, as they stood in the shadow of a nearby tree. 'He is checking the Gate for any traps left by the Dark.'

Alma looked at him in alarm, liking the idea of going back to the strange valley less and less every minute. 'What happens if he finds one?' she whispered back, her face paler than usual.

'Oh, don't worry – Thorion will disarm it. Nothing can touch him – that is part of his power as High King.'

Caleb was watching the proceedings with increasing interest. He couldn't believe his luck. First a visit to the Crystal Chamber, now a secret trip to the Other World.

And Alma. She had ridden with him, holding him close. For that he would face a thousand traps from the Dark.

Lord Meredan had finished his check of the Gate. 'It is safe, my Lord,' he told Thorion. 'I have checked it and there is nothing here now.'

'Nothing here now?' said Lord Artos. He had picked up on the subtle wording used by Meredan, as had Thorion, Caleb could see. It was also clear that Meredan was angry – his jaw tight as he faced them all, burdened with news he did not want to tell.

'Ah... no, my Lord,' he said, his usually strong voice sounding darker, almost pained.

'But there was something?' said Thorion.

Meredan looked away for a moment, obviously trying to control his anger before speaking, his expression fierce. 'A Galardin passed through here. At least one.'

The effect of this announcement was immediate. Adara cried out 'No!' a hand to her mouth, while Lord Artos turned away, his shoulders bowed under some heavy weight of pain. Thorion closed his eyes for a moment, sorrow and anger crossing his handsome face and Meredan became anguished, regret writ large upon his expressive features.

Opening his eyes, Thorion reached out to lay a hand on Meredan's shoulder. 'Do not distress yourself, my friend. This was not of your doing. It is right, though, that we should know of this.'

'No, it was not your doing – but it was that of the Dark!' spat Lord Artos, furious. 'Foul creatures of their creation – they have been banned these many long years and still they make them! Thorion, you must act on this,' he challenged the High King.

Thorion's eyes flashed blue for a moment but he just shook his head, regretful. 'The Dark, it seems, ignore my pronouncements on such matters. There is not much more I can do, for we do not know whose creature these were – what is important is that it is no longer here.'

'I have a fairly good idea whose they were,' muttered Lord Artos, but Thorion shut him down with a sharp glance.

'As do we all, friend,' he said. 'But we cannot waste time on idle speculation without proof. The most important thing now is to retrieve the Sword.'

'And Gwion,' said Adara softly, 'if he still remains.'

While this conversation was happening, Alma and Caleb waited under the trees. Alma had no idea what a Galardin was but was sure she didn't like the sound of it.

'They are servants of the Dark,' said Caleb, keeping his voice low. 'This Gate was closed years ago because it leads to a part of the in-between, a piece of the Old World that has become separate from both realms, a drifting space of mists where humans and Elders alike can become trapped. Only those of the highest levels, such as Lord Gwion, can travel through safely.'

'Well, that explains why I'd never seen the place before,' Alma whispered back, half distracted by the discussion taking place before them.

'Yes,' said Caleb, his face solemn as he watched Thorion and Artos. 'You were lucky you didn't enter the valley, that the scream stopped you. You might have been trapped there, perhaps even been taken to be made into a Galardin.'

Alma looked at him aghast, her mouth open. 'You mean the Dark...'

'Yes,' said Caleb, giving her an I-told-you-so look. 'The Dark take humans who have become lost in the mists, luring them with offers of help then keeping them to turn into their servants, mutations with one purpose only: to kill all those of the Light. And the worst part? You know what's happening to you, the whole time, but you can't do anything about it once you're... changed.'

'Stop.' Alma put her hands over her ears, closing her eyes and shuddering. It was too horrible to think about.

'That is why Thorion closed this Gate,' continued Caleb, 'so that no one else could be lost here and transformed in such a way.'

'So who do they think...?' asked Alma, wrapping her arms around herself. She felt sick to her stomach.

'Who made the creature? Why Lord Denoris, of course.'

Open mouthed, Alma could only stare at Caleb. Deryck's father. Why did all paths she took seem to lead back to him, to the constant reminder of what he was. It was too unfair. She went to speak but was hushed by Caleb, who gestured towards Thorion. He was opening the Gate.

Dark Valley

Thorion stood before the Gate with his eyes closed, feet slightly apart. His breath was deep and strong, his focus absolute as he tapped into the power of the land. Alma and Caleb watched in awe as the air around him started to shimmer, pulsing like a heartbeat. Slowly the symbols graven on the tree trunks began to glow, pearl and grey against the knotty bark, pulsing with their own light in time with the glow surrounding the King. As the intensity increased Alma found she was holding her breath, transfixed by the display of power. The pulsing reached a crescendo and Thorion slowly lifted his arms and spoke a single word; to Alma it seemed as though he said '*Agorendith*', though she was never sure when she thought about it afterwards. The signs glowed hot with a sudden burst of brilliant light, then gradually dimmed until they resembled the ones on the Oak Gate, gleaming softly. Thorion lowered his arms. He was breathing hard and beads of sweat gleamed on his brow. But he had done it. The Gate was open.

Wiping his brow with one hand, Thorion beckoned to Meredan.

'Will you go through first?' he asked and Meredan nodded. 'But be wary. The woods run deep on the other side.'

The brave Lord, saying nothing further, drew his sword and passed through the Gate. Adara came up to Alma and took her hand. Alma looked at her as though just waking up and Adara gave her a gentle smile.

'We shall cross together, Alma, for we do not wish to lose you, and I'm afraid your bracelet will not help you here.'

'Oh!' said Alma, then swallowed hard. 'OK, let's do this.'

'You are ready?' said Adara. Alma nodded, and together they walked through the Gate. Air and light twisted around them as they emerged on the other side. Alma was dizzy and stumbling as usual, while Adara remained unruffled, holding onto Alma until she regained her balance. They were in a place of mists, white tendrils swirling through the trees that surrounded them, silent and dark. Artos was next through the Gate, the flash of light that heralded his arrival brighter than usual in the shifting gloom. Thorion followed with a stumbling Caleb, held up only by the High King's strong arm. Relieved to see him, Alma stepped forward only to grab hold of Adara again. Her head was still spinning. The Elder looked at her compassionately, her golden eyes soft.

'Just wait, Alma,' she said, her voice slightly muffled

by the fog. 'Thorion has him – he will be fine.' Caleb was bent over. Thorion's hand rested on his back as he comforted the boy, who was coughing and shaking his head. Adara smiled gently to see Alma's concern. 'He is not used to it as you are, and this crossing was more difficult than most. It will be easier, I hope, on the way back.'

Alma nodded in agreement. Breathing deeply, she looked into the swirling mist and saw a crimson-clad figure, his sword raised as he moved through the shadows. She tensed in fear before she realised it was Meredan patrolling the small clearing. He looked worried, beckoning for Thorion to join him. Taking another deep breath, Alma caught the scent of pines. The feel of the cool air took her back to the last time she was in the valley. Letting go of Adara, she made her way gingerly towards Caleb, who had managed to straighten up but still looked green.

'Oh Caleb,' she said, laying a sympathetic hand on his arm, 'are you all right?'

'Uh, getting there,' he managed to say. 'Is it… always like this?'

Alma shook her head and Caleb let out a relieved sigh. 'Well, here we are then,' he said, his voice sounding stronger. Then he looked around. 'But, where are we, exactly?'

Alma looked around as well, trying to get a sense of their surroundings. She opened her mouth to answer Caleb but as she did so his face changed and he shoved her, hard enough to send her sprawling onto the pine needles, spiky beneath the palms of her hands. Scrabbling to get her footing she heard a grunting hiss of breath and smelt a sharp musky scent. She looked up in horror to see a dark shape towering over Caleb, furred and scaled, black and metal. Then everything happened very quickly.

Caleb ducked as a taloned arm swept the air where his head had been a moment before. He bent back to avoid another swinging strike, twisting his body, but the metal tipped claws caught him on the shoulder with enough force to knock him down. Alma screamed his name as he rolled to the side, barely evading another blow, his arms shielding his head. Adara ran to Alma, helping her to her feet and pulling her away, a knife unsheathed in her delicate hand.

Artos, his sword drawn, advanced on the Galardin. But then another sword, glittering as it whirled through the air, sliced through the creature's arm before it could strike at Caleb again. The monster threw its head back and shrieked, a broken sound full of pain. As it turned, Alma saw the creature's sorrowful dark eyes and she held its gaze for a moment, transfixed. It was as though she could feel its agony, deeper than a wound. There was a buzzing in her feet, then a pulse, as though energy was coming through the ground to her. Time seemed to slow and she watched as Thorion drew his arm back, the motion crystal clear, saw as Artos half turned to her, his face incredulous. Then Thorion slashed at the creature again, drawing it away from Caleb and the strange moment passed.

Artos darted in and grabbed Caleb, pulling the boy to his feet and away from the fight. Caleb was holding his shoulder. Alma could see his tunic was torn, bruises visibly darkening on his skin and felt sick at how close he'd come to being killed. She was gasping out sobs, clinging to Adara as Meredan moved to join in the fray, supporting his King. Not that Thorion needed him. His sword flashed, dark hair flying as he wove a deadly dance around the creature, striking at it, his face contorted with what looked like pure fury. Another arm was sliced away and the creature fell to its knees. Alma retched as she saw the dark blood splash on the ground, turning away with her hand to her mouth. The creature screamed again. Then she heard a thud and a guttural groan followed by silence, final.

She felt a hand on her shoulder and turned to see Caleb. He was pale, his cheek smudged with dirt and she'd never been so happy to see him in her life. Without thinking she threw her arms around him, burying her face in his shoulder, so glad that he was all right.

'Are you OK?'

He hugged her back, but only with one arm, his body tense against hers. She drew back, not wanting to hurt him any further. His tunic was ripped down one arm, his shoulder scored with reddish purple lines turning to black, as though the skin had been burnt. Feeling sick at the sight of it, she reached out gentle fingers to touch the wound. He winced and she pulled her hand back. 'You're hurt…oh, Caleb.'

'It's nothing, I'm OK,' he said. 'See?' He flexed his fingers and moved his shoulder but she could see how it hurt him, her hands fluttering around him as she tried to help. If she looked at his arm she didn't have to look at the creature lying humped in the clearing and see the fur and scales, the pooling blood.

'Oh, Caleb, don't,' she said, her voice catching. But he just shook his head and smiled at her, his eyes blue-grey.

'I'm fine. As long as you are,' he said, his voice low as he leaned in close to her. She wiped her face with her hands, vaguely aware of Thorion and Meredan both cleaning their swords on the creature's fur before sheathing them. Meredan knelt down next to it, pushing the huge shoulder so that it rolled onto its back. She glanced over then wished she hadn't. She could smell death, hot metal blood and musky fear. It made her gulp again.

Then Thorion was there, his handsome face spattered with dark blood, his eyes so grey they were nearly black. He pulled Caleb into a strong hug, his eyes closing. Strong emotions played out on his face as he briefly touched the boy's blonde hair with one hand, holding him close. Then he released him and began examining his injured arm.

'Are you all right?' He sounded so worried, unlike his usual calm self, his hands gentle on Caleb as he probed the injured shoulder. Caleb looked stunned, though he managed to respond.

'I am fine, my Lord.' But he flinched as the King touched him and Alma saw him grit his teeth, trying to hold it in. Thorion saw it too, his hands pausing in their investigation.

'There is damage here,' he said, his hands hovering

over Caleb's arm. His face was raw with pain, as though he felt the boy's wound as his own. 'I am so sorry I didn't see the creature coming, didn't get to you in time.' Alma saw a glance pass between Adara and Artos and the Elder Lord went over to them.

'We can get Marlin to attend to this,' he said, laying his hand on Thorion's arm, 'when we return. But for now, I may be able to help.'

The King looked at him as though just realising he was there, then around at the rest of the group. His expression grew more reserved, and he wiped his hand over his face, smearing the blood. He took a deep breath and smiled at Caleb, who still looked bewildered. 'Lord Artos will be able to ease the pain for you,' he said. 'At least till we return. Please let him do so.' He nodded then stepped back, his hands hanging loose at his side as though he didn't know what to do with them. Adara left Alma's side to go to him. Using the hem of her sleeve she wiped his face clean, drawing him away from the group as she did so and murmuring something that Alma couldn't hear. Artos, meanwhile, had laid gentle hands on Caleb's shoulder. Alma watched as he closed his eyes and breathed deeply. After a few moments, Caleb's expression changed from wary to relieved and some colour came back to his cheeks. Artos opened his eyes and looked at the boy.

'Better?'

Caleb nodded, then cleared his throat. 'Um, yes. Thank you, sir.'

'No, thank you,' said Artos, looking at him with

affection. 'It was a brave thing you did.'

'It was indeed,' said Meredan, emerging from the trees. 'There are no more,' he went on, in response to a questioning look from Thorion. 'It was a female, but quite old. Lucky for you,' he said, nodding at Caleb. 'And for us all.'

'Female Galardin are more vicious than the males,' said Artos, seeing Alma frown. 'So it is fortunate indeed that this one was so old. I wonder how long she's been here?'

'Does it matter?' said Adara in her light voice, coming towards them, Thorion following behind. She took both Alma's hands in hers, meeting her eyes with her own golden gaze. 'Come now,' she said, her voice gentle as she rubbed Alma's hands. 'It is over, and we must move forward. Can you still do this for us, Alma?'

Alma stared at Adara, then nodded, slowly. She was shaking all over, the adrenalin wearing off, but she knew if she didn't do it now, there was no way she could ever come back here again. Holding her breath so she didn't have to smell the dead Galardin, she slid her hands from Adara's grasp then turned to look around the clearing, trying to get her bearings. She could feel everyone waiting for her and her resolve faltered, not sure if she could do it. But then, through a gap in the trees, she saw the track leading up to the ridge and she knew. 'There,' she said, pointing. Despite her best efforts her voice shook and Thorion moved to stand on the other side of her, his strong hand on her shoulder.

'Alma, everything is fine now. Meredan has checked

and there is nothing more here that can harm us.'

Alma looked at him and nodded, only slightly comforted. Reaction was still thrumming away inside her, wanting to come out as tears or screaming or something else. She wasn't sure how much longer she could keep it at bay. Fighting for control, she forced herself to focus on the task at hand. 'We need to go on to the track,' she said. 'Through there,' she pointed, indicating the rough gravel road through the trees.

Thorion inclined his head, his face serious. 'Thank you, Alma,' he said. Then he called the others to him. 'Follow Alma,' he said. 'And remember, stay together. It is easy to become lost in the mists.'

Great. Alma looked at Caleb, wanting his warm reassurance. He was looking much better, the bruises on his shoulder faded to purplish yellow.

'Come on,' he said, He nodded his head, encouraging her, a smile in his eyes. 'You can do this.'

Taking a deep breath, Alma moved forward. Caleb came up close behind her and Thorion beckoned the others to follow. Through the trees she led them, until they reached the track that ran through the centre of the forest, cutting it in two. The sky above them was a watery yellow-grey, the peculiar half-light of a winter's day.

'Alma, can you show us exactly where the incident took place?' asked Thorion, his tone calm as though nothing had just happened, no blood or death in the clearing. Alma looked around, then up to the ridge beyond. Her heart was pounding in her chest and she felt like she might faint. The trees seemed full of shadows and it felt as though a thousand dark eyes were watching her, waiting to pounce. Ugh. For a moment she felt sick, then Caleb placed a gentle hand on her back and she took a deep breath. Adara was right. It was over, and she needed to move forward. Focus, Alma.

'I think I need to go back up there to where I was standing, when I was here before.' But she still couldn't seem to move.

'Come on then,' said Caleb in a challenging tone. 'Let's go.' Inclining his head, he started to run up the track. His movements were slow at first, favouring the injured shoulder, but he soon picked up the pace, his boots kicking up puffs of dust from the dry ground. 'Catch me if you can!'

Alma stared after Caleb in surprise, then looked at Artos, who winked at her. She shook herself and started to run, leaving her fear behind. She raced after Caleb, her legs pounding and red hair flying as they scrambled up the rocky slope to the ridge. They both reached the top at the same time, panting, and took a moment to catch their breath. Alma looked at Caleb, his face red, hair tousled from the wind.

'Thanks,' she said. It was only one word, but it held a world of meaning.

Caleb smiled back. 'You're welcome.'

She held his gaze a moment longer, then straightened up. Looking down into the pine valley she felt a sense of déjà vu roll over her. There was the track running through the centre of the woods, the tall pines of the Gate visible to the far left. But it was in the woods to the right of the track that she had seen the strange light and so she focused her search there, trying to figure it out. All at once it was as though she were ten years old again, standing there with her hair in her eyes, straining to see into the dark under the trees. She tensed for a moment, expecting a scream to rise up as before, but there was nothing, only the expectant group on the track below and beside her the warm comforting presence of Caleb. Narrowing her eyes, she tried to remember where she had been standing that day.

The messenger knocked cautiously at the door of Lord Denoris' study, for the Dark Lord could be notoriously testy when disturbed. Still, this was a matter of great importance. A group had been seen, heading to the closed Gate. Lord Denoris would be pleased with this information, would perhaps even pay for it, if delivered in a timely fashion. Hearing a voice bid him enter, the messenger slowly opened the heavy wooden door and walked forward to stand before the large desk, which was wondrously carved with dragons. Behind it sat Lord Denoris, his blonde head bent forward, pen scratching on paper as the fire crackled in the fireplace. A clock on the wall above marked out the hours. The messenger, his boots sinking into the rich carpet, waited for the Dark Lord to finish what he was doing, clearing his throat in preparation of the news he had to deliver. This was, perhaps, a mistake. The golden brows drew together and Lord Denoris slowly raised his head from his papers, turning the full force of his famously green eyes on the now terrified messenger. Hastily, he presented his news in a garbled fashion, relaxing slightly only when he saw the expression on the handsome face change from murderous to thoughtful. Tapping the fingers of one hand on the leather blotter, Lord Denoris seemed to be considering his options. The messenger hoped fervently to himself that they did not involve him. Finally, Denoris spoke, his voice curt.

'Bring me my son,' he said, waving a hand to dismiss the near-to-fainting messenger. Bowing, sweating, he backed out of the study, grateful to be leaving with all his limbs intact. Outside, the door closed behind him, the messenger sank down with trembling knees onto a wooden bench seemingly placed there for the purpose and wondered, not for the first time, whether another profession might be less stressful. But he could not linger long – Lord Denoris had asked for his son, and so the message had to be delivered. With a sigh he stood, straightening his tunic and wiping his damp brow before setting off to the gardens where he had last seen Lord Deryck.

Moving a little further to the right, Alma sighted a gap between the pines and it all fell into place.

'That's the place, I'm sure of it,' she said, turning to Caleb.

'You're positive?' he said, his face slightly awed. Alma scowled at him and he grinned, raising his unwounded arm to indicate to the watching Elders that they had marked the spot. Treading carefully so as not to slip, the two made their way back down the slope, dislodging small stones that rattled down below. Thorion and the others had already left the dusty track, moving around the edge of the wood to meet up with Alma and Caleb at the gap in the pines.

As the small group moved slowly among the trees, Caleb turned to Thorion, his genial face perturbed. 'Lord Thorion,' he asked, his voice quiet, 'I do not understand. Surely others would have been here, and could have taken the Sword?'

'It is a good question, Caleb,' he said in his deep voice. 'In a normal forest, that would certainly have been the case. But this, as you may already be aware, is no ordinary woodland.'

'Ah,' said Caleb, realisation dawning on him. 'Yes, my Lord, I see what you mean. Because this place moves so much between the worlds, it's unlikely to have had any other visitors since Lord Gwion came through.'

'Yes. That is what we are hoping for, anyway,' smiled Thorion, obviously pleased by Caleb's answer. 'And are you quite recovered?' he went on, reaching out his hand as if to touch Caleb's arm, though he didn't make contact.

'Er, yes, my Lord, thank you,' said Caleb, his cheeks going red. 'Lord Artos was very helpful.'

'Good,' said the King. 'Make sure Marlin looks at it when we get back.'

'I will, my Lord,' replied Caleb.

Thorion nodded then moved forward to catch up with

Meredan, who was scanning the woods as he walked. The group moved further into the chill dank of the wood, their feet disturbing small puffs of dust from the forest floor, mist swirling around them. Then Meredan stopped, raising his hand. 'I have it,' he said, his voice low. Pointing ahead, he indicated an area where the ground had been disturbed, although some time ago, judging from the fine dust lying on the ridges and furrows scored in the earth. The marks bore witness to some terrible struggle. Footprints dug into the soil interspersed with terrible clawed grooves, while ominous darker patches still stained the pine needles that covered the forest floor. The wood lay silent and heavy as the group moved to stand at the patch of ground with its silent message of violence past. Adara, especially, seemed affected – slowly she walked around the battle site, stopping finally at a depression in the soil where it seemed something heavy had fallen and lain. One hand to her mouth, she bent and picked up something small from the displaced earth. Her expression anguished, she turned to Alma, who was closest to her.

'I gave this to him.' She opened her hand to show Alma a small charm, a silver flower, still with a scrap of blue ribbon attached. Alma could only look back at her, speechless in the face of such sorrow. 'A forget-me-not,' she continued, her voice breaking so Alma could barely hear her. Closing her hand, she stepped away from Alma and the rest of the group. She stood under the trees with her back to them, her shoulders hunched and arms wrapped around herself. His own face full of pain,

Thorion went to her, gently placing his hand on her shoulder. She turned to him, stepping into his arms and weeping against his shoulder as he sought to comfort her.

'*Heart's love the Sword will lay down,*' whispered Alma to Caleb. 'So now we know who the first heart was. Oh, this place is so sad.' He only nodded, his blue eyes shifting to the grey of a stormy sea. 'I still can't believe this is real. It's so strange to be here again.' She wanted to keep talking, to somehow ward off the bad feelings the place aroused in her. Meredan moved past them both, his red cloak swirling around him as he tracked the last movements of Gwion in his battle with the Galardin.

'He was ambushed here,' he said, his voice a low rumble in the chill mist. 'It would have been quick – he fought hard, but had already taken a fatal blow.' Lord Artos looked at him, his face impassive. Alma bit her lip. 'He fell here,' Meredan went on, indicating the hollow in the ground. His eyes narrowed as he knelt down, moving his hands to trace the shapes in the earth. 'He hit hard – it may be because he was struck again. Then the Galardin stood over him.' He frowned. 'It looks as though the creature left suddenly – I don't know why.' Laying his hands on the soil he closed his eyes to focus, breathing deeply. Alma frowned at Caleb and he leaned in, lips close to her ear, his breath warm as he whispered to her. 'He's trying to access the moment Gwion's soul passed to the Realms of Light.'

Alma's eyes went wide and she turned to Caleb but he put his finger to his lips, jerking his head in Meredan's direction. She turned to see the Lord still kneeling, his focus absolute, while Artos stood nearby with arms folded, his expression unreadable. Watching in awe, she saw Meredan move his hands away from where Gwion had lain, as though following a trail no one else could see. A little to the right of the depression he stopped, his hands hovering several inches above the ground.

'It is here.'

'The Sword?' said Caleb, startled into speech.

Meredan, opening his eyes slightly to look at him, nodded. 'The Sword.'

'Why have you not yet brought me the girl?' The words sliced through the air as Deryck stood before his father's desk in the same place as the messenger before him, though with quite a different attitude.

'You told me I could do this my own way. So leave me to do it!'

Lord Denoris stood, both fists clenched as he regarded his son. 'They are on their way, even now, to the Closed Gate of Penwyth Gawr,' he said softly. 'Do I need to remind you what that means?'

Deryck did not need reminding, nor was he fooled by the softness in his father's voice. He had heard about the Gate, what they might find and what they hoped to find on the other side. What he could not understand was how Alma had known to take them there. He still remembered the nightmarish sight of the blood-smeared Galardin returning to his father's estate from the Gate some years past. Twelve years old he had been, supposed to be sleeping but instead peering through his bedroom window at the commotion in the yard below. His father had strode out to meet the hulking creature, cloak billowing behind him in the fitful light of the torches, and forced the Galardin to kneel, holding it by the hair as it relayed its news. Once finished, Denoris had run the monster through with his sword and Deryck could still hear the strangled cry it had let out, whether in pain or release, he was never sure. He'd had bad dreams for some weeks after, waking screaming from sleep to find either his valet or, on rare occasions, his mother there to comfort him.

'I left another Galardin there,' said Denoris, cutting into his thoughts. Deryck stared at his father, unable to conceal his shock. Denoris came out from behind his desk, one hand stroking his chin as he paced, green eyes fixed on his son. 'So it will not be easy for them... Still, their numbers are enough. They will protect the girl, of course.'

Deryck pulled himself together and nodded, adopting what he hoped was a serious expression. But, a Galardin! Thinking fast, he spoke. 'I almost had her the other day. She will be mine before too much longer. Just let me do it, sir, I know I can succeed.'

'Almost isn't good enough,' his father shot back. 'If they find the Sword today...'

'You couldn't find it!' Deryck blurted. Seeing his father's expression, he backpedalled hastily. 'What I mean, sir, is that if they find it, then we will get the Cup and the Crown!' he went on, his face earnest. 'With two thirds of the Regalia in our hands, the balance of power will still lie with the Dark.'

Lord Denoris looked at him a moment, his expression calculating. Pursing his lips, he blew a breath out through his nose. 'Fine. You may have your way in this. But only for so long, Deryck. Time is of the essence.' Staring hard at the boy, his eyes narrowed, he waited until Deryck bowed his head in acknowledgement. 'You may leave,' Denoris said, with a hint of a smile. 'But make sure you are there to greet her when they return. If they return.'

He waited, studying his son and Deryck nodded. He bowed to his father and left the study, closing the door behind. Sinking down on the same wooden bench so recently vacated by the hapless messenger, he leaned forward, resting his head in his hands. He knew that he owed it to his father and the assembled Dark to use every wile he possessed to bring Alma to their cause. The problem was that there was a large part of him that no longer wished to do so. He wished to have Alma on her own terms, to be with her because she wanted to be with him, not because he had tricked her in any way. He regretted ever coming up with his plan to seduce Alma, for he knew his father would expect him to succeed. And now all he could do was hope she would make it back into Ambeth in one piece. Standing, he made his way slowly to his rooms to get changed. There was nothing else he could do and, if he was to meet Alma on her return he wanted to make a good impression, to at least give her the chance to make up her own mind.

Meredan knelt down, holding out his hands over a patch of ground. Alma realised that if she squinted she could see something like a faint shimmer in the air. She looked up as Thorion came to stand next to her. 'You are sure, Meredan?' His tone betrayed his excitement.

'Yes, Thorion,' he replied. 'I can feel its presence, even through the concealment spell he laid on it.'

'It must have been the last thing he did,' said Adara, her voice thick with tears. 'I wonder how...' She trailed off, but her question was obvious. How had Gwion, wounded and under attack, found the time to shape a spell? Then Alma spoke, in a voice of wonder.

'I think it was me.'

All eyes turned to her. 'What do you mean?' Thorion asked, a curious expression on his face.

'I-I can't explain it, really. I just remember feeling, somehow, drawn to what was happening under the trees. It was as though everything stopped when I stood here. I'm sorry, I can't explain it any more than that.'

'I can,' said Artos unexpectedly. 'It was your presence that stopped the creature.'

'Artos,' said Thorion sharply, a warning tone in his voice.

'But, how is that possible?' said Alma. She was still unsure of Lord Artos, though she liked the Elder and he was always kind to her.

Lord Artos looked at the High King. 'Thorion, it must be told!'

'Artos, you know my wishes here. *Our* wishes, if you remember. It is what the Council decided.'

Alma turned to Caleb, her eyebrows raised in query. Nonplussed, he shook his head. 'I have no idea,' he whispered, for the two Lords had now stepped to one side and were having what looked like a heated discussion. Adara, her face still stained with tears, saw Alma's confusion and came over to her.

'It is nothing,' she said, taking Alma's arm and rubbing it gently, as though to warm her. 'Lord Artos is Gwion and Galen's father, you see. Being here is hard for him, it is hard for us all.' Her eyes were red and her voice caught as she spoke. 'I think all he means is that you disturbed what was happening here, caused the creature to take fright. It is what gave Gwion time to hide the sword, so for that we are grateful.'

Alma nodded, putting her hand over Adara's where it rested on her arm. She was sure there was no way she could possibly have frightened off a creature like the one that had just attacked them but, seeing the sorrow still on Adara's face, she decided not to push the issue. She wished with all her heart that she had some comfort to offer her, here in this place of anguish and death.

'I'm so sorry' she whispered. 'for... for everything. It must be so hard for you to be here.'

Adara half-smiled in response then, to Alma's surprise, gave her a hug. 'Thank you,' she murmured. 'That means more to me than you could ever know.' Then, standing back, she touched Alma's cheek gently. 'Do not worry about Lord Artos. He has had much sorrow, losing both of his sons. He means well and is a powerful member of the Light. Plus, I think he might like you.' Alma frowned in disbelief, but looking at Adara's mischievous elfin face marked by grief, she did not have the heart to disagree. 'Come now,' the Elder went on. 'Let us watch as Meredan breaks the concealment spell.'

'What's a concealment spell?' Alma asked. But it was Artos who answered, breaking off from his discussion with Thorion to come nearer, his normally rich voice rough with emotion as he spoke.

'It is a simple thing, but also one of our most effective workings,' he said, resting his hand on Alma's shoulder for a moment. She turned to look at him, surprised to see affection in his ice blue eyes. She nodded, and he went on. 'It takes only a few moments to set, but once done, no one not of the Light can detect or break it, no matter how they try. My son was... skilled in such things,' he said, turning his attention to Meredan. He was murmuring words of power as he moved his hands across the patch of earth where the Sword lay, his eyes closed and concentration complete.

'And he knew the Dark well enough, that they would have come through to find it,' said Thorion. He paused, his face dark with sorrow as he contemplated the hollow in the soil. 'Rest well, my friend.'

Alma said nothing, taken aback, her heart twisting with sadness. A shimmering began to emanate from the ground, a golden light that gave all of them pause. Thorion stepped back and Caleb moved closer to Alma, all of them watching as the glow increased in intensity, then dissipated. Slowly, a beautiful sword came into view, wrought of gleaming silver metal that shone with a pearly sheen like moonlight. Alma recognised it immediately – it was the one from the Seer's document. The hilt was fashioned like twisting vines, amethyst stones gleaming amongst the silver leaves. It was a thing of beauty, yet the story it told was one of pain. Frozen in time since Gwion laid it down, blood was still fresh on the blade and spattered on the hand guard, while more pooled around the weapon itself. Adara made a choking sound, turning away, and Alma went to stand with her, part in sympathy, partly because she couldn't look at the sight for long herself. Lord Artos stepped forward and gently lifted the sword, cleaning it on his cloak. The thick dark fabric soaked up the blood and restored the weapon to its former shimmering beauty. A sombre Caleb stepped forward to scatter a handful of pine needles and earth onto the remaining blood, covering the last traces. Lord Artos turned to face them all, blood on his cloak and his face a mask of pain as he held the sword that had led his son to his death. He handed it to Thorion who took it from him, bowing his head. Then Artos moved to Adara, who was weeping again, and placed his arm around her shoulders. 'Come, my dear,' they all heard him say. 'Let us leave this place of sorrow.'

'Yes,' said Thorion, his voice quiet. 'Let us go.'

He and the rest of the little group fell in behind Adara and Artos as they moved out to the path that would lead them to the Gate, Caleb and Alma bringing up the rear, arms linked and walking close. Alma, shaken by what she had seen, fought back tears. Caleb put his arm around her shoulders, hugging her to him. Looking at him, wiping her eyes, she nodded in thanks, unable to speak.

'It's OK,' he murmured, his own eyes suspiciously bright.

As a group they reached the Gate, and, without any further words, started to cross back through to Ambeth. Artos went first, his blood-stained cloak swirling around him in the mists, followed by Adara, who paused a moment before crossing to look back at the desolate valley, her lovely face pale and drawn. Then Meredan, a crimson shape in the increasing mist and gloom, stepped through strong and tall. Thorion, Alma and Caleb stood together for a moment in the mists.

'It has not been easy for any of us,' Thorion said, his voice gentle and deep, 'to see this and to learn of poor Gwion's fate. Do you realise now, Alma, what it was that you saw that day under the pines?'

'The scream, it… it was Gwion, wasn't it?' said Alma, her voice choked with unshed tears, pain in her chest. 'And the dark shape was the creature. But, what about the silver light?'

'It was Gwion's passing, dear one,' Thorion said in his deep voice, his eyes shifting to stormy grey. 'When he died, his spirit passed to the Realms of Light and his body, no longer needed, turned to light and disappeared. So it is for us all, Light and Dark, when we pass.'

'Oh,' said Alma, no longer able to hold back her tears. 'Oh, that is so sad.' Her voice trailed to a whisper and she wept as she thought of Gwion, dying alone in the dark woods and Adara grieving his loss these many years.

Caleb nodded in agreement, dashing away a tear of his own as Alma wiped her eyes. Seeing their distress, Thorion laid a strong hand on Alma's shoulder. 'But Alma,' he said, his glorious face close to hers. 'You did it.'

Alma just looked at him, not knowing for a moment what he meant.

'The Sword, Alma,' said Thorion, his face lighting up. 'It is as was foretold. You have found the Sword and made the first strike against the Dark.'

Alma's eyes widened at this and she shrank into Caleb's side.

'Do not fear, dear heart,' said Thorion. 'None can harm you, not with us around you. Your name will be feted in our realms and beyond for what you have achieved this day.'

Alma gulped and nodded, the enormity of what had happened sinking in. She wasn't sure she wanted to be feted, but it seemed there was no help for it. She shivered again, the cold starting to seep through her clothes.

'Yes, let us go from here,' said Thorion, noticing her discomfort. 'Take my hands, both of you, and do not let go.' Holding out his hands, he waited until he had both Alma and Caleb secure in his grasp before breathing deep and closing his eyes. Alma felt the power move through her, heat travelling up her arm from where her hand touched Thorion's, warming her through. Opening his eyes, the High King looked at them both. 'Now,' he said, and they stepped through the Gate together.

Deryck nodded to the guards as they opened the double doors for him to enter the Great Hall. It was almost empty, just a few members of the court moving through on their own business. Deryck made his way to one of the alcoves and took a seat on the bench, his hands loosely clasped in front of him as he watched the passing traffic. But his mind was elsewhere. If Alma succeeded, if the Light retrieved the Sword, it would be a blow against his father and make him more determined than ever to have control of the girl. Nodding to a passing acquaintance, Deryck pushed the thought away, tired of worrying about it. Let him get through today, and hopefully talk to Alma. Whatever was going to happen tomorrow could wait until then.

The Sword

As Thorion, Alma and Caleb came through the Gate, the forest seemed greener and more beautiful than ever, especially after the wintry gloom of the pine valley. While Alma and Caleb both paused to recover, Thorion turned to close the Gate. The light faded out of the carved symbols as the way was sealed once more. Her head still spinning a little, Alma saw Meredan, Artos and Adara standing together in the shade of a large tree. They looked so much brighter than they had in the valley, the colours of their robes and armour no longer muted by the mists. Adara came over, looking concerned.

'Are you all right?' she asked both Caleb and Alma. 'We forget how hard it is for you to cross.' She placed a gentle hand on Alma's arm and Alma looked at her, surprised to see that she was restored almost to her old self.

'I'm all right,' she replied, 'but... are you?'

Adara smiled, though sorrow still shadowed her eyes.

'I am better,' she said quietly, 'though I will always miss Gwion.' She looked distant for a moment then returned to Alma. 'The hardest thing was not knowing,' she went on. 'Not knowing if he was out there, somewhere, unable to get back. At least now I can grieve for him.'

'I am so sorry,' whispered Alma, stricken. Adara stopped her before she could continue.

'No, there is nothing to be sorry for. You gave me this gift, Alma, and I will forever be grateful.'

'As will we all,' interjected Lord Artos in his rich voice. He came over to Alma and placed his hands on her arms, looking at her as though inexpressibly proud. 'For you have also given us back the Sword, which means that not all is lost.' Alma was surprised to see a twinkle in the older man's eye as he leaned in closer, saying, 'I knew you could do this.' Then, giving her a wink, he stepped back, leaving her astounded.

Thorion had mounted his horse and now sat waiting, the Sword gleaming bright in his hand. 'Let us go now,' he said, excitement thrumming in his voice. 'It is time to move. Let us ride!'

Adara and Artos went to their horses, while Caleb wheeled his mount around and Meredan, smiling broadly, offered his strong arm to boost Alma as she scrambled onto the patient horse's back. Once she was steady, holding tightly to Caleb, he smiled up at her. 'You did well today,' he said, his face full of admiration.

'Th-thank you,' said Alma. 'For the boost, as well,' she called after him, hearing him laugh as he swung himself easily onto his own horse's back. His broad crimson back disappeared down the path with Thorion following behind, calling to the rest of the group.

'Come on!' he cried. 'We must hurry now! Let the word go out, that the Sword has been found!' He sped forward, forcing the others to keep up as they raced through the woods, a much different ride than that of earlier in the day. Even Adara, who had been so sorrowful earlier, laughed as she rode through the glowing green of the wood and Alma felt joy within her, an easing of the worry she carried inside.

'Is it the Sword?' she asked, clinging to Caleb as they galloped through the trees.

'Yes!' he cried. 'It is starting, the return of joy to the world!' He put his head down, riding so quickly that Alma closed her eyes and tightened her arms around him, scared they would smash into a tree at any moment. Still, with that irrepressible bubble of joy growing inside her it was hard to care, so she opened them again, laughing along with the rest of them. It was a thrilling, madcap, exhilarating ride – any one of them could have been knocked off by a passing branch at any time, yet it didn't seem to matter, as though a greater force guided them through the woods. They burst from the trees in a blaze of light and colour, Thorion holding the Sword high as he rode across the field to the nearby village, bringing people running to their gates.

'The Sword!' they cried. The word travelled through the small community, bringing more and more people outside as the group rode through. 'It is the High King and he has the Sword!'

Thorion laughed out loud as he rode, his dark hair blowing back from his face, the Sword gleaming in the sun. 'Yes!' he cried. 'It is the Sword! To the Great Hall! Let us celebrate!'

Shouts of jubilation went up as they rode through the village, hooves clattering on the cobbled street. Circling around, they cantered back through the green field to the gardens, drawing a crowd that grew as the news spread. As they hurtled up the Long Walk, scattering people to left and right, Thorion kept up the cry. 'Spread the word, the Sword has returned to us!' Alma could see the news spread through the gardens, with people who had heard running to tell others. Most reacted with joy at the news. But not all. She had seen Lord Denoris, standing like a living statue at the junction of one of the paths, watching the group as they raced by. His eyes met hers and there was no warmth in his emerald gaze. In spite of the joy that filled her, she felt cold for a moment. It seemed she had succeeded in completing the first part of her quest without even trying. And, despite all of Thorion's assurances, she knew now that she was well and truly marked by the Dark.

Magnificent in his triumph, the High King reined in his horse at the entrance to the Palace, still holding the Sword high, his dark hair flowing back from his brow and his blue eyes ablaze.

'Let the word be spread!' he cried, his voice ringing out over the excited chatter of the growing crowd. 'The Sacred Sword has returned to us!' To the sound of cheers he dismounted. The others followed suit and the guards took their horses. Thorion led them through the Foyer into the Great Hall, which glowed with colour, the sun streaming in through the stained glass.

Caleb grabbed Alma's hand before she got swallowed up in the crowd. 'Come on,' he said, 'you need to stand next to Thorion.'

'Wait, what?' began Alma, pulling back a little. She did not want to be singled out.

'No, come on,' insisted Caleb, his expression amused as he took in her reticence. Adara, a little ahead of them, turned and beckoned to Alma with a smile.

'Oh, OK,' sighed Alma, giving in to the inevitable. She hated standing up in front of crowds and could feel her blush starting already. The Hall filled with noise as the mass of people followed them inside, the members of the Court and villagers all craning their necks and jostling for position as they sought to see the Sword. Stepping onto the dais at the end of the room, Thorion gestured for calm. Once the crowd was mostly silent he spoke, his handsome face more glorious than ever.

'This is a momentous day for all who live in Ambeth and the world beyond,' he said, his voice ringing in all corners of the room. 'Thanks to Alma-' he gestured to her where she stood nearby, flanked by Caleb and Adara, blushing furiously '-we have been able to retrieve the Sacred Sword of the Regalia from where it has lain hidden these many years. May it mark the return of Balance to all our worlds.' His face radiant with joy, Thorion turned and with great reverence went and placed the sword into the empty recess. A faint glow began to emanate from the rocky alcove, serene and golden, and a sigh of rapture came from the crowd. Thorion stepped back, slowly, and turned once more to face them, gesturing for silence. His face had grown solemn.

'On a more difficult note, we have learned of the fate of Lord Gwion. As he passed through the Gate from Ambeth he was ambushed and most foully murdered by a Galardin. We, too, were attacked, and one of our group injured.' At this he paused, fixing several Lords of the Dark with a hard glance. A gasp of horror ran round the room. 'Let us all take a moment to remember him, that his spirit hear us and feel joy that there is still love for him in this world.'

With these words, the majority of those assembled bowed their heads, silent in grief for one gone too soon. Alma was one of the only to notice when Adara, overcome with sorrow, touched Thorion lightly on the arm and slipped out through a side door, the public outpouring for Gwion too much for her. Finally with ritual words Thorion signalled an end to the moment of reflection, although many still looked sorrowful as they turned, quietly, to talk with their neighbour.

Along one side of the Hall, Alma spied an efficient team of servants setting up a long table full of refreshments. She had been so caught up in the events of the day, she hadn't realised how tired, hungry and thirsty she was. Caleb seemed to be thinking the same thing. 'Let's go,' he said, jerking his head towards the buffet. 'I'm starving!'

But Thorion stepped in, stopping him with a gentle

hand on his arm. 'First we need to fix that shoulder of yours,' he said, gesturing to a nearby Elder. Tall and bearded, dressed in dark green, he came over and drew Caleb to one side, examining the boy's injured arm. Thorion turned to Alma.

'Shall we eat? You can bring something for Caleb, if you like.' He smiled at her and Alma nodded back before following Thorion across the Hall, pausing only to look back one more time at the Sword glowing in its sheltered space.

The Great Hall was filled with members of the Court, both Light and Dark, in a splendid display, many of them coming up to congratulate Alma and shake her hand. Still in her regular clothes, and somewhat the worse for wear after the wild ride through the woods, she felt quite drab and wanted to slip away to her room and get changed. She was also still embarrassed at being singled out by Thorion in front of the assembly; she hadn't done much, only been in the right place at the right time and still wasn't sure this meant she was the one from the Prophecy, no matter how much Caleb went on about it. Dear Caleb. Right now he was surrounded by a group of his friends, all listening as he told the story of finding the Sword and his part in it. He smiled at Alma before returning to his tale, flushed and animated with excitement.

As the crowd around her dispersed, Alma started towards the doors, weaving her way through the jubilant throng. Here and there knots of people stood with serious faces, talking quietly amongst themselves. Only by the heat of her bracelet did Alma know they were of the Dark. She avoided them as best she could, knowing she would be no favourite of theirs - although she didn't know why they couldn't see that the return of the Sword was good for everyone. She was almost at the doors when a voice called her name and she stopped, feeling her heart skip a beat. Deryck. Tall and handsome, clad in embroidered ivory and brown, he leant against the wall, his relaxed beauty taking her breath away. She faltered, unsure he had spoken to her. Seeing this, he smiled and said her name again, lifting his chin and beckoning her with his hand. Alma's mouth dropped open and she hastily closed it. She could feel the resentment from the nearby group of girls as she moved towards Deryck, her bracelet blazing against her wrist, heart pounding. She still couldn't believe he was Dark - sometimes she wondered if the bracelet worked properly.

Across the crowded Great Hall, Lord Denoris, deep in conversation with one of his advisors, paused for a moment. He watched as his son beckoned the girl over to him, saw the pleased look on her face as she realised he had spoken to her. A half smile crossed his handsome features as he watched Alma with Deryck, seeing his hand touching her arm, the excited look on her face as he spoke to her. So the plan had changed, the girl turning out to be more than expected – that was manageable. He just needed his son to do his part successfully. So he would let him have this moment, see what he could achieve. One way or another, Alma was to be brought to the Dark. If she was seduced across to their side, if she *chose* to ally herself with the Dark, Thorion could do nothing about it. After all, he was always going on about choice – what irony it would be if the whole thing backfired because of his insistence on the girl having free will. Lord Denoris' smile deepened. When the girl was theirs she would have no choice about anything she did any more – he would personally see to it.

'Congratulations, Alma,' said Deryck as he straightened up and moved towards her. 'I hear that they would not have found the Sword without you. There is to be a celebration tomorrow night, did you know?'

'Yes, I-I had heard,' said Alma, completely at a loss. Deryck always did this to her, made her feel like a dolt. She could feel herself blushing and sought desperately for something else to say.

'So, will you be going to the dance?' she asked, then made a face as the group of girls nearby giggled at her. Deryck, however, turned and glared at them, shocking them to silence. He returned his attention to Alma.

'Yes, I'll be there. Will you? Or does your life in the other realm require…'

'No! I mean yes, I'll be there. I can come back here, I wouldn't miss it.'

'Well then,' said Deryck, his hand coming to rest on her arm as he leaned in closer. 'Will you save me a dance? I imagine you'll have many wanting to dance with you after what you have achieved today, but I hope you can put one aside for me.' He grinned at her, a lock of his golden hair falling forwards. He was so beautiful Alma just stared at him, feeling the warmth of his hand on her arm, trying to keep breathing normally. Then she realised that he was looking at her, amused, waiting for an answer. The nearby group of girls were positively squirming with jealousy.

'Oh!' Flustered, she went on. 'Well, of course, I mean, I hadn't even thought about it, um, yes, that would be great.'

Laughing now, Deryck took her hand and raised it to his lips, kissing it gently. 'Well, it's a date. Isn't that what they would say in your world?'

Alma's mouth fell open and she felt like she would faint, or scream, or do something else entirely uncool but was saved from embarrassing herself further by Lord Denoris, who had come to stand nearby and now signalled to his son. Deryck relinquished Alma's hand with seeming reluctance before turning to his father, who nodded at Alma. 'I must speak with you,' he said to his son.

'If you'll excuse me, Lady Alma, I will see you tomorrow,' said Deryck, bowing to her before leaving to follow his father to the doors. The knot of girls, throwing furious glances at Alma, moved in his wake.

Alma was still standing in the same spot when Caleb found her a moment later.

'Are you all right?' he asked, looking at her curiously.

'What? Yes, er, I'm fine thanks,' said Alma, still distracted. 'Are you?'

Caleb grinned. 'All fixed up.' He turned to show her his shoulder. The marks were almost gone, just faded pink lines. Alma's eyes opened wide.

'Wow. So was this, um, Marlin?'

'Yes, he's a Healer. A pretty good one, too. So, um, hey, I was thinking, I'm going to get changed and then perhaps we could-'

'Sorry Caleb,' said Alma, her cheeks flushing hot. 'I just think I need to go home now. I'm pretty tired.' Caleb's face dropped.

'Why not just stay?' he asked, frowning. 'Your room is ready, and I'll make sure you get to the Gate in the morning, I promise.'

But Alma shook her head. 'I really just need to go home for a while,' she said, hoping he would understand. Apart from the fact that she was exhausted, she needed to have some time alone, to think about what had just happened. She couldn't discuss it with Caleb – what she needed was the peace and sanctuary of her own bed where she could go over and over again what Deryck had said and how he had said it. *He had asked her to dance!*

'But you'll definitely be back tomorrow, won't you? For the celebration?' pressed Caleb, his pleasant face hopeful. 'It's for the Feast Day, as well as the Sword,' he went on. 'So you need to be here.'

Alma nodded her head. 'Sure, I mean, yes, of course I'll be here. Wouldn't miss it.'

'Good,' said Caleb, smiling into her eyes. Then, as she tried unsuccessfully to conceal a yawn, he sighed.

'Come on then,' he said reluctantly, shaking his head as he looked at Alma. 'I'll take you to the Gate, but you should let Thorion know you're going.'

'Thanks, Caleb,' said Alma, stifling another yawn. She really was tired. Linking her arm with his, she smiled gratefully at him as they moved through the crowd to find Thorion.

Denoris and Deryck walked through the fragrant gardens in the fading light, Deryck trailing his hand along the hedges, deep in thought.

'I saw you speaking with the girl,' said Lord Denoris with a smile, his voice unusually warm. 'It seems your plan is working after all.'

'Her name is Alma,' replied Deryck, feeling the need to defend her in some obscure way.

Lord Denoris looked sharply at his son. 'Don't tell me you're developing feelings for her?' he asked.

'No!' Deryck shot back. 'But, I think, perhaps she is for me. We will see, tomorrow night.'

'Well, be sure that you do not fall for her.' They were nearing their apartments. Golden light streamed from the long windows across the gravel. 'You know what our plans are. There will be no time for romance once she is with the Dark.' Denoris smiled broadly and laid a hand on Deryck's shoulder. Deryck looked up, surprised.

'Oh yes, of course,' he said, forcing a smile. He

walked the rest of the way in silence, only speaking to bid his father good night once they reached their rooms. Lord Denoris considered him for a moment before placing both hands on his son's shoulders.

'Remember, Deryck, you hold all our hopes. Do not fail us.' Deryck just nodded, hoping his face would not reveal his indecision, before turning to enter the solitude of his room.

Denoris turned away, his expression thoughtful. Well, if the boy got his heart broken, he couldn't say he wasn't warned. He had to learn not to let his feelings get in the way of a job that needed to be done. Entering his own rooms, the Dark Lord found Gwenene waiting, her beauty illuminated by the glow from the fire. She smiled at him as he stepped forward to embrace her, twining her arms around his neck to pull him close for a kiss, biting on his lip in a way that pleased him.

'How goes it, my Lord?' she asked, her voice low and husky, her eyes bright in the firelit room.

'It is better, now,' allowed Denoris. 'And you, my Lady?' he asked, his hands sliding on the silk of her light gown.

'I am in need of some comfort after a difficult day,' replied Gwenene, her crimson lips curving in a smile as she looked at him from under her lashes. 'Your lady wife is at your estate, is she not?'

'She is,' said Denoris, one hand coming up to caress her soft dark hair. Lifting it away from her neck he kissed her throat. 'So I am all yours, for tonight.'

'And what of the girl? When will she be yours?' purred

Gwenene, closing her eyes as he kissed her again. 'I saw her today with your son, in the Hall.'

Her hands moved down Denoris' chest, and he grabbed them tight in his own, stopping their descent, growling deep in his throat as Gwenene pouted. 'Yes,' he said, his lips curled in a half smile, half snarl, 'the boy has promise. In fact, if all goes to plan tomorrow night our bird may well be ensnared without even realising it.'

He smiled at Gwenene, green eyes gleaming in the firelight and she raised her eyebrows briefly before deliberately letting her dress slip off one shoulder. Yes, thought Denoris, bending his head to the eager Gwenene, the game was still in play.

After she had made her farewells, Caleb walked Alma to the Gate, wanting to make sure she got through in one piece. Thorion, of the same mind, despatched two guards to escort them through the woods, over Alma's protestations.

'You underestimate your own importance,' he said, looking at her affectionately. Caleb nodded in agreement. 'We could not have done this without you. Your role in finding the Sword has marked you as the one from the prophecy. Therefore your safety is more important than ever.'

So Alma had accepted the escort and Caleb's insistence on accompanying her, but was quiet as they walked along, saying she was tired. At the Gate, she kissed him goodbye on the cheek. The scent of her hair and skin as she did so was intoxicating to him. He watched as she went through, his heart full, the sparkle of light letting him know she was safely across. After the day they had shared he thought he might finally be able to tell her how he really felt. After all, she had ridden with him, had linked her arm with his as they walked in the Great Hall. *She had kissed him on the cheek!* Today, thought Caleb, walking back through the woods with a smile on his face, had been a great day.

Alma came through the Gate to the park, reeling from the events of the day and completely exhausted. She staggered to her bench and sat down, needing a few minutes of just sitting and breathing before she felt equal to the task of getting home. All she could think about was Deryck, the way he had smiled at her and kissed her hand, asking her to promise him a dance. Eventually she got up slowly and started to walk home, wishing more than ever that she could call Sara and talk to her about what she was going through. She needed her advice. Reaching her driveway at last, almost stumbling with weariness, Alma quietly let herself in the side door. She could hear the hum of the television in the sitting room and knew her parents were in there, but was too tired to say more than 'Goodnight' as she went past the door. In bed a short while later, Alma found herself unable to sleep despite her exhaustion, the events of the day playing over and over in her mind. She tossed and turned, trying to find a comfortable position. Finally, she drifted off into a restless slumber. 'Tomorrow,' was her last thought, 'I'll see him again.'

Celebration

The Great Hall hummed with music and conversation as people filed in. Members of the Court and residents of the nearby village mingled with others from the distant hills, all come together to celebrate the Feast Day and, now, the return of the Sword. Even the Dark put a brave face on things, making their presence felt and taking advantage of the event to cement alliances and pursue flirtations as they worked the room. Alma, dressed in gold silk, her hair in waves around her flushed face, was thoroughly enjoying herself. She had never been to anything like this before. As she entered the Great Hall on Caleb's arm, she smiled at him in excitement. He grinned back, squeezing her arm, his amiable face glowing with pride.

'Come on. Let's find the refreshments, before all the good things are gone.'

Alma chuckled as she trailed through the crowd behind him – typical Caleb, always thinking with his stomach. While she hadn't made any official plans to attend the ball with him, she was grateful to have him at her side as they moved through the crowd and people came forward to congratulate them on their achievement. The long windows were open to the warm summer air, letting in the scents of myriad flowers to mingle with the heated atmosphere. She saw Thorion standing with Meredan, both magnificent in ornate tunics and breeches, Thorion in his customary blue and Meredan in red and gold. She waved as she went past and was rewarded with broad smiles from them both, Meredan raising his glass to her.

Alma waited by a nearby pillar while Caleb fought his way through to the refreshment table, emerging a few moments later with drinks for them both and, balanced on top, a plate piled high with chicken legs, salad and savoury pastries, all in imminent danger of falling. Alma burst out laughing, taking the plate from him before he dropped it. She then swapped it for a drink which she sipped as she scanned the room, pleased to find it was the cordial she liked so much. She tapped her foot to the lively beat of the music and Caleb offered her some food. She waved it away.

'No thanks,' she said, smiling. 'I'm really not hungry – too excited tonight.'

'Really?' said Caleb, looking surprised. 'Are you sure?' All around them people were stuffing their faces, exclaiming with pleasure over the delicious food. Couples started to fill the dance floor, whirling around as the music played. Alma just nodded, looking around – she loved to people watch, and when the crowd were all so good-looking, it was even more fun. Though if she was being honest, there was only one person she was looking out for and she hadn't seen him yet.

'Will you dance with me, Alma?' asked Caleb suddenly. He had finished his meal and set the plate aside, looking expectantly at Alma who looked back at him in surprise.

'Oh! Well, that is, I'm not a very good dancer, I don't know the steps,' she babbled, not wanting to hurt his feelings. Looking downcast, Caleb tried to hide his disappointment without much success and Alma sought to reassure him. 'I'm not saying I won't dance with you, I just need a minute to watch what they're doing.'

'I can help you,' Caleb replied, cheering up a little. 'I'm not a bad dancer, you know,' he continued, executing a step. Alma laughed out loud, she couldn't help it, then tried to cover it up as she saw the hurt expression on his face.

'Oh, Caleb, I'm not laughing at you, I promise,' she said, still smiling. 'You are a good dancer, it's just I've never seen you like that before,' she went on, draining the last of her drink.

'So, then - later?' asked Caleb.

'Later,' agreed Alma, 'but only if you promise to help me with the steps. And not laugh at me,' she called out, for Caleb, noticing her empty cup, had taken it from her and, with a little bow and a wink, had gone to refill it. As soon as he went, Alma scanned the room again. Where was Deryck?

Denoris entered the Great Hall, the guards bowing as he came through the double doors, magnificent in dark brocade that set off his golden good looks. Gwenene was exquisite in silk and lace at his side. He scanned the room, nodding to acquaintances, his handsome face smiling as he moved through the throng. Inside, though, he was still seething, and he knew Gwenene could feel the tension in him as she held his arm.

'Denoris,' she murmured, and he turned his head to look at her. She raised one dark eyebrow at him. 'We do not have to stay long.'

'We need to be seen,' he said through his teeth. 'And I need to make sure the boy does his job. But where is he?'

He frowned as he scanned the crowd again. Gwenene stopped a passing waiter and took two drinks, handing one to Denoris. She waited, her blue eyes on him until he met her gaze again, then she smiled.

'To catching birds.' She raised her glass and clinked it with his. He smiled at her again - this time a real smile that reached his eyes. He took a drink then leaned in to kiss Gwenene, tasting the wine on her lips, her slender arm coming around his neck as she laughed against him.

'To catching birds,' he murmured against her mouth. Then he raised his head, looking around the room again. Where was the boy?

Alma moved through the glittering throng, oblivious to any admiring glances thrown her way. She smiled at the occasional person she recognised but didn't stop, not wanting to be diverted from her goal. Caleb had gone to find drinks for them again and last she saw had been waylaid by one of his friends, no doubt having to tell the story once more of how he had been there when the Sword was found. So Alma was left to her own devices and she had one thing on her mind. Deryck. Since arriving through the Gate she had been in a whirl of nervous excitement, unable to share it with anyone. As she put on her beautiful gown and brushed out her hair, all her thoughts had been on one person and how she would look when he saw her. Now she was determined to find him and claim her dance.

Peering around a tall man in a rose tunic she thought she glimpsed Deryck's golden hair near the edge of the dance floor. Perfect. Slipping past, she darted around a couple attired in matching shades of violet and purple then stopped dead, almost knocking into another dancing couple. Frowning, they moved around her but she didn't notice. It *was* Deryck, immaculate and splendid as usual in midnight blue velvet. But he was otherwise occupied. A tall slender girl stood close to him, her long dark hair trailing down the back of her embroidered pale green gown. Her hand lay on his arm as he smiled down at her, his green eyes warm and full of affection. She said something to him that made him throw his handsome head back and laugh and Alma felt it like a blow to the gut. The two of them were so obviously close, so obviously suited for each other – how could she have thought for one moment that he liked her? The usual crowd of giggling girls congregated around Deryck, each vying for his attention but he only had eyes for the mysterious girl in green. Devastated and shocked by how much he was affecting her, Alma turned away and, pushing blindly through the crowd, headed for the glass doors to the gardens. She needed some fresh air.

Deryck turned his head as he noticed a slim figure in gold run from the room. Alma. He had been looking for her since he arrived, had been waiting to see her all day and now it seemed he had almost missed her. Excusing himself from his conversation, he made his way to the long window where he had last seen her, stepping out onto the terrace in time to see a flash of golden gown disappear down one of the gravel pathways. Quickly descending the steps that led into the garden, he followed down the same path, hoping to find her. He did not mean to miss his chance with her again.

Alma walked along the gravel path winding through the garden beds and down to the river, where gaily-coloured boats bobbed at their tethers, waiting to take passengers wherever they wished. The gravel that crunched under her feet was whitest quartz, while around her sweet-scented flowers in all the shades of the rainbow waved and nodded in the warm evening breeze. Exquisitely carved benches invited the wanderer to sit in shadowy alcoves, while in the distance the soft sound of a fountain could be heard. All of this beauty was lost on Alma, caught up as she was in her own sadness. *The way he had smiled at her!* It was all she could see, Deryck smiling down at the dark-haired girl as they stood close together on the edge of the dance floor. Alma had been sure he was interested in her but saw now he must just have been humouring her, another of the girls who clamoured around him, desperate for the smallest sign of affection. Caleb had warned her, the Elders had gently chided her, but she hadn't listened – now she just felt like an idiot. Wallowing in self-pity, Alma didn't hear the footsteps behind her until they drew close. 'Caleb' she thought and, without turning, spoke.

'I don't need you to feel sorry for me-' She stopped in shock as her bracelet started to burn against her wrist.

'I don't feel sorry for you. In fact, sorry is not how I feel about you at all.'

His voice was warm velvet and Alma turned around slowly to see Deryck smiling at her in a way that made her knees go weak.

'Deryck!' she gasped. Then, not knowing what else to say, she turned away again, wanting to hide her burning cheeks. He moved up behind her, standing close enough that she could feel the warmth of his body and gently brushed her hair aside to kiss the side of her throat. Alma thought she might die. Turning, she found herself in his arms – she felt nervous for a second but then it didn't matter and she was kissing him, heating up, her arms around his neck as he pressed against her, increasingly intense. His hands moved along her back, holding her hard against him, then came to cup her face as they stopped, both panting, standing close with foreheads touching.

'Where did you go?' he murmured. 'I've been looking for you – one moment you were there, the next you were gone. And you had promised me a dance, remember?'

Alma struggled to calm her breathing, still overwhelmed by the rapid turn of events. 'I… it was… well, you seemed otherwise occupied,' she said lamely, not wanting sound jealous but unable to help it, despite her situation.

Deryck smiled, moving his head back to look into her eyes. 'When I was talking to my sister?'

'Your sister?' queried Alma, curious.

'Yes, the dark-haired girl I was talking to – I presume that's who you mean?' He looked at her quizzically, one corner of his mouth crooked into a smile. Alma could only nod. Deryck tightened his arms around her waist, pulling her close.

'She is my half-sister, to be correct. My father sired her on a trip to your world, so she is half-human. She spent some time there but has recently come to live back here.'

'Really?' said Alma, interested in the mysterious girl. Hell, she was interested in anything to do with Deryck – he could talk to her about shoe leather and she would be enthralled.

'Yes, really,' he laughed, mimicking her tone. 'I'll introduce you to her. I think you might get along.' This last he said with a smile that hid something deeper, as though he were privy to some joke Alma was not. 'But first,' he said, leaning closer, murmuring in her ear, 'let us walk together for a while. I would show you more of these gardens, if you would like.' His lips brushed the side of her cheek, moving to her neck and Alma was lost. She would happily go wherever he liked.

Walking with Deryck through the darkened gardens, Alma felt as though the night had burst into bloom. The beauty that had eluded her before was now all around her, overwhelming her senses. Her only distraction was the stone at her wrist – rubbing her arm she tried in vain to alleviate the pain from her bracelet, which burned hot against her skin. Deryck, seeing the movement, stopped and took Alma's hand in his own, careful not to touch the stone as he gently pushed her bracelet up her arm. He frowned as he saw the red mark on her skin, visible even in the moonlight. Reaching into a pocket of his tunic he brought out a square of pale cotton, which he handed to Alma. 'Here,' he said, 'put this around the stone. I dare not do it myself, in case I touch it accidentally.'

Thanking him, Alma folded the soft handkerchief and twisted it around her bracelet, tucking the ends securely through the tiny links that held the stone in place, relieved to no longer feel its heat against her skin. Then she looked at Deryck with a slight frown.

'Why don't you want to touch the stone? I mean, you are of the Dark, and...' She trailed off, not sure how to ask the question without seeming rude, not wanting to rob the night of any of its magic. But Deryck seemed to understand what she was getting at.

'You mean, why don't I touch the stone and break the power of your bracelet?' Smiling, he moved closer to her, taking her hands in his own and bringing them around his back so she was forced to move towards him, to feel the length of him against her. Not that Alma minded at all. She managed to nod as he bent to kiss her gently before releasing her. She took a step back, needing to take a breath, amazed at how lightheaded she felt. Laughing a little, Deryck reached up to touch her face, his thumb sliding along her cheekbone and across her lips. Alma closed her eyes, overcome with her feelings for him. She felt his arms slide around her again, his body against hers, his voice soft as he murmured against her hair.

'You really have no idea how much I like you, do you? If I destroy your bracelet, you won't be able to come and see me anymore. So we need to protect it, and you, from me.' He bent his head to kiss her again, effectively silencing her. Not that she minded.

Deryck was completely taken, his desire for Alma coursing through him, feeling her arms around his neck, her body against his. As she kissed him, soft and warm in his arms, he knew he wanted nothing more than to be with her. All thoughts of the Regalia and his father were pushed to one side. Surrendering to the moment, he kissed her hard, his lips moving to take in her jawline and neck, then moving downwards and making her gasp. Realising with his last shred of rational thought that they were in a public place, that they needed to slow down, Deryck pulled back from Alma reluctantly. Still holding her close, his hands moving gently across her back, he whispered, 'We should get back.'

Alma nodded but didn't move, her head resting on Deryck's shoulder. She was tall but he was taller still and her head fit perfectly under his chin, her cheek resting on midnight blue velvet as his breath slowly calmed. His hands played with her long red hair as they stood there together.

'Besides,' she whispered, her voice sounding shaky, 'you said you would introduce me to your sister.'

'That I did,' replied Deryck. He really didn't want to go back to the ballroom – instead, he wished he could take Alma back to his own chambers to continue what they had started. He wrenched his mind away from that line of reasoning – there was still a plan to follow and it was vital he kept that in his head. Whatever his heart was feeling had to come second. With a sigh he let go of Alma, feeling cold as he did so, both of them shivering a little in the night air. Wrapping one arm around her shoulders he kept her close as they walked back towards the light and noise of the celebration.

Stepping into the ballroom with Deryck was like entering a kaleidoscope, with people swirling in colour and beauty through the warm perfumed air, and candles and lanterns casting a golden glow across the revellers. Alma thrilled at the feeling of Deryck's arm around her waist. She smiled into his green eyes and he smiled back, expertly weaving his way through the crowd. They crossed the dance floor, attracting more than a few curious glances and one of concern from Thorion who stood with Artos and Adara. He broke the conversation to stare at them both as they passed, oblivious to anyone but each other.

But it was poor Caleb who had the worst shock. Still searching for Alma, drinks in hand, saw her enter the room, her cheeks flushed and eyes bright, more beautiful than he had ever seen her before... entwined with Deryck. It was like a knife to the heart. Stumbling a little, he put the drinks down, pushing through the crowd to get away so he didn't have to see them anymore. Thorion took leave from the other Elders to go after him, hoping to stop him from doing anything foolish. He knew, they all knew, how Caleb felt about Alma and how this turn of events would hurt him.

But Alma had eyes only for Deryck. Laughing as they twirled and stepped around the other dancers, Deryck guided Alma to the other side of the room where his mysterious sister waited, talking animatedly to another girl. Alma could see her now – the slender back with waving dark hair seemed strangely familiar. Deryck reached out, touching her on the shoulder and she turned, her beautiful green dress swirling around her. Alma's mouth dropped open in shock as a pair of green eyes that she recognised met her own. It was Ellery.

'Thorion should have done more to protect her.' Lord Artos, his face hard, watched as Deryck and Alma crossed the dance floor together.

At his side Adara, radiant in lilac silk and velvet, nodded. 'It is important to him that she has choice.'

'And look what she has chosen!' said Artos forcefully, the disappointment plain in his voice. 'She is all but lost to the Dark now – that whelp of Denoris will get his hooks into her and then it will all have been for naught. Galen, Gwion and now Alma, all lost to the Dark!'

Adara, frowning, shook her head. 'I do not think Alma will turn to the Dark, Artos,' she said in her gentle voice, her hand on his arm. 'She saw how it was at the Gate – I think it affected her more than she admits. I believe she will stay with us, though I confess the situation with Deryck does have me worried. Perhaps Thorion…' She trailed off and Artos looked at her affectionately, the emotion softening his face and showing a trace of the handsome young man he had once been.

'You will say no word against him, will you.'

Adara blushed a little, trying to dissemble. But Artos knew he had her. 'I wish you only happiness, my dear. I know, more than anyone, what you have been through,' he said, patting her hand. 'But you must admit that Thorion should have bound her to us! Only then could we be sure of her allegiance.'

'Perhaps,' was all Adara would say, her loyalty to Thorion stopping her from voicing her concerns. But her face as she watched Alma in Deryck's arms was worried, the joy of the celebration gone from her.

Alma's stomach lurched with fear and she took an involuntary step back, Deryck's arm the only thing stopping her from going any further. What the hell was Ellery doing here?

'Alma! It's so nice to see you!' cried Ellery as she embraced her, kissing her on one cheek. Alma was so shocked she couldn't even speak. She turned to Deryck, her blue eyes sparking with outrage.

'Alma, what's wrong?' He looked at her in surprise.

Ellery touched her arm. 'Alma, let me talk to you. I'm- I'm sorry.'

Deryck looked from Alma to Ellery. 'What's this, sister? Do you already know each other?'

Ellery gave him a look that Alma couldn't see. 'Yes, brother, we know each other. From the Human Realm. And, well, I was not so nice to Alma there.'

'Not so nice!' Alma had found her voice and it was angry. Furious, as a matter of fact. 'Are you kidding me? You were a complete-' Then she stopped, conscious of Deryck next to her. He looked at her, then his sister, face full of confusion.

'How about I get both of you a drink?'

'Fine!' said Ellery, starting to sound annoyed.

'Thanks,' nodded Alma, frowning. Deryck walked away and Alma watched him go, unable to help herself.

She didn't know what to think about anything anymore. Turning back to Ellery she was surprised to see a smile on her lovely face, as though she was amused by something. This made her even more annoyed.

'What the hell is this, Ellery?' she hissed, leaning in close, not wanting to make a scene. 'Why are you here? And why did you push me through the Gate?'

Ellery's green eyes narrowed. 'I did not push you!'

'You did, and you knew what would happen. Do you know how scared I was?' Alma was actually trembling, she was so angry. Ellery glared at her. Then she took a breath, her face relaxing as she touched Alma's arm.

'Alma, I'm sorry for the way I treated you,' said Ellery. 'Okay? I was just having a bad day, that's all. And there's no way I knew you would come through to Ambeth.' She was starting to look worried, but Alma didn't care.

'Oh, a bad day! Am I supposed to believe that?'

'Yes! A bad day. You know who my father is, right?'

'Yeah, and?' Alma was not impressed. Folding her arms, she raised her eyebrows.

'Well, he tolerates me at best, I guess. I had just been to visit him, and it hadn't gone well.' She looked down. 'So, I wasn't feeling too great and-'

'So you decided to beat me up.' Alma's tone was full of derision and Ellery's face twisted, as though in pain.

'Yes! I mean, no – you were just in the wrong place at the wrong time. I really am sorry.' She looked pleadingly at Alma, who shook her head.

'But what about the Gate? This just doesn't make any

sense, Ellery.'

Deryck arrived just then, drinks in hand for them all, giving one to Alma first, then his sister. Pausing for a moment to thank Deryck, Ellery tried to explain.

'Oh, Alma, you have to understand – of course I knew there was a Gate there, but never in my wildest dreams did I think you would go through it!'

'But... it kind of felt as though you pushed me through,' said Alma. 'I mean, I didn't imagine that, did I?'

Ellery seemed at a loss for words. Alma could almost hear her thinking frantically. Deryck looked amused and, as she glanced at him, smiled and raised his eyebrows at her. Oh, he was just too annoyingly gorgeous, thought Alma, momentarily distracted. Turning her attention back to Ellery, she saw that she seemed more collected now. Hmmm.

'Well, did I?' she continued, determined now to get a response. Ellery sighed. She really was beautiful, thought Alma, but then it made sense now that she knew who her father was.

'All right,' she said. 'We were trying to move you into the woods.' Alma gasped, but Ellery continued. 'It was only a game.' She sounded desperate now. 'We just wanted to scare you a little, we wouldn't really have hurt you and, like I said, there was no way I thought you could go through to Ambeth. Please, please forgive me, I'm so sorry.'

Alma looked from Ellery's pleading face to Deryck, who had added his own begging expression to the mix. Then she started to laugh. This was all too much, really it was. All of a sudden she was tired of it, tired of arguing with Ellery. She just wanted to get back to being alone with Deryck. Ellery and Deryck looked taken aback but Alma just couldn't help it. Her hysteria finally subsiding, she decided to end the conversation, sensing she had the upper hand.

'Fine, I believe you. Let's not talk about it anymore.'

'So you forgive me?' said Ellery, smiling now. Stepping forward, she gave Alma a hug that surprised her, squeezing her hard for a moment. 'Friends?' she asked, pouting a little.

'Friends,' conceded Alma, not wanting to deal with it anymore. Deryck put his hand on Ellery's arm.

'Now, my dear sister, if you will let Alma go, I would very much like to dance with her. Alone,' he added, looking at Alma in a way that made her blush.

Ellery leaned in and kissed her on the cheek again. 'Look after him,' she whispered, then was gone, drifting across the dance floor, elegant in her pale green silk.

Deryck came close, putting his hands on Alma's waist as he gazed into her eyes. 'Shall we go outside? There is a walk, by the river, where we can watch the stars.'

Alma found she could hardly breathe. 'Yes,' she managed. Taking her hand, Deryck led her once more through the swell of dancers to the long windows. Stepping through, he turned to help Alma negotiate the low sill. She tripped on the hem of her gown, laughing at her own clumsiness, and Deryck took the opportunity to pull her close and kiss her again. The music changed and Deryck stepped back to offer his arm.

'Will you dance with me, Alma?'

Laughing, Alma moved into his embrace and Deryck began to twirl her across the lawn; he was an excellent dancer and made it easy for Alma to keep up with him. The stars above seemed to be wheeling in the sky and she had never been so happy, never felt like this before. All her concern about Ellery, her fears about the Prophecy, were swept away with the force of her feelings for Deryck and, as they danced on the velvety grass, Alma felt she had never seen anywhere, been anywhere, this beautiful. As the music ended they stopped, engrossed in each other, and kissed where they stood in the light spilling out of the long windows onto the green grass below. Alma could not imagine a more perfect moment. She did not see the green-clad figure standing at one of the windows, watching her with an anguished expression. A taller figure in blue stood next to him.

'Do not despair, Caleb, she is not yet lost.'

Caleb turned sorrowful eyes to Thorion, replying in a voice broken with pain. 'But she is now – she is lost to me.'

At this the High King could only nod, laying a sympathetic hand on Caleb's shoulder as they watched the entwined couple, each thinking their own troubled thoughts.

Standing in a corner of the crowded ballroom, Lord Denoris slid a warm hand along the curve of Gwenene's back. She smiled. 'It seems your son has done his job.' Her blue eyes, the same colour as her gown, gleamed in the lantern light as she turned to Denoris.

'He has,' said the Dark Lord, one corner of his mouth lifting. His emerald gaze followed Deryck and Alma as they crossed the dance floor towards the long windows. 'I expected nothing less.'

Gwenene slid her hands over his chest, twining her arms around his neck. 'So shall we celebrate?'

At this Denoris smiled, his arms coming around Gwenene to pull her close against him. 'We shall,' he said, bending his head to hers. 'And I'll let him have his fun for a while. For it won't be long until she is mine.'

Here ends Volume One of The Ambeth Chronicles

Volume Two, *No Quarter*, now available on Amazon.

Volume Three, *Hills and Valleys*, coming March 2016

If you enjoyed *Oak and Mist*, please consider leaving a star rating or review, or visit me at my blog, www.journeytoambeth.com

Thank you for reading.

No Quarter

Volume Two of The Ambeth Chronicles

Things couldn't be better for Alma. She's returned the lost Sword to Ambeth and is finally with Deryck, Prince of the Dark. But what's really going on? Deryck is struggling with his father, who wants to control Alma, while Alma is struggling with her best friend Caleb, who doesn't trust Deryck one inch. Plus it's getting harder and harder to keep up with her life in the human world. Falling in love shouldn't be this difficult. But things are about to get much worse…

ABOUT THE AUTHOR

 Helen Jones loves to write. That's all there is to it. Growing up in Coventry, she then lived in Canada and Australia before returning to the UK some years ago. She now lives in Hertfordshire with her husband and daughter and spends her days writing, thinking, cleaning and counting cats on the way to school.

Blog: www.journeytoambeth.com

Facebook: Author Helen Jones

Twitter: @AuthorHelenJ